Tanners Dell

A Darkly Disturbing Occult Horror

Trilogy - Book 2

S. E. England

ISBN: 9780993518355

1st Edition: EchoWords 2016
www.echowords.org
www.sarahenglandauthor.co.uk

About the author

Sarah England is a UK author. Originally she trained as a nurse before a career in the pharmaceutical industry, specialising in mental health – a theme which creeps into much of her work. She then spent many years writing short stories and serials for magazines before her first novel was published in 2013.

At the fore of Sarah's body of work is the bestselling trilogy of occult horror novels – *Father of Lies, Tanners Dell* and *Magda*; followed by *The Owlmen*.

You might also enjoy, *The Soprano*, a haunting thriller set on the North Staffordshire Moors, or *Hidden Company* – a gothic horror set in a Victorian asylum in the heart of Wales. *Monkspike* is her latest novel.

If you would like to be informed about future releases, there is a newsletter sign-up on Sarah's website. Please feel free to keep in touch via any of the social media channels, too. It's good to hear from you!

www.sarahenglandauthor.co.uk
www.facebook.com/sarahenglandauthor
www.twitter.com/sarahengland16

Prologue

Drummersgate Secure Forensic Unit
December 2015: Ruby

The banging noises started around 3am. At first they were pinprick taps and scratches, just enough to crawl into the sleeping mind. Now though, there's an unmistakeable, rhythmic thudding – kicking against locked doors and foot-stamping – with momentum gaining until the corridors echo and the floor judders. I put my hands over my ears. *It's just a dream...not really happening...*But it's getting louder. *Boom, boom, boom, boom...*the beat of an adrenalin-fuelled mob.

I'm lying here, eyes wide: something or someone is coming. And then I sense him, shrouded in the dank, foggy yard outside, willing me to find him, to see him: a lone drummer boy announcing the death of prisoners lined up for hanging. Through his ragged clothes, open sores weep; wet hair dripping down his sightless face as each diseased man shuffles closer to the noose.

Inside the unit the hysteria is spreading – a contagious primeval dread. Does each caged soul see what I see? Are they drawn to their cell window to watch the filthy waif, barely perceptible in the mists of a grey dawn, beating time to each inevitable doom? They know something bad is here, for sure. But I am alone with my vision. It is only me whose insides curl and loosen in terror as, vomit lurching into my throat, I stumble up the steps to the hangman's noose. *'Sorry...sorry, Anna...'* Who is Anna? A woman left behind at home? And it is only me who hears the guttural screams before each neck cracks; terrified eyes bulge and blackened tongues loll out.

I'm sick with it, curling up on the cold linoleum floor in a tight ball as iciness crawls over my skin like death itself. The rancid stench of fear is overwhelming, and still the animalistic

1

thumping inside the walls continues. I can't breathe... *Make it stop...make it stop...it isn't real. Celeste said it isn't real. Won't somebody help me? Anyone?*

Then abruptly everything ceases; and a suffocating blanket of total blackness descends, snuffing out the madness.

Silence.

Not even the sound of my own breath.

✳✳✳

<u>Chapter One</u>

Doncaster Royal Infirmary
Sunday December 27th, 2015

She had been here all night.

The young officer, DC Toby Harbour, who was sitting with her, rubbed his hands together. "It's bloody cold in 'ere, I've lost the feeling in me feet. I wish that lamp'd stop flicking on and off an' all – it's giving me the creeps."

Outside the room in which DI Callum Ross lay unconscious, the rest of the ward was bathed in the gloom of a few night lights. Strands of tinsel glittered darkly where it hung in loops from the ceiling, and most of the patients were fast asleep with just the occasional snore to rattle the peace. A sleety December rain spattered across the windows.

On the bedside table a digital clock glowed. *3.33am*

"It's probably an old generator," Becky suggested.

"What? Just for this room? Hey, maybe it's haunted? That's what happens – the temperature drops. I've heard some right spooky stories about 'ospitals. And people die in these side wards, don't they?"

She smiled weakly. God, he had no idea. Let's hope he thought ghosts were just spooky tales kids told each other for a joke, and that it always stayed that way for him. She really ought to send him either home or back to the station for his own good, except he'd been instructed by the top brass to stay until Callum woke up – probably to begin the interrogation straight away. Time was of the essence, she appreciated that.

He was right though, there *was* a crypt-like chill ascending from the floor; her legs were freezing. It must be a heating failure and yet – she looked over towards the rest of the ward – the other patients had kicked off their excess blankets. She huddled more deeply into her coat.

"See, it *is* cold in 'ere," Toby said, noticing her shivers. "I bet there's a ghost coming."

Hmmm, ghosts she could cope with.

People died and that was natural. Imprints of fear and emotional trauma were well documented: olfactory, visual and auditory experiences apparent to those sensitive to them, but that was all. She had worked in hospitals all her life, even some of the old Victorian asylums before they were razed to the ground, and her opinion was you couldn't encounter serious illness, madness, fear and death and not feel that some of it lingered. Very few of her colleagues were without a tale to tell on that score and it had never fazed her. In fact, in some ways she had always found it quite comforting to think the human race wasn't consigned to eternal ashes and dust. But that was before recent events. And now there was nothing comforting at all about a darkness that could neither be seen nor understood.

A sudden movement caught her eye: a dark shape about the size of a large rat skittering on the edge of her vision. She winged round in time to see a long tail disappearing under the bed. Then another shot up the wall behind the headboard. *Ghosts don't do that. This was no ghost. Oh God, please don't let it be starting up again...*

Had Toby seen it? He had his head down, rapidly pressing keys on an iPhone again. Good, well that was something.

Shaking slightly, she leaned forwards and took Callum's pale hand in her own. Hands often gave her a skip of the heartbeat. Maybe it was because hands are so vital to us and when we we're ill, especially unconscious, the sight of particularly strong, capable hands like Callum's, piggy-backed with cannulas, bruised and inert, brought it all home. She stroked his bruised and swollen face, praying he wasn't reliving whatever had happened during the week he'd been missing in Woodsend. Hopefully he was having peaceful dreams or, preferably, remained entirely dreamless while his mind and body recovered from whatever ordeal he'd been put through.

4

And please God, when he wakes up let him remember who and what he saw before the Deans and their black arts stopped any hope of finding Alice.

The police wouldn't know what they were up against: the threat of dark forces wasn't something any of them were exactly going to take seriously, was it? To them this was the case of a young girl who apparently existed but was not officially registered, and that was it. In the cold light of day the facts were hard ones: a police officer had been assaulted and left for dead in the vicinity of Woodsend; and the image of a young girl had been caught on that officer's mobile phone during the attack. That was what they were working on.

The rest, Becky thought, presented a vague, albeit disturbing, picture, but only if you put all the jigsaw pieces together. And would they? Somehow she thought not. For example, few had believed Ruby even had a real daughter. Not surprising really when you considered Ruby was a mental health patient with dozens of different personalities. Who was to say Alice wasn't yet another of her alters just like her sister, Marie, had turned out to be? When Ruby had attacked local man, Paul Dean, in Woodsend two years ago, there hadn't been a single person who even recognised her: she was just a mad woman, said the locals – no one they knew – substantiated by the fact there were no school or GP records for her in the area. Even Ruby herself was clueless as to who she was or where she'd come from. The police had subsequently wrapped up the case and Ruby had been duly incarcerated in a secure unit at Drummersgate Hospital, where she remained.

The fact that everyone who had then tried to help Ruby had suffered a serious psychological or physical repercussion would be seen by any rational person as pure coincidence. Unless you've experienced it yourself, Becky thought. Unless you've been to hell and back you wouldn't even contemplate another, darker, reality. So what *was* real then? What could she honestly say to the investigating police officer due in later this morning? That Dr Jack McGowan had hypnotised a mentally disturbed woman and was now a shell of a man back home with his parents in Ireland, instead of the medical director, top psychiatrist and family man he was just over a month ago? That she herself had witnessed Ruby's bizarre, demonic behaviour during the hypnosis and subsequently been persecuted by a hallucination, which threatened her sanity until she was physically dragged into a church? That Dissociative Identity Disorder Specialist Dr Kristy Silver was now sectioned in Laurel Lawns Private Hospital under the mental health act? And steady, reliable social worker, Martha Kind, who had gone to investigate matters in Woodsend had collapsed and died suddenly, as had her predecessor? Hardly police business. What could they do about any of that?

Now though, at last there was something concrete to go on: photographic evidence that a young girl really did exist in Woodsend without any registration at the school or with the GP, exactly as Ruby claimed; assuming she was Ruby's daughter, of course, which would no doubt be contested. But there would be Callum's testimony too, when he woke up. All of which the Deans would be aware of. Not that the Deans per se frightened her personally – they were a pretty nasty bunch of abusive, child-molesting men who could be caught, surely? It was the other stuff - intelligently targeted towards the very fabric of your sanity and sense of self - sent to dismantle your humanity and plummet you into an isolated world of fear and depression, madness and confusion; ultimately designed to leave you helpless in a mental health unit trying to explain that it was real to people who simply wouldn't and couldn't believe you.

"What time's DS Hall coming in again?" she asked Toby.

They both looked at the clock. *3.51am.*

"Sid? First thing…it'll be just after six…" Toby broke off as the room suddenly plummeted into coalface blackness. Not a single thing was visible and for a moment the two of them sat in stunned silence.

A shiver crawled up her spine as if someone had crept up behind her and Becky lunged for the bedside lamp, just as a

6

sneering, mocking voice shouted loudly into her ear, "*Well howdy, little sister…long time no see…*"

She leapt from the chair, knocking things over in her rush to the door. It was jammed and a panicky voice she realised was her own, called out. *It was happening again, yes it was, the same thing. Oh God…* Someone on the other side rattled the handle and from the black interior it was possible to make out the silhouette of a man, behind him the night nurse. All of them pushed and pulled at the door for what seemed like several minutes, until suddenly it gave way and the night light flicked back on.

"Flaming 'ell," said Toby, the colour drained from his face. "What 'appened there?"

Becky slumped back down, sitting on her hands so no one could see them shaking. "I don't know. Wedge the door open, will you, Toby."

He stood towering over her, motionless.

"And then go and get us some coffees, eh? We're as spooked as a couple of alley cats!"

All she had to do was get him through the night, send him to the canteen for a long break or something, and he'd never know about this stuff, as she now called it in her head – just stuff – why acknowledge it as anything else – because once he knew he'd be marked.

He was way too young for this – a fresh-faced lad with designer stubble and a rooster haircut – he should be knocking on doors and carrying out routine enquiries, or going out on a Saturday night with his mates; queueing up for pints and chatting up girls.

"What? And walk past the mortuary on me own?"

"You'll be fine. And you don't have to walk past it, take the lift. Trust me. Go."

The night nurse bustled back with some more blankets. "It's freezing in here. I can see my own breath! Why didn't you say?"

"Thanks, I don't suppose you've got one of those for me too?"

The nurse handed her one, a frown etched deeply into her face.

'I'm not surprised she's pissy', Becky thought: some of the other patients were now awake and calling out when she'd been happily knitting and chatting with the Orderly. Now she was busy and it was still only four in the morning. She watched her potter round taking bed pans and fetching paracetamol.

Oh, to just be a bit narky because your shift was busy. At least you were still sane, your mind balanced and undisturbed. Like the innocence of childhood, once it was gone it was gone but you wouldn't know that until you lost it. Because that was the thing, Becky realised, pulling the scratchy NHS blanket tightly around herself – once you'd crossed that line you couldn't uncross it. The horror, when it came for you, was all your own: a black terror you couldn't see, explain, or ever share. And worse – perhaps the worst thing of all – was that you never forgot and it would always, always haunt you.

The room was still cool, but now normalising. She leaned over to touch Callum's icy cheek. Whatever just happened had been purely to scare her and warn her off, but she would not be leaving Callum alone while ever he lay here helpless, and she would see this through right to the end, no matter how tough it got. Even so, it would be wise to start praying. The Deans had their backs against the wall now and they would play every low down, dirty, black arts trick in the book. Callum would have seen at least one, maybe several members of their sect.

And they still had Alice. Oh God, poor Alice. What would she be now – ten? Twelve? Her fate was unimaginable. The problem was, she could almost hear them laughing.

***

Chapter Two

Woodsend Village

June 1972

Seventeen year old Rosella Locke closed the caravan door softly behind her and padded barefoot across Drovers Common into the woods. An ethereal mist lay across the valley below, while stars and the scythe of a new moon still glittered over the moors, the fuchsia streaks of dawn yet to break through.

Ahead lay the gloom of a dormant forest, and fleetingly she looked over her shoulder. Good. No one had seen her leave. She picked up pace. This must be done before the sun came up.

The dew on the grass beneath her feet tingled icily. Pale-faced from sleep, she carefully picked her way along the path looking for a suitable place. Eventually she came to a small clearing and her eyes widened: a ring of stone boulders shone in the moonlight, a summer canopy of leaves rustling overhead as silkily as a duchess's gown. It was as if the scene had been set just for her: a magical place and host to a thousand pagan rites. Rosella swung around and around, checking repeatedly for watchers – one in particular – but all was quiet; without even the disturbance of a bird at this perfect veil in time between the dark and the light.

Quickly she set to work, etching a circle into the ground with a stick, before arranging the necessary herbs and a few nettles onto a large, silk shawl, along with scribbled-on notepaper, candles and various other artefacts. The midsummer sun would soon dawn and there was no time to lose. Hopefully, please God, it wouldn't be too little too late. She sat down cross-legged, checked the immediate area once more and then began to meditate.

By the time gentle warmth bathed her shoulders in misty light, the deed was done, and a few moments later she opened her eyes to a cacophony of crows exploding into the dappled treetops.

A damp chill had seeped under her skin, seizing the muscles, and she stumbled slightly, hurrying to brush away evidence of the circle she'd drawn, scramble together her belongings and hasten back to the camp. She would say she'd been gathering herbs for dinner tonight. In that case she ought to find some…down by the river path there should be plenty, although it would have to be lightning quick because that's where the witch, Ida, collected hemlock. She pulled a boline from her skirt pocket in readiness as she walked, hoping for parsley and garlic. Mala, her mother, would be pleased. God, how she hated deceiving her and the rest of the family – it left a bad taste casting spells and spying on people – but what choice was there with someone like Ida in the camp?

***

As true Roma gypsies they had a strict code of honour and should never have taken Ida in, but it was too late now. Ida had been evicted from another camp, or so she said – abandoned to fend for herself due to the unfairness of a quarrel with an elder. Thrown out, more likely, Rosella thought sulkily, but she'd given Mala a sob story and Mala had a soft heart. Said come along with us! She'd thought her mother was smart. Obviously not smart enough… *Unless Ida had played dirty tricks on her too?*

Right from the off there had been something suspicious about that woman, who could have been anything from fifteen to thirty with those dark, watchful eyes and gleamingly strong, peasant skin. Fit and muscular looking she could turn on the charm in the flash of a smile and just as quickly snuff it out. She flitted in and out of different personas to suit the company she kept: creeping from caravan to caravan at all manner of hours; dancing for the men at night; ingratiating herself next day with the women by fixing their hair or helping with the cooking, until they began to wonder how they'd managed without her – sitting back in the sunshine while she boiled, fried, baked or stirred one delicious meal after the next. And then there were the herbal remedies for pain relief in childbirth, calming asthma, and soothing swollen joints. In a very short time she had made herself invaluable. It seemed everyone was fooled except herself.

One morning shortly after dawn, Rosella followed her, watching from a distance as Ida selected flowers, leaves and stalks. But then, and it was most peculiar, the scene in front of her had frozen as if it was a video-still, and the air crackled with static. She tried to move but her feet were leaden, stuck fast in the ground; nor could she breathe in. But just as the panic rose inside her the spell was broken. Birdsong burst into her ears again and her legs crumpled slightly.

A voice directly behind said, "Hello Rosella!"

Rosella swung round to find Ida directly behind her. Those eyes – she would never forget those eyes as long as she lived – had no irises, no pupils and were entirely white. Rosella stared open mouthed, transfixed… *No, no, this couldn't be…it had to be an illusion or magic…* Gradually she backed away, and then she was running like hell with the sound of echoing laughter ringing through the forest.

There was something so not right about Ida. No one knew where she'd come from, which camp she'd been with before the last one, or why she was alone in the world; and the longer it went on the more the others deemed it ungrateful to ask.

Why couldn't her mother, Mala, see through Ida? The woman was no good and bore them ill, Rosella was sure of it; some of the women had become ill – new mothers with impaired vision, nausea and headaches, causing them to snap at and shun their husbands. There had been more arguments recently too, with several of the women in low spirits and a couple of fights breaking out amongst the men. And all the while Ida flirted and danced and glowed more radiantly than ever, serving up meals and administering medicines or poultices. One evening shortly after the incident in the woods, as they sat round the camp fire, something – she couldn't quite say what it was – caused Rosella to glance across the flames to where Ida sat smoking roll-ups and laughing. A tall shadow was hovering over her like a dark-cloaked gatekeeper. Mesmerised, she watched as it then coiled into a plume of black dust and vanished into the wood smoke.

She had always been able to see auras, right from being a small child – and mostly people had white or misty fields of energy around them, sometimes a hint of blue or green, occasionally yellow or gold. But Ida's was a cloud of sludgy, dark brown that clung to her like a bad smell. If she tried to talk to her mother about any of this, though – anything to do with the occult, in fact – Mala would fly at her in temper. And so for weeks Rosella had lain awake at night alone with her suspicions, haunted by a creeping fear that traced her skin like cold water on a hot day. *What was it? What was coming?*

And then the nightmares began, her dreams becoming spiked with terror. At first it was an inexplicable feeling of dread that would build and build until the need to get out of the caravan became overwhelming; yet any hope of escape was impossible because she was unable to move so much as a limb, much less wake up. Very rapidly this then escalated to visions of black shapes forming from the darkness into demonic creatures with faces that peered directly into her own, false pity oozing from cavernous black eyeballs in a stench of human excreta that made her retch even as she slept. When finally she came to, it would be in the early hours, coated in sweat and gasping for air. Night after night this continued, wearing her down until the days became drugged stupors, her appetite dried up and her energy drained away.

And how Ida grew rosy on it.

Something had to be done.

The answer came on a day Mala had been shouting at her for lying in the long grass again instead of doing her chores. Overhead a biplane hummed and the sun warmed her body on the scent of a summer breeze. *Do something…* Her drowsy mind turned over the facts: if Ida was poisoning her then how? Rosella only ate her own food and she watched the woman like a hawk.

Was there a hex on her then? Is that what the woman had done?

Above her a kestrel hovered and far, far away a children's nursery rhyme carried on the wind.

'Ring-o' Ring o' Roses…'

And then the solution came riding in.

A night not so long ago she'd gone to a fairground with some other girls and they'd got drunk on cider, hiding behind one of the caravans to the drone of the generators while they swapped ghost stories and tried to scare each other. One thing you could do if attacked by demons, said one of the quieter girls, was to put anise seeds in a little pouch under your pillow at night; another was to smudge sage smoke and hang white heather and holly outside the caravan. She'd spoken as if she believed it and become upset when the others hadn't taken her seriously and said it was old gypsy women's rubbish.

Well it was worth a try, so that night she put anise seeds under her pillow.

Next day though, she could almost see the smirk on Ida's face as she walked past Mala and herself hanging out washing. *Nice dreams, Rosella*?

None of the other stuff had worked either. And so Ida's hex - because that's what it must be - had to be reversed.

***

And now the deed was done.

They were not supposed to do these things. Apprehension and guilt prickled away at her conscience as she walked ever quicker towards the river… *The sun's coming up… Hurry, hurry…* Pagan worship, Christian worship, any religion in fact – was fine. But witchcraft, no. Never.

When she'd learned about it from those girls that summer, and subsequently told Mala who had been skinning a rabbit at the time, her mother had turned on her with a knife still dripping in blood. "Don't you ever, do you hear me, don't you *ever* bring that kind of dark magic into our home! It doesn't leave you once you've invited it in, Rosella. Ever. Don't play with what you don't understand or it'll haunt you for the rest of your days."

Her mother still spoke in a heavily accented Yugoslavian tongue. The family had been in England for most of Rosella's life but the memory of densely wooded hills and richly fruited orchards still rolled in on blue sky days like that one. Rosella had nodded, chastised, and backed out of the caravan. The day had been sunny but clouds scooted in from nowhere, chilling the air, and she'd heeded the warning.

Until today.

She stepped out of the woods onto the river path. The mist had now lifted to reveal crystal clear water, which bubbled and sparkled as it surged over shiny rocks. For a shard of a second Rosella's mood lifted. It was so beautiful here. She almost smiled, when suddenly the crack of a twig stopped the breath in her chest. Turning, oh so slowly, in the direction of the sound, her eyes straining into a myriad of tree trunks still shrouded in mist, she held herself rigid. *Someone was there.*

With heightened senses her nostrils flared, every nerve-ending static with alertness while she scanned the scene. But there was nothing – just the softly lit canopy of trees and a few crows cawing in the distance. For a full minute she waited.

Gushing water.

Nothing else.

Time to get back.

Then came the faint but unmistakeable whiff of tobacco on the air. Her heart rate picked up, thudding loudly in her ears. Was it Ida?

Run…run now…you need to run…

But exactly as before, her feet failed to move. In fact both her legs were completely paralysed and no sound would come from her throat. Once again the atmosphere seemed electrically charged, the scene before her playing out in slow motion. A man had stepped out of the shadows onto the path - an old man with a white widow's peak and the palest ice-blue eyes imaginable. She stood hypnotised. He had a look about him that was older than time, exuding an almost inhuman chill; his skin wizened like a reptile's, lips wet and full as they pulled back from yellowing teeth into a leer. The smell of him was rank like he hadn't washed in months; the white hair combed back in greasy strands. But there was something a whole lot worse than any of that. Far, far worse than the way he looked…

Revulsion lurched into her throat, her insides loosening as he walked towards her. *Don't look down… Oh God, don't look…*

His trousers were undone at the zip.

Helpless, she kept her eyes fixed on his, unable to move or utter a single syllable, yet knowing precisely how this was going to unfold. There was a splinter of a second, just a sparkling flash in time, as a brief image of Nicu, her eighteen year old fiancé, with his shiny brown hair and dancing green eyes, faded from her mind as any kind of future possibility… before the stinking old monster moved in, one hand snatching at her skirt, the other smashing her throat with staggering force. And as the powerful shove rammed her spine into a tree trunk, cracking her head, a searing pain shot through her body. After which she lost consciousness.

***

When she woke up it was night. From somewhere outside an owl hooted, and there were little scratches and rustles like trees scraping at a window. *Where was this? Back in the caravan? Doesn't smell the same…mould…*

She drifted in and out of consciousness. Next time she surfaced it was to the sound of boots thudding heavily upstairs – workman's boots – coming closer and quickly. *Not the caravan then…* She leapt back, slamming into the wall behind, the sudden movement causing a sickening pain to rip through her insides so violently it took her breath. Hot liquid gushed from between her legs – blood? – and cold sweat surfaced all over her body as she fell sideways onto the bed clutching her tummy. With pressure swelling inside her brain like the worst of hangovers she struggled to open her eyes. *Was someone there? Who was it? What was happening?*

15

He stood framed in candlelight at the doorway.

Gradually her eyes adjusted to the gloom. The room appeared to be devoid of furniture apart from a heavy oak wardrobe in the corner by the window. Her fingers felt around: on top of her lay a scratchy coat, and underneath she was naked. Tracing down her body with fluttery fingers she winced to the slightest touch. Had he broken her bones? She tried to wiggle her toes…no feeling… Panic shot into her veins as he strode towards her. She tried to scream but nothing came out.

"Here's something you've to drink. Get it down. Stay put or you'll be somewhere you like even less."

She looked at the proffered cup of evil-smelling stuff and attempted to knock it away but his hand was like an iron girder and all she got was another bruise smashed into the side of her face.

"I said drink it, you stupid bitch." He held her head back with one hand and threw the liquid down her throat.

Blinding pain shot up her neck and into her head as if the arteries had been squeezed shut, and she gulped in shock when the liquid fired into her stomach wall a second later like it was red hot whisky boiled with chilli pepper.

He left her with a brain pulsing so hard she thought it would burst from her skull. Overhead the ceiling began to rotate, swirling around like a dizzying, nauseating carousel; and each breath was iron-rigid, stuck in a vice grip as she struggled to gasp in the icy air…*Oh God she was going to die…*before a sudden eclipse plunged her from consciousness once more.

Quite when the hallucinations began it was impossible to say – maybe minutes, hours or even days after she had been brought here – to wherever 'here' was. At first it was just an awareness of whispering and a light breeze against her skin. But when she opened her eyes it was to see a monk draped in a hooded robe, observing her from the corner of the room. She blinked and blinked again, slowly grasping the fact that he was actually floating several feet off the ground. Staring for several disbelieving seconds she was in the process of trying to rationalise this when suddenly it rushed towards the bed at speed.

A silent scream knotted in her throat. Shutting her eyes she turned onto her side and curled into a tight ball. *No, no, no – it was just a dream; a drug-induced hallucination.* But after that, every time she opened her eyes there would be more of them. Sometimes they loomed over her as if peering into a cot at a baby, other times they cackled and whispered in the corners before fading into the walls like ghosts.

None of this could be real. It had to be because of whatever concoctions he was giving her, like LSD or something. Or maybe she'd gone crazy and this was a mental hospital? Soon she'd be told these were just bizarre opiate-dreams because she'd been attacked but was now on the mend.

The cold though…the fridge cold of the place…and the perpetual rushing of water. And the smell too - of mould and wood smoke and some kind of sweet tobacco – not the same as her father's roll-ups but not too dissimilar either: there was something familiar about it, but what? This was no hospital…Her weary mind repeatedly collapsed in on itself with the effort of thinking. All she could do was try to stay sane: it was all she had left. And so whenever the dark hooded figures came calling, she would close her eyes and cite the Lord's Prayer over and over. *Please God, make them go away.*

Still the echoing laughter grew, as did the colicky pain, which shook her to the core, leaving her sick and exhausted, lying in a pool of her own sweat.

But now…now there was something new. A raw burn cut into her ankles and wrists.

One time, a voice she thought might be her own asked who the monks were.

"Shut her up."

A heavy hand clamped something foul-smelling over her nose and mouth, before the dark claimed her once more.

The next time she surfaced the air was as freezing as a mortuary and her body was stretched out in a star shape. Rope seared into her skin and a cold slab permeated her spine.

A different place this time – wetter. Drip…drip…drip… *A cave?*

Cloth had been shoved into her mouth, tied so tightly it cut into the corners of her mouth, and a thin dark fabric covered her eyes, although there were shades of light and dark visible through it. A low chanting echoed in monotone and through the veil she could see hooded figures circling around her. Directly in front of her stood a macabre figure in a horned mask, with a cape of fur and feathers billowing around him. Her eyes battled against the blindfold. *Oh God, what's going to happen to me? What is this? A ceremony? What was coming?* Her dulled mind lapsed in and out of consciousness, vaguely registering the escalating chanting, and a heady, intoxicating aroma of burning herbs. She forced herself to open her eyes in response to being repeatedly shaken. *Oh dear God, there were children here too. Really young ones.*

Suddenly a woman's face loomed inches from her own in a hazy blur, and old dog breath assaulted her nostrils as it seemed she was climbing onto her chest. Rosella turned her head this way and that to avoid what she now realised was a hissing snake being pushed into her mouth, thrashing in vain against metal clamps clicking into place around her arms and legs. Then suddenly excruciating, intolerable pain – white hot or ice cold – was thrust up inside her, accompanied by a bloodcurdling scream she realised was her own.

When she next came to, it was to the smell of cauterised flesh. The soles of her feet were screaming as if she'd danced on fire.

Not real. Not real. Not real…

"Oh but it is, my dear."

Something was forcing open her eyes, a hand holding her head back by the hair.

"Look at me. You have our child now, dear."

No.

How long had she been here? Hours? Days? Weeks?

"She can stay down here 'til she gives birth," said a male voice.

How long? How long had she been missing? Where was Mala? Where was her father? Her brothers? Wouldn't they find her in this house by the river?

Give birth?

***

Chapter Three

Drummersgate Secure Forensic Unit
Sunday December 27th, 2015

Noel stared at the woman standing in front of him in Reception. As a mental health nurse he'd seen some sights over the years, but this one was quite something and certainly put a twinkle in his eye. Wearing a furry green coat she was short and stout, and sported a crown of permed hair dyed a similar shade of red to Jessica Rabbit's. Crimson lips bled into white powdery skin etched with wrinkles, and each breath seemed an effort even though she had only walked a few yards to the door. Her eyes, though...her eyes were a rich conker brown, gleaming with angel kindness. He smiled.

"I'd like to see Ruby, please," she said, holding onto the desk while she got her breath back. "Becky phoned and said she'd asked for me but it was Christmas Eve and at the time I was up to my armpits in sprouts and whatnot."

Noel indicated a couple of armchairs next to a potted plant and she tottered gratefully towards it.

"Did Becky say what it was about? Only Ruby's visitors have to be pre-approved and I've got nothing down saying anyone's coming." In fact, Ruby had never had a single visitor in all the two years she'd been here so it was more than unusual. This woman couldn't be family either. Ruby *had* no family.

The lady plonked herself firmly onto a chair and shook her head. "Oh dear, I'm sorry, love, but I did hope it'd be Becky who'd be here and I wouldn't have to, you know, explain?"

"Normally she would be, but she's currently off on a personal matter. We work closely together though, so I hope I can help. Could we start with who you are, do you think?"

"Celeste Frost, love. I met Ruby many years ago and became a friend. We lost touch until I found out from Martha Kind, the social worker who used to work here—"

"Oh you met Martha, did you? God rest her soul."

Celeste nodded. "Yes, shocking business that, wasn't it – to just collapse and die so suddenly? She seemed perfectly well and looking forward to retirement too."

"Yes, I know. We were all very upset. Anyway, sorry, you were saying…"

"Yes, well Martha came to see me just before Christmas. She was digging around, trying to find out what was going on in Woodsend. She'd seen the reports in the papers about how I was supposedly hounded out of the village for being a witch. Anyhow, I told her straight – I'm a medium and I didn't want to be neither. I helped folk with healing and that was it. Anyhow, I had, 'Get out Witch' scrawled across my front door and folk causing trouble so me and my husband left soon after. He was ill with it, nearly died with the stress. It was bad that place, had a bad feel to it. Any road, I'm getting off the subject. I told Martha and I'll tell you – Ruby came to see me years ago because she was living in that old mill in Bridesmoor and the poor lass was spooked out. I only saw her once after that and it wasn't good. Then I read in the news a couple of years back she'd attempted murder on Paul Dean. Well anyhow, if she's sent for me I'm guessing I'm her only friend."

"Wow, you're a medium?"

She eyed him for a few moments before continuing. "I don't expect it to be taken seriously – especially in a place like this… although it might help…" She looked into the middle distance, breaking off the conversation.

"Are you alright?" said Noel.

She jumped visibly. "Oh sorry, love. It's just there's a lot of unrest in this building, did you know?"

He laughed. "Oh yes!"

She smiled. "I daresay. Anyway, I've come here instead of being at home with my poorly husband for one reason and one reason only, and that's because Ruby asked for me. That's it. And I'm not going until I've helped her."

"Okay. Look, I'll be back in a minute. Do you want a cup of tea, Mrs Frost?"

"Celeste. And yes, I'd love one please."

When he returned he sat next to her and leaned forwards, his voice low. "Sorry about that, Celeste, but I'm sure you can imagine that with the sort of patients we have here, we have to be ultra-careful with regard to who visits. Anyway, I've checked with Becky and she says it's fine and she'll take full responsibility. She did pass on a warning, though. I don't know how familiar you are with people who have Dissociative Identity Disorder?"

Celeste shook her head.

"Okay, well it used to be called Multiple Personality Disorder and it basically means a fragmented personality. It's usually caused by trauma growing up. But here's the thing, Celeste: Ruby can switch into alter personalities and it can be very alarming, so I'm going to get someone to sit in with you and we haven't got many staff on. She's a trainee mental health nurse and her name's Emily. Is that okay?"

Celeste sipped her tea and nodded. "Of course."

They sat quietly for a moment before Noel asked, "Is Ruby psychic? Only the other patients seem to think she is. So does Becky. And Claire, our doctor, so there must be something in it."

Celeste drained her cup and placed it down with a clatter. "Oops-a-daisy. Oh yes, definitely. She's more than that, though. Lots of people have strong intuition and we call them clairsentient, but Ruby is most definitely clairvoyant; and she's also mediumistic."

Noel frowned. "But wouldn't that make her spectacularly vulnerable if she started trancing out? I mean, presumably being a medium involves spirit guides and contact with the dead, or at least a belief you're in contact with the dead? You have control over your own mind, Celeste, and presumably know what you're doing, but Ruby's a very poorly girl. How does she know which spirits are there to help and which are there to you know…?"

22

"Possess her? She doesn't and it's terrifying. That's why she needs my help, Mister…" She peered at Noel's name badge.

"Noel. Call me Noel."

"You've seen a bit of the dark side, yourself, haven't you, love?"

He stared at her, the pit of his stomach plunging. *How the hell did this woman know that?*

"So you'll understand then? That I've to help her?"

***

Celeste found Ruby sitting on the window sill, idly tracing raindrops across the glass with a badly bitten fingernail as she hummed to herself. The view of wild, windswept moorland was a bleak one at this time of year, with a mass of thunder grey cloud parked over miles of sodden turf.

The trainee nurse, Emily, shut the door behind them both and indicated Celeste should take a seat. "There's a friend here to see you, Ruby," she said in a chirrupy voice. "Do you remember asking her to visit? Her name's Celeste."

Ruby turned around so quickly it made Celeste's heart skitter.

"Hello, love. Remember me?"

Ruby's eyes were a startlingly pale blue, lighting up gaunt features old before their time. Her hair, the colour of weak tea, was worn tucked behind her ears, a slight smile playing around her lips. Tap-tap-tapping her feet, which were drawn up to her chest, she stopped humming while she examined Celeste from the tips of her sensible shoes to the top of her scarlet hairdo. "Never seen you before in me life," she said in a contemptuous voice. "Love!"

Emily interjected. "Ruby!"

Ruby smirked. "Sorry you've got *me*." She turned back to the view and resumed humming the tune, '*Four and twenty blackbirds baked in a pie…when the pie was opened, the birds began to sing…*'

"She means Eve," Emily whispered to Celeste. "Eve's the teenager who steps in to protect Ruby. She's pretty bolshie."

"That's a nice nursery rhyme," Celeste said. "Where did you learn it? At school?"

Ruby threw back her head and laughed. "Ida used to sing it all the bloody time."

"Who's Ida?"

"Supposed to be our dear mother, only she weren't. Anyway, what do you want?"

"Ruby asked me to come. She came to visit me once while she was living in a mill near Woodsend. I helped her and thought I could maybe help her again?"

Emily interjected again. "Eve, do you think we could talk to Ruby? Celeste is a friend and she's come a long way to see her."

She turned to Celeste and whispered, "She's been doing ever so well, you know? Her alters talk to each other now. Becky and Claire have done a fantastic job – Ruby knows what's going on and who's speaking inside her system. It's amazing."

Celeste focused on Ruby, who had turned to stare at her again. The girl's expression was so oddly blank and her demeanour so still, she had the appearance of one who'd been lobotomised, almost like a waxwork. "Ruby?"

After what seemed like an age, with only the sound of the overhead fluorescent lights buzzing and the wind buffeting the window, a light finally flickered in her eyes.

"You alright, love?"

Ruby blinked and nodded. All three sat in silence for a moment, until Ruby said, "Got a fag, Emily?"

Emily shook her head.

"Go get me one, eh? I'm alright, I promise."

Emily raised her eyes to the ceiling. "You'd better be. Okay then, but don't move, do you hear me?"

Ruby smiled.

Finally, after a moment's hesitation, Emily stood up and with just one nervous little glance over her shoulder, walked over to the door before closing it behind her.

The second she'd gone Ruby darted over to Celeste and threw herself at her knees. "Oh God, thank you so much for coming. I can't stand it. I don't want them lot to know 'ow bad it is, especially that bloody Isaac – the stupid git pumps me with sedatives and they make it bloody worse – if I'm out of it you see, I can't protect us...but he doesn't get it and never will…"

"Slow down, slow down," Celeste took Ruby's hands in hers as images began to form in her third eye. "What's really bad?"

Ruby nodded, searching Celeste's face. "You know. You can see."

Celeste closed her eyes, still holding Ruby's hands: *a line of dirty faced, wretched looking men in the yard outside. It was gloomy and grey, a faint rain spitting on the cobbles, the beat of a drum echoing around the walls.* Fear stabbed at her stomach and she tried not to gag on something tightening around her neck. "Oh dear, yes - restless spirits…" She broke off and forced the images from her mind. "You can't switch it off, can you?"

"No. It's at night that it's the worst. About three in t' morning. I wake up to drumming noises and the whole place starts thumping. Thing is, if I tell the doctors they'll just say I'm psychotic again and inject me with that stuff that makes me nerves tick and me legs shake, it's horrible, knocks me out for days after and I still get the bloody visions. But it's real, isn't it, Celeste? You've seen it. You know. Thank God. I mean it's every night. I wake up on the floor being sick and the room stinks like putrid flesh. I can't stand it anymore. I'll top meself, I swear. Well anyway, when Becky came in and found me on the floor again I remembered you."

Celeste was nodding furiously. "Spirit wants you to work by the sound of it."

"What do you mean, work?"

"There's a lot of unrest in here, but you're afraid and I'm not surprised."

"Please help me. Make it stop. It's like torture all the time. What have I done to deserve this? It just goes on and on and on."

"Nothing – it isn't your fault and you mustn't think it is. Now calm down and tell me more about what you're seeing and—"

Emily breezed back in with a lit cigarette. "Got you one, Ruby, although I really shouldn't have done this."

"Ah, fuck it," said Ruby, snatching it from her. "We'll not tell anyone, eh?"

"Ruby," said Celeste. "Tell me more about what you see and feel?"

Ruby took a long drag on the cigarette and turned to Emily. "Don't you dare tell them lot what I'm saying to Celeste or you'll be sorry!"

Emily's face registered a flicker of fear, and she nodded.

"I mean it."

"Yes, I know," said Emily in a small voice. "I give you my word you have total confidentiality."

Ruby eyed her for a bit, then satisfied, moved so close to Celeste she was whispering into her hair. "Right, well, just that really! There's this young lad drumming and he's standing there in t' yard all sopping wet in rags, sores on his face. I get the feeling he wants me to see him and to see what he sees." She took a deep breath and then it all came out in a rush. "There's a noose on a platform that the men shuffle towards and then I'm one of them and I can see this woman back home looking through a window crying, and I'm hearing the words, 'Sorry Anna' over and over, and I'm feeling sick to my stomach cos I've got to walk to that rope, and the pounding is getting worse in my head…" She bent over, crouching on the floor and Celeste stroked her hair.

"Yes, I see what you see," said Celeste. "It isn't your pain though, Ruby. These poor men don't know they've gone and so they keep reliving it – they're locked in eternal torture. You can help them, though – by showing them how to pass over." She shuddered. "There is so much madness and confusion here, disease and wrongful death sentences – the whole building is full of deep unrest. I'm not surprised you're tormented. But peace will only come with acceptance and that's where you come in – you must take them to the light."

Ruby lifted her small, pale face to hers. "I'm scared."

"I know. And ideally you would not be alone to do this but in the dead of night with no one to either help or believe you, the only thing I can do is offer guidance to try and ease your suffering. And because of your illness this is all particularly dangerous so you do need to take control – we have to do something! So first you *must always, always, always* – I can't stress that enough – pray and ask for protection before you begin."

Ruby nodded miserably.

"Okay, now do you remember how to fill yourself with light from the top down like I showed you? You will see and hear the spirits because you are very mediumistic, and you must tell them what to do. Afterwards you will be exhausted but it's very important you close all the channels down again. If anyone bothers you from the spirit world you must tell them to go away very firmly. You wouldn't have anyone gate-crashing your home so you mustn't have them gate-crashing your mind! Imagine the doors to your chakras snapping shut like traps behind you when you've finished." She demonstrated with her fluttery little hands from her forehead down through the rest of her body. "It will take a while but afterwards peace will come."

"I can't do it, I'm too scared."

Celeste stroked her hair some more. "Have courage, love. It is very frightening at first but I will come back and help as often as I can if the staff will let me. You shouldn't be doing this alone but it really is the only way because if you don't use your power it shines like a beacon to the underworld, and it will grow and grow until you can't control it. You have to channel it away, do you see? I know you're scared – I used to be too, and still am sometimes; but those spirits won't let you alone until the job's done. It's just the way it is."

Ruby was nodding with resignation. "What if *he* comes back, though? One of the other younger ones might let him in again."

"Him?"

She clamped shut.

"Who is *he*? Who do you mean?"

Ruby turned her face away.

"Who do you mean?" Celeste repeated.

"This place was a prison, you know?" Emily said.

Celeste sighed at the interruption.

Ruby had stood up and begun to pace around the room in an agitated fashion, muttering to herself, the cigarette waving wildly around in her fingers.

"Sit down, Ruby," said Emily. "There's a good girl."

Ruby stopped stone dead, her face a mask of shocked horror.

Emily flushed. "Oh no, I shouldn't have said that, I just forgot." She rushed towards Ruby but couldn't move her. "Ruby? You're in hospital and you're safe, now." She put an arm around her shoulders and tried to lead her to the bed. "Ruby?"

Celeste heaved herself up but even between them they could not move Ruby's slight seven stone frame. The girl's eyes had rolled back in her head and her muscles were set to stone, her body as rigid as a statue. "We need to get help," said Emily in a shaky voice, reaching for her panic button. But just as she was about to press it, Ruby's body crumpled into Celeste's arms, her lips trembling and tears dripping miserably.

"It's okay I'm here, love," said Celeste, leading the woman-child to the bed and lifting up her feet so she could lie down. She pulled a blanket over her. "Ruby, are you alright, love?"

Emily stood in the middle of the room holding Ruby's cigarette, unsure what to do next. "I've never been alone with her before. Perhaps I should fetch Noel?"

"She's thirteen and they'll baptise her soon…it's all black dark by the river…that's where they do it..." Ruby whispered, focusing on Celeste. "Once she's marked she's gone. He knows where it is but he can't talk – they paralysed him."

"I don't know what you mean, love."

The blue of Ruby's eyes was fading to colourless, the expression one of slight surprise as if she was falling backwards.

Seconds later the blank stare was back.

"Is she okay, do you think?" Celeste said over her shoulder to Emily.

"Um, I think I'll get Noel."

Celeste nodded. "Well it might be best…"

"No!" Ruby was struggling to sit up. "No. I'm okay, I don't want any more drugs." She rubbed at her neck. "God, me neck hurts."

"You know the more I think about this, the more I'm sure you shouldn't do medium work alone. If you can hang on for another night I'll arrange to come in and we'll work on it together."

Ruby started to nod. "If it's the only way it's going to stop."

"I'm afraid it is unless they move you from here, although there will always be something else until you start work as it were: it's what you're supposed to do – what you need to do. Are you alright now?"

Tear stains had dried on her cheeks but she smiled weakly. "My throat hurts, and my head."

Emily sprang into action. "I'll go and fetch Noel – she needs some paracetamol after switching like that."

After Emily had left the room again, Celeste looked hard into Ruby's eyes. "Now I'm being shown a man – swarthy with big, brown eyes – he's coming through you. He's standing outside a stone building and I've seen him before. Who is he, Ruby?"

Ruby frowned, rubbing her forehead over and over. "Sounds like Jes."

"Jes? Who is he? How did you meet him?"

Ruby shrugged. "Gypsies used to camp on Drovers Common, so I suppose he turned up that way and kept coming back. I don't know 'ow I met him, really. Anyway it were 'is mother who'd said you were, you know, like a real medium and not a fake."

"Were you close to his mother? Did his family live there?"

Ruby screwed up her eyes. "Jes were just fed up of me going on about the place being 'aunted and driving him nuts. He said it were all me being a mad witch, stuff like that, cos it never 'appened when he were there. Just me on me own."

Her own private hell. It was always the way. And who would a woman like Ruby have turned to? Who in the sane world would have believed her? Perhaps Jes wasn't heartless after all – he knew he couldn't cope and found her a friend.

"I wonder if I knew his mother? Perhaps she was one of my pupils?"

"Doubt it. She said she'd never to set foot in Woodsend again as long as she lived."

***

Chapter Four

Detective Sergeant Hall's booming voice woke her at just after 6.15am. "How is he?"

Becky jolted from a fitful doze in the chair by Callum's bed and rubbed her stiff neck. The ward was beginning to clatter awake with the lights switched on for a new day, although outside it was still winter dark. Gently she touched Callum's shoulder while the officer pulled up a chair beside her. "Still spark out by the look of it."

"Has he said anything yet?"

She shook her head. "No."

"Has he woken up at *all* since he was brought in?"

"No. Not so much as the flicker of an eyelid."

For a few moments they both watched Callum's chest steadily rise and fall.

Frowning, Becky asked, "Where was he exactly when you found him?"

Sid Hall took off his anorak, briefly glanced over his shoulder and then leaned in close. "Actually, I was on my way home when I noticed someone staggering about on The Old Coach Road. At first I thought it was a drunk who'd fallen out of The Highwayman, you know, and got lost, but as it was such a rough night up there I thought I'd just make sure the bloke got home safe. Anyhow – got level and that's when I saw the state of him! Coated in black soot like he'd just come off a shift at the pit, blood caked all over, not to mention delirious and muttering all sorts of mumbo-jumbo. Anyhow, I called out to him and bugger me if it wasn't Callum. To be honest I'd given up hope of us ever finding him."

"So it looks like he *had* been down a mine shaft? And he *had* been left for dead!"

"Well we don't know that he'd been left for dead. He might have fallen. When did you last see him, Becky?"

"You know I'm surprised you knew about me, Sid – you know, to call me? His children will be here later, by the way, but Callum and I were supposed to be a secret. It doesn't matter now but…"

"Your name was the only thing I could make sense of: Sister up at Drummersgate, he said. Wanted to um…marry you… Anyway, I've a lot of gaps to fill in. His last job had him attending a meeting at Drummersgate on the night of the…"

He thumbed through his notes while Becky reeled from the information she'd just received. *Marry her? Really?* Her glance flicked over to Callum lying in the hospital bed – hooked up to a drip, attached to a catheter and a cardiac monitor, and with an oxygen mask over his face. His forearms, neck and face were covered in cuts and bruises, and there was a large patch of matted blood in his closely cropped hair. It seemed he'd hauled himself out of an underground tunnel despite several broken ribs and a shattered right patella. He must have been in agony.

Marry her?

"…Right here we go – the night of December 18th. What can you recall about that meeting? What was it for? As the nurse in charge, I take it you were there?"

Her stomach turned in on itself just thinking about that night. "Sort of."

One of his eyebrows raised in query. "What do you mean, sort of? You were either there or you weren't there, surely?"

"Yeah." She turned away for a second. There really wasn't a cat in hell's chance of ever being able to tell the police about hers or any of the doctors' experiences. *Just stick to the facts, ma'am…* "Yes, I was there although I was officially still off sick after an accident. Dr Silver asked me to attend because we have two cases of patients who've very likely suffered child abuse in Woodsend; and one of them – Ruby – we believe has a daughter, Alice, who's

32

still there. On top of that there were some odd things happening to the team and we were pooling information. Callum came along at Dr Silver's request and then decided to have a look around the area. I didn't know he was going that night and I wasn't in a fit state to…" She broke off and looked away for a second. "Anyway, that was the last we saw of him until you picked him up. The rest you know because of what you've seen on his mobile. Alice is in a lot of danger and I think Callum must have stumbled on the truth and been left for dead, like I said." Irritation flared up from nowhere. "You know, I don't understand why there isn't more urgency about this!"

"What sort of accident did you have?"

"What? Um, a head injury. It happened at work."

"I see. And can we contact Dr Silver or any of the other witnesses present that evening?"

"Dr Silver is seriously ill in Laurel Lawns."

Sid Hall raised both eyebrows this time.

"Dr Isaac Hardy could talk to you, though – he's the consultant on our unit at Drummersgate. He's standing in for Dr Silver and Dr McGowan. Oh, and so could Noel, my staff nurse. The other person who was there that night was Martha Kind but she's now dead so good luck with that one. I'm afraid like both Callum and Dr Silver she made the mistake of asking questions in Woodsend. It never ends well going there."

Sid Hall appraised her for a few moments before putting away his notebook. He had the look about him, she thought, of a patient father who'd had just about enough of a recalcitrant teen.

"Well, we've been knocking on doors in that area for over a week and not found anything untoward. Nor have we any reason to be suspicious about Alice Dean's circumstances. As far as the police service is concerned, we're just waiting for Callum to wake up and tell us what happened. It's likely he fell down a mine shaft after a head injury from the car crash. It was pitch black out there and those moors are lethal with old mining tunnels. Have you ever been up there when it's foggy?"

"Pardon? Car crash? On his own when he's a good driver and it was a clear night? Not to mention that his car was upside down!"

"Picture it Becky. The car hits a bank of fog or there's sheep on the road and he swerves, breaks, hits a rock and off it goes at speed, rolls over and he hits his head. Then in a delirious state in thick fog he falls down a shaft—"

"That night, I remember it because I went to a church after the meeting. It was freezing but all the stars were out. Good visibility, Sergeant!"

"You said yourself you'd just been off sick with a head injury. Can you really remember? And high up on Bridesmoor…"

"It's bloody high up at Drummersgate. Stars are stars, and they were out."

"Quite a few miles away – fog rolls in and off the moors in banks."

"Even so, assuming things happened as you say, you still can't possibly leave Alice in Woodsend. She's not safe."

"Why?"

"Sergeant Hall, we have two cases of seriously traumatised young adults who suffered child abuse there. Another girl of around the same age, again from the Dean family, has been in a psychiatric unit since she was fourteen. Both Martha, our social worker, and her predecessor Linda, suffered sudden deaths after asking questions in the area. Two doctors have had mental breakdowns – again, after asking questions. And there's no way Callum would have just gone off the road. He didn't drink and he was an advanced driver who knew the road well. And it was a crystal clear night, I'm damn sure of it."

"Why isn't Alice safe?" he repeated.

"With Paul Dean? Are you serious? That was the man Ruby was arrested for attempting to murder-

"She suffers from mental illness, does she not?"

"She's lucid a lot of the time and she definitely gave birth. He's got her daughter. Alice is Ruby's daughter."

"He has stated that Alice is his own daughter."

"So who did he say was the mother? And have you checked she goes to school and that she's registered with the GP? Where's the birth certificate? Did anyone ask? "

"Her GP was there when one of my officers visited. Alice was in bed with a nasty case of measles, apparently."

"What about school attendance?"

"Apparently she has learning disabilities and she's being home-schooled. His wife, Ida, was very helpful on that one."

"And you're buying that?"

"Becky," he said kindly. "What you're describing is a series of coincidences. Frankly, I'm just here to sure there's nothing more to add to the investigation before it's closed. Callum is safely in hospital after his accident and the girl, Alice, we're satisfied is not in any danger. She's with her parents. CS Scutts has instructed us to close the file as soon as possible."

"Close the case? Are you joking? What about what Callum has to say?"

"Well yes, of course we'll be asking him what happened as soon as he wakes up."

"I don't believe this! And did one of you ever actually see or speak to Alice?"

Sid Hall sighed heavily and not for the first time Becky thought he looked overweight, a tad weary, and ready for retirement. "No," he said. "But like I told you – the doctor was there and the child had the measles. The thing is, between you and me, when Scutts is personally involved—"

"Why? Why is he personally involved? Shouldn't he be at a higher level than that? "

"I take your point, but with a detective inspector missing and an accusation of child abuse he did get personally involved, so we can't ask for more than that."

"No, I don't suppose." Her spirits plummeted. They had no social worker now for Drummersgate except a busy temp. And the police had closed the case. *Jesus wept.*

"If you don't mind me saying so, you look exhausted, Becky. Why don't you go home and rest and I'll wait for Callum to come round?"

Not bloody likely. "What happened to his photos, by the way – the ones on Callum's mobile, which would dispute the fact he crashed his car and fell down a mine shaft?"

Sid shook his head. "His empty wallet and keys were found in the area too. I'm just guessing, but someone must have found the car and robbed him, maybe dropped the phone?"

"Lame."

Neither of them said anything for a few moments. Callum's oxygen hissed and crockery clattered from beyond the side room where breakfasts were being handed out on trays.

She shuffled closer so that she was inches from his face and levelled her gaze to his. "You know this isn't right, Detective Hall. You damn well know there's something very wrong in Woodsend."

His steady brown eyes looked straight into hers. Eventually, under his breath and so softly she'd wonder later if he'd said it at all, he replied, "Yes but I can't do a damn thing about it. Scutts has closed the case and you wouldn't want to cross Scutts if your life depended on it, Becky."

***

Chapter Five

Bridesmoor

June 1972

Cora Dean was down by the river when the pit siren went up. The day was still sunny with cotton wool clouds perfecting a picture postcard day. Sparkling water washed over her toes as she watched her three eldest children – Paul, Derek and Ricky – splashing around on the rocks. They all looked so like their father with those pale blue eyes and shocks of dark hair. Sometimes the resemblance was quite uncanny – there seemed nothing of herself in them.

She looked over at Bridestones Moor to where the pithead wheel was silhouetted against the skyline, and her heart didn't miss a beat.

That gypsy girl…you knew it would be him…you knew and did nothing…

Desperately worried wives and girlfriends would be tearing out of their houses by now, revving up cars and making frantic phone calls, already rushing up to the yard to see who was being brought out on stretchers and who was unaccounted for. Many would be left without husbands after today, or fathers for their children. Not herself, though. She would not be one of them – Lucas would be just fine. The devil looked after his own and all that. Still, it would look odd if she didn't show her face. It might be best to at least put on an act.

Although reluctant to leave the warm grassy bank and the hypnotic tranquillity, she heaved herself up and put babies Natalie and Kathleen into the buggy. "Come on, we're going!" she shouted to the boys. Still in their infancy, all three ignored her. "I said, 'Come on!' Pit siren's going off. We need to see if your dad's okay."

Paul Dean, aged nine, dead-eyed her. "We're stopping 'ere."

The little shit was defying her again, blatantly, and in front of the other two. "Now!" she snapped.

He grinned, clearly relishing the stand-off. "I said, 'no', *Cora!*"

Fury shot through her veins and she ran to grab him and slap him, but skilful as a fly-half he dodged her and plunged further into the river, egged on by the other two. "Drown then, you little bastard," she said.

"*You* drown, you old witch."

Cora staggered back onto the bank, the hem of her skirt soaked through, and yanked the buggy up towards the path. *Hell and hell again.* They were more like their dad than she cared to admit. All those women in the village eyeing her with pity, gossiping so she could hear: *What were the Deans doing with that great empty mill as well as a terrace when they'd got five kids to feed? What did her Lucas want with it? Don't talk rubbish about it being renovated when they'd had it years and not done a thing to it. And those kids backchat like she shouldn't stand for. And now that young girl missing, have you heard? It must be something to do with him...*

She fought back the tears. It would be better for her if Lucas was one of the men trapped inside the mine – better for everyone, in fact – but he wouldn't be. And even if he was stone dead it wouldn't end there, would it? Paul was going to be just the blasted same. Give him another few years and he'd be every bit as nasty, especially since Lucas now had him tagging along at night. She'd begged him not to take the lad out so late, but with Paul standing there laughing at her, there'd been no point railing against it. He was 'going to the bad' just like his father.

The thought was horrific.

Surely Lucas didn't take him to Tanners Dell?

***

She'd followed Lucas once – the night every last vestige of pretence between them was finally dropped. Her mother had

38

offered to babysit so 'they could have an evening out together.' She'd had to lie about why Lucas had gone out first, spinning her mother a line about Lucas preferring a couple of pints with his workmates before she arrived – and that she'd join him a few hours later in the clubhouse.

"Oh yes?" Her mother wasn't fooled – had never disguised the wary contempt she felt for her son-in-law – but eventually she went to bed and Cora let herself out of the back door sometime around ten o'clock.

For a long time she kept out of sight, lying low in the shadows of the churchyard for the pubs to empty and curtains to be drawn. No one, absolutely no one, must see her. Perhaps she'd dozed off a little, huddled with her back to a gravestone, because she'd jolted awake to find the night inky black and her limbs stiff with cold. She looked at her watch – it was gone midnight.

The track down to the mill was off the public footpath and unknown to anyone aside from the locals; and most of those wouldn't venture into Carrions Wood even in daylight. There was an unearthly stillness in what was ancient woodland, reputedly planted on top of an Anglo-Saxon burial ground. Birds didn't nest in the trees here, apart from a few rooks, and even those who liked to put traps down for rabbits complained there were never any takers. No signs, in fact, of life. At midnight the light was an ethereal blue, the only sound her own breathing as she tramped further and further in. After every half dozen footsteps she stopped to scan the myriad of tree trunks on either side, then behind, doing a three hundred and sixty degree reconnaissance before continuing; until eventually there came the unmistakeable sound of rushing water. Not far now. Once the mill was in view she darted off the path and hunkered down under the protection of a large oak. *Now let's see what the old devil gets up to…*

History had it that a miller had beaten his wife to death here and now it was haunted. Various tenants had come and gone but there had been no buyer, so by the time it lay in ruins Lucas had been able to purchase it for a song. Word spread that he planned to turn it into an idyllic retreat and sell it to a Londoner for a fortune;

but that was four years ago now and not a single improvement had been made. In fact, part of the roof had caved in, one of the ceilings downstairs was propped up with an old tree trunk, and several window panes were missing.

So that was another lie she'd bought into. Every time she'd asked about the mill, though, it ignited the rage in him that never seemed far from the surface. Not for the first time she asked herself just who she had really married at Doncaster Register Office all those years ago. She'd been a sixteen year old virgin with no qualifications and he was a well-paid miner with a sharkish grin and wandering hands. *Stupid, stupid, stupid…* With no preparation for the sadistic, painful sex she would subsequently be subjected to, not to mention the perversions, the trap had been set and dressed in a catalogue bridal gown she'd walked right in. Wherever possible she avoided his sexual attentions these days – not that it mattered anymore because clearly he was being satisfied elsewhere, which was, quite frankly, absolutely fine as long as it wasn't herself.

She should have vanished the night she followed him and found out just who and what he really was: the lost opportunity would haunt her for the rest of her life. But the chance had come and the chance had gone. *Where would she go?* He'd find her, seek her out and make her pay like others had paid. You didn't hitch your wagon to a man like Lucas Dean and ever expect to be able to unhitch it again. The man was capable of inflicting the most unimaginable torture on someone who crossed him, but like most of the horrors revealed to her that night, the realisation came way too late.

In the end it was a three hour wait and she'd been about to give up and go home. If Lucas wasn't going to turn up he might get back before her and there would be hell to pay. Indecision pulled her both ways. But then just before 3 am, a line of black robed figures emerged from a forest swathed in dawn mist, and silently entered the mill.

Cora's eyes widened as she counted – ten, eleven, twelve, thirteen of them, gliding across the ground like spectres.

Once they'd disappeared inside she took off her shoes and hid them inside the roots of the tree, then keeping low, skirted around the periphery of the trees before scooting over to the rear of the building and skulking into its shadows. Her heart was thumping hard in her chest by the time she slid down beneath a window to catch her breath. Again her ears strained to hear anyone but there was nothing other than the cascading water, so after a few more minutes, slowly and carefully, she stood up and peered inside.

The filthy window pane was jagged and broken, providing a clear view into what was quite definitely an empty room. From the centre of the ceiling a wire hung down and bare floorboards, illuminated by slivers of moonlight, were clearly rotting. Puzzled by where the group could have gone, she crept around to the side of the mill. Not a glimmer of light broke the gloom here; the ancient ivy roots so thick, gnarled and twisted they'd cracked the mortar and pulled away stones.

Partially hidden by the creepers there was a side door. *They'd gone in that way, they must have done...*Cora peeped through the keyhole half expecting to meet with another eye, but was met instead by the ghostly interior of a large farmhouse-style kitchen, with a range, a stand-alone cooker, and the outline of a butler's sink with a cupboard underneath it. She nudged the door and surprisingly it opened without so much as a squeak. Hovering in the doorway for several minutes she waited, shivering and listening, scanning the full radius, checking over her shoulder again and again...

Then she stepped inside.

With her back to the wall, ready to run out at the drop of a hairpin, she inched further and further into the building. *Jesus Christ, where had they gone?* The air was icy, the atmosphere brooding and oppressive. Again she checked over her shoulder, convinced there were eyes on her, stopping after every couple of steps; until something caught her attention. Riveted to the spot her ears strained to hear. Yes, there it was...definitely...the low hum of chanting. *Coming from underground?*

On tiptoes she flew across the flagstones towards the arched hallway and the cellar door. *Were they down there, then?*

She hesitated: this was seriously dangerous. If she went down those steps there was a distinct and very real possibility she'd never come back up again. *Surely though, surely he wouldn't kill his own wife? He'd threaten her, hurt her badly, but as the mother of his kids she was his veneer of respectability.* Something, she thought later, must have instilled her with enough courage though, because in the end she had pushed open the heavy wooden door and gone down.

With each cautious step the air became ever colder, and the darkness intensified until it was impossible to see anything at all. Finally at the bottom, she groped blindly for a wall to flatten her back to, happening on an iron hook that dug into her spine. There was a key on it. Instinctively she slipped it into her pocket while her eyes adjusted to the darkness. The chanting was louder now and in the far distance firelight flickered in a corridor arched with stone – enough to decipher the vague outline of a vast water wheel; a great dinosaur that creaked and groaned with rust and age. She looked back at the way she'd come. It was coalface black and the floor beneath her bare feet was slippery with damp. *Could she run if she had to*? The lure though, of wanting and needing to see for herself, in the end, proved irresistible.

Using the wheel to feel her way across the room, she ventured closer to the flames; padding silently down the passageway under archway after archway towards a chanting that was beginning to escalate, the words indecipherable like nothing she'd ever heard or could try to describe later. She looked at her watch but it was impossible to see the time, guessing that maybe an hour or so must have passed since she'd left the relative safety of the woods. The smell of smoke and incense was stronger now, and there was something else too….something disgusting like a sewer…although strangely sweet. Only a few more yards to go…

Then all at once it was there in front – what she had craved to know. Cora pressed her back to the wall and peered around the corner into what was a huge, dark cavernous room. And almost vomited in shock.

The scene turned out to be nothing like anything she could ever have prepared for; any expectation of a witches' circle or a pagan ritual being instantly erased. Set against the far wall stood an altar draped in dark cloth and adorned with stinking, black waxy candles that flickered, oozed and spat, their mustardy light licking the dripping chamber with lunging shadows; and above the alter hung an upside down cross. Her horrified stare quickly took in a trestle table set with goblets of dark liquid, together with plates weighed down with food – no doubt for a feast later – and a powerful, musty incense smoked in the air, drugging the senses.

The whole atmosphere fizzed with frenzied anticipation, and fear gripped her stomach. In the centre of the cave the robed figures had formed a circle, at their head a man in a goat-headed mask wearing a cloak of feathers and fur. The chanting now was much more guttural and becoming louder by the second as they whipped themselves up into a crescendo of excitement. The energy was palpable and her eyes widened and kept on widening as they began to dance around like savages and howl like wolves…

Oh dear God there was something live in the middle of the floor.

Mesmerised and unable to move she watched stricken. The thing in the middle had been bound in ropes and was thrashing around inside a sack, squealing like a stuck pig. Then without warning the howling ceased and they all turned to face the bestial figure at the head of the circle. An inhuman roar tore from his throat as he raised a knife above his head and lunged towards the creature in the middle, plunging the blade into the writhing, screaming flesh.

She must have gasped out loud or even screamed because one of the hooded figures shot a look over his shoulder. She slammed a hand over her mouth. *She was in the dark and he in the glare of torch light so he couldn't possibly see her…he couldn't!*

But it was in that split moment her world tipped on its axis and the full impact of what was happening in this small village truly hit her. The unusual cut of the man's jutting jaw combined with the bend of his once broken nose gave him away. *God in heaven please help us all.* There was nothing she could do about this now or ever. Nothing. A drinking buddy of Lucas' for years, Ernest Scutts was in the sodding police force. It was time to run like hell.

For the rest of that night and every one subsequently, she would lie awake staring into the darkness wondering what to do. Any escape route she might choose was fraught with danger. Losing the children to him and the physical fear wasn't the worst of it, though – it was the strange things that had happened to people who crossed him. It had been all too easy to overlook individual instances, but piece them together and a disturbing pattern emerged – first there'd been a bloke up at the mine who'd challenged him about fire damp and shortly afterwards been fatally electrocuted using machinery he operated every day. Another man had confronted him over an incident involving his wife, and a row had erupted. A week later his teenage son had been struck blind in the classroom. Out of the blue. No reason. No warning.

Each event taken in isolation could have been put down to bad luck, but the coincidences, now she started thinking about it, were stacking up. She began to count them.

***

When Cora reached the mine, there were ambulances, fire engines and police cars everywhere. A huddle of women turned to glare at her as she stood on the fringes, watching as Lucas helped with stretchers and gave interviews to the local radio station. They'd been mining a deeper seam than normal. It must have been a gas build-up due to ventilation failing, he was saying. Heavy electrical equipment was being used and it was almost the end of the shift. Tragic. He shook his head. *Tragic.*

Cora, standing on an embankment at the edge of the yard, met his pale blue gaze over the top of people's heads as he spoke. Inside he'd be laughing. He'd shut them up, hadn't he? Someone

44

must have been talking about him and the missing gypsy girl, and he'd shut them up. Just like he always did.

***

Chapter Six

Sunday 27th December, 2015

Celeste heaved herself into the back of the waiting taxi, resolutely refusing to look back at Drummersgate as they trundled away down the drive. The depressingly austere image of a gothic prison façade would be what she'd see – not the modern day L-shaped brick unit it now was. Out here on the wind-flattened moors, well away from the towns, those prisoners would have been left to rot or hang, and their rabid fear was still imprinted in the atmosphere. No wonder Ruby suffered such torment.

Glancing neither left nor right as the taxi driver waited for the electric gates to open, she shuddered inwardly. That Ruby held the key to the horrors going on in Woodsend, there was little doubt. The problem was, someone had to be either naïve enough or brave enough to open the door to her mind; and after what had happened to herself and her husband Gerry, not to mention a few well-meaning medical staff… 'Well, you'd have to want your head looking at for even setting foot in that village! Still, there was a little girl in the midst of it apparently – was she the one about to be baptised? Did Ruby mean by the Satanic sect? Oh Lord, what to do?'

Ruby had actually been quite calm when she'd talked about living in the old mill; despite being haunted by ghostly apparitions and physically attacked with nips and pinches, having the bedclothes pulled off and her name hissed nastily when she lay sleeping - so she was tougher than she looked. But the second the conversation strayed onto her childhood, that's when her character began switching in and out of different personas – that's where it became far more than supernatural torment, crossing the line into both mental and sometimes physical illness.

It was also pretty alarming to observe.

No, all that psychological damage was far beyond her own personal remit; she would never take Ruby down the path of seeing what had really happened to her as a child – not ever. The day Ruby had asked her to read her cards was not a day she would wish to repeat. Frankly, there are some things a person just shouldn't know.

As Noel had reasonably explained, she herself was in possession of a rational mind, whereas Ruby was coping with a fragmented personality on top of a clairvoyance she couldn't control. Imagine the fear of being mediumistic but not in the driving seat when the spirit arrived! Who could step in to possess you?

She didn't believe in the devil as an individual entity, but most certainly she'd had first-hand experience of a dark energy hell-bent on destroying humanity; and frankly it was the only thing that scared her because it did real harm. That people raised it out of bravado, ignorance, or a mean desire to hold power over others she had no doubt; that it used these people as a gateway and progressed to channel fear and destruction through them she also had no doubt; by which time, of course, those concerned would have no say in what happened afterwards because it would be far too late. By definition then, the mentally ill must surely be perfect instruments? She frowned. No wonder the evil entity inside Ruby had chosen psychiatrists to attach itself to.

At least the spiritual part of things she *could* help Ruby with: she could teach her how to shut down unwanted psychic visits and protect herself; and they had, in fairness, made a start on that. Hopefully Ruby now felt less alone with her torment and was reassured that it wasn't simply her own madness. Again, her heart went out to the girl. What a journey some poor souls had on this earth. She'd been lucky really – married for love, been relatively safe and content, had a normal childhood on a sprawling estate on the edge of Doncaster. Not privileged in any way, but certainly not abused, or terrified of her own father.

But here was the next question: was there anyone she either could or should talk to about what she'd learned today? What about Becky – the one member of the original team left standing? Ought she go and see her?

As the taxi sped over the moors, Celeste popped a toffee into her mouth and clipped her handbag shut again. She chewed and closed her eyes. She was far too old to go opening up this box of horrors, but who else was going to do it? She was here on this earth for a reason and had been given the gift of mediumship by spirit – this was her task and she had to face up to it.

All at once the life force seemed to drain away from her. It was often the way after using a lot of psychic energy; there were so many lost souls in that prison – such a negative, depressing and angry atmosphere. Fancy building a psychiatric unit on top of it! That was the thing – very few people today would even listen to what they'd describe as 'mumbo-jumbo' or 'nonsense'. So now here were some of the most disturbed and vulnerable people on earth housed on top of a prison where terrified men had been hanged and others had lain dying from disease. And poor Ruby relived that suffering every single night.

At least she could take some comfort from knowing she'd helped her a little today. Many mocked all she did and all she stood for; a fact repeatedly borne out by the sceptics who attended her classes just for a laugh. But if they were worn down on a constant basis like Ruby was she'd take a bet they too would use prayer and white light and whatever else they could lay their hands on. In her experience few believed in the dark side until it was way too late, anyway.

Some people swore by black tourmalines to ward off bad spirits, or smudging white heather through every room, burning sage, or ritual psychic cleansing. She'd used them all in her time. It probably wouldn't be allowed in Drummersgate though, or she'd be accused of witchery, but if she could, she'd advise Ruby to use the whole lot: sometimes it was the power of taking an element of control, of faith, and stoking up positive energy – maybe that's how these things worked? Celeste's mind wandered on…at least the doctor in charge of Riber Ward, Claire Airy, was happy for her to visit, so that was one less obstacle. Claire was apparently also against the use of heavy sedatives. All good. Maybe she'd take Ruby some crystals next time she visited then – a black tourmaline or some shattuckite, which would help protect her from possession.

An unbidden image suddenly shot into her mind's eye and she sighed with annoyance… *Darn it! Even now it wasn't always controllable…* A blonde lady was being shown to her: a young woman with alabaster skin so translucent that a map of blue veins could be seen underneath it. She was lying on a bed, staring dull-eyed at a barred window. The woman's intense fear and loneliness was washing over her to the point of overwhelming sadness; the anguish transmitting itself directly into Celeste's heart, wringing out a surge of despair as the drip, drip, drip of tears crawled down the woman's cheek, trickling into her hair; tears she couldn't wipe away because her hands, it seemed, were tethered. And so she lay, unable to do a simple thing like brushing away her own misery. Hopelessness lay heavily on Celeste and she hung her head… *Oh it was like the flu…like being a rag doll…* Inwardly she called for help from her spirit guides but the air had become soupy and static and no words formed in her mind. Something was coming… Nausea rose upwards from the pit of her stomach like travel sickness. She kept her head still, hoping not to have to stop the taxi driver.

He glanced into the rear-view mirror. "You all right, duck? Want the window down?"

She nodded, lying back against the seat and breathing through her nose, concentrating totally on not being sick; when suddenly a diabolical face reared directly into hers – a red-eyed girl with lank hair and dead-white skin running with sores.

Her heart jolted and she shut her eyes tightly in an effort to regain her composure. C*lose down… close down…okay, okay…it's all okay…*

A moment later the air cleared, leaving just the sonorous hum of the car's wheels resonating into her spine, the countryside flashing past as it had before. *Oh it would sure be nice if these things stopped happening, it really would. Especially when nothing seemed linked. What on earth was that all about? Someone wanted to tell her something, anyway.*

The taxi began its descent from the moors and the driver leaned forwards to switch on the radio. Apparently a young girl reported as 'at risk' in the Bridesmoor area where a police detective had recently gone missing after a car accident, had now been accounted for and was safe and well. Police were satisfied there was no link between the two events and the case was now closed. Celeste closed her eyes.

Lies….

There were links here but she was missing them. That officer was lying in hospital – the one Becky was with. And wasn't the little girl they were talking about, Ruby's daughter? No, the case could not be closed. But what could she do?

You need to talk to Becky.

Yes, yes… Celeste nodded to herself, aware she was twisting her handkerchief into ever tighter knots. She popped another toffee into her mouth. Talking to Becky was now imperative if they were to piece things together.

Time…time running out…

Yes, yes…

Ruby. Ruby's boyfriend, Jes… Why would he keep coming back to a village his mother wouldn't set foot in ever again? What had happened to his mother? How exactly had he managed to meet Ruby when no one in the area knew her? And where was this man now? Maybe he could fill in some of the blanks?

Think, think… She cast her mind back to that day she'd gone to Tanners Dell to find Ruby – what had it been, seven or eight years ago now? The whole place had brooded with a menace so cold and merciless it crushed her with its weight the second she walked in. It had been difficult to draw breath as she walked upstairs calling Ruby's name; a feeling of impending doom building with every step. She'd had to fly downstairs and out into the fresh air after only a few minutes; the sickness staying with her for days afterwards.

Ruby had described floating entities in long cloaks, which lurked in the darkened corridors. Some had red-eyed dogs with them, others swung long sticks or clubs and threatened to kill her. Ghosts didn't deliberately frighten people – although unwittingly they did if they wished to draw attention to their plight. No, this was demonic activity without a doubt. The whole place was riddled with bad energy – probably from dabbling with the dark arts. Reluctant as she had been to conduct research into Satanism – because even showing an interest in such things could result in the door being opened to demonic forces in the same way as using a Ouija board, particularly for one such as herself. She'd forced herself to find out more in order to see what they were up against. It hadn't made for easy reading and having the books on her shelves didn't sit well with her either; but she'd persevered. One of the biggest shocks though, had been that these things were still practised all over the world – often under the guise of respectability – and generally speaking a blind eye was turned.

The rites involved invoking dark spirits, and the people who carried them out believed, truly believed, doing so would give them superhuman power over others, notably their enemies or rivals. In the main however, they relished the actual rituals – getting thrilling kicks out of letting blood from terrified animal or human sacrifices; from having violent, sadistic sex; raping their victims, inflicting excruciating pain and feeding off the fear. But most of all they really believed the rites gave them magical powers, especially if they harnessed all that energy in one place at the same time. Sleep paralysis, known as a night crusher, was one of the nasty curses they liked to inflict on a victim; another was interminable black depression, a poisoning of the soul and withering of the mind – otherwise referred to as insanity. Psychic attacks most often occurred in a person's dreams, leaving them sleep deprived and terrified out of their wits. Another was blindness. Add in some poisonous herbs and it wouldn't be long before an arch enemy would either capitulate or take their own life.

The scene Ruby had described, of an old woman peeling skin off babies in the bath in order to cut out the fat, was also borne out in various satanic practices. Baby fat was mixed with ash to fashion candles for a black mass. Urine, or well water in which babies or infants had been drowned, was used instead of holy water, and the wine used in communion was sacrificial blood. The entire thing was diabolical beyond belief and the images she had seen as she researched the subject would now stay with her forever. Those books she had burned, their very presence in the house serving only to taunt… *We're here now…you can't ever turn back the clock…we're here…*

How could you prove this kind of thing existed on your doorstep, though, when you were a medium and the only other person who knew about it had been sectioned? Quite simply there was no evidence, and Ruby could easily be accused of having false memory syndrome – that's what a clever lawyer hired by someone like Paul Dean would say, and most people would agree. In fact, the said clever lawyer could be recruited from the sect itself. Many satanic worshippers were professionals, the kind of people who held great sway over others and who no one would ever suspect. And once sworn in to a satanic cult, there had to be something extremely serious to ally them into the group forever, such as murder. Once in, always in. It was also possible the whole village knew, or had a strong suspicion about what was going on, but kept the secret for fear of what might happen to them or their families.

This girl had escaped though, hadn't she? Insane, drugged and lost until recently, Ruby was now the most dangerous adversary this satanic sect had ever had. Somehow she had protected herself for all those years with that whatever it was Noel had said she'd got. Dissociative something? By whatever means, Ruby had saved her soul and kept it glittering and pure. Clever girl. Because in the end that was all that mattered and that was all the detestable inhuman darkness wanted to defile – our pure, clean souls.

Celeste crossed herself as the taxi passed the local church, from which people were streaming out from the Sunday afternoon service. However, Ruby was in a weak position, so in reality the only two people, since the police had apparently closed the case, who could save Alice from her fate, were herself and Becky.

***

Chapter Seven

After Sergeant Hall had left, Becky sat with Callum for several more hours. *Would he ever wake up? What if he didn't?*

It would be just her luck after all those years of being without him, to have him back and feel all the lights on again inside, only for them to be snuffed out once more. There wouldn't be any point really, in going on.

No, she couldn't and mustn't think that way – this was just his body's way of recovering from a terrible ordeal. He would surface any day now. He would! She held his hand, turning it over and over in her own, wondering if he could hear her voice. Apparently the last thing to go and the first to come back was the hearing. It was worth a try.

She took a deep breath. "Callum, I want to tell you some things. I suspect you went off to Woodsend that night on your own because you thought I was excluding you and maybe, oh I don't know, maybe some bad memories were being stirred up? I wish you hadn't but... well anyway, if you can hear me I need you to know that Noel is just a colleague. Actually he's gay, if you must know. But I was ill that night and had been for weeks. I didn't want to tell you just how ill or what was happening in case you freaked out on me, and after all the time we'd been apart because of a misunderstanding I didn't want you flouncing off again. Sorry, I know you don't flounce." She smiled sadly, knowing that if he could respond he'd object at being accused of such a thing. "Look, I didn't want to lose you again, okay? And I had some horrible, off-the-wall stuff to deal with."

She stopped. Outside the wind was whipping up and dead leaves swirled around the windows. Callum's chest rose and fell with each oxygen-assisted breath. Should she tell him about the hallucinations she'd had, and the church visit? After all, he knew nothing of it. He'd spent the week trying to escape from an underground prison by the looks of it and almost lost his life. What truck would he have with the supernatural? Although, to be fair he'd had experience of it once…Okay, it would be best to tell him.

"Right. Look, now I'm going to tell you some things you're going to have a hard time dealing with, but we go back a long way and I'm asking you to trust me on this. Deep breath…okay, well I asked Noel to take me to a church that night because I'd had some disturbing things happen to me following my accident, and after the meeting with Kristy it hit home that the same thing might be happening to me as it did to Jack McGowan, and I was scared to death… See I told you it was a difficult one…anyway, we prayed all night in that church and afterwards I collapsed. But I was well again. Oh God, Callum, I didn't want you to have to see me like that. Please understand!

"Anyway, I stayed with Noel in his spare room until I felt better: I couldn't face going back home and having to explain things to Mark. I just couldn't cope with all that rowing and stuff. To be honest, I put Noel through a lot and he risked his professional standing to help me. He's a good mate. The best."

She traced a pattern on the back of Callum's hand, running a finger down the forked vein that bulged from the cannula.

"I asked about you every day, you know, until they found you."

Tears surged hotly and she wiped them away.

"Stay with me."

Another gust of wind buffeted the windows. "I wish you'd wake up and tell me what you saw. Why on earth did you go out there on your own at that time? Did you come across the Deans? Paul Dean? My guess is you got too close and discovered something or recognised someone; and now you've been stopped. It sounds barmy, doesn't it? Somehow they do that, though – something nasty happens to anyone trying to investigate Woodsend; and the worst part is that the police have just closed the case. According to them you had a car accident and Alice is safely with her loving parents. Did you hear Sergeant Hall say that? Bloody unbelievable!"

She gazed out at a row of trees lining the car park like soldiers at the far end of the field. Skeletal branches forked against a stormy sky boiling with angry clouds, and a low whistle sounded through the vents.

"Do you believe in evil, Callum? That an inhuman intelligence can be raised to destroy us? Sounds nuts, doesn't it? And here's the really clever bit - the part *they* like the best – you can't tell society what's happening to you because if you say you're being possessed or psychically attacked you're going to get locked up for being a lunatic. And so it goes on - they're still at it. Not that I know how they do this to us. All I know for sure is that I'm the only person left who's onto them, and the only one who can get Alice out of there, because what happened to Ruby is absolutely sodding real and I'm determined it's not going to happen to her daughter as well.

"Thing is though – it means a trip to Woodsend on my own: I can't even tell the police because…" A twitch of Callum's hand caused her to stop speaking for a moment. "Callum?"

But he made no further movements and it seemed, depressingly, as if it had just been a nerve jumping around.

She stroked his forehead. "I'm not happy there's a little girl out there at the Deans' place. And I'm not convinced you had a car accident either. I've got to do something. No one else is going to."

Again a twitch of his hand. His eyelashes fluttered.

"Your children will be in later, I hope. They've been told you're here. Anyway, I've got to make a couple of calls now so you can reflect on just how bonkers your own private mental health nurse is! Oh, by the way, you should know that Mark has filed for divorce, which I'm fine about. I just feel sorry, really sorry, that you and I didn't get to spend our lives together, and I put him through some pain. I didn't mean to you know? But in the end you can't force yourself to love someone, can you?"

Leaning over, she kissed Callum's cheek. "Please come back to me."

She stared into his face for several intense seconds. If only his eyes would open and he'd smile that wide smile of his. If only she wasn't so alone. "I'll be back tonight, don't worry."

***

Outside in the car park the winter wind was icy, blowing people across the tarmac and snatching at litter. Becky hurried towards the bus stop, checking her mobile as she walked. There was a message from Noel, and also one from Celeste. It would be best to call them back en-route.

With the bus full, though, that proved awkward. It didn't seem to bother other people, who cheerfully discussed their most private affairs in public, but this was somewhat different. With the mobile clamped to one ear and a finger in the other, she strained to hear what Noel was saying – it sounded like he was speaking from the ocean floor.

"I can't really talk, but how did it go with Celeste?"

"Really well. Ruby seems happier, anyway."

"Oh, that's good, then."

"Same can't be said for our little trainee!?"

"Why? What's happened?"

"Now if I tell you, promise you won't freak!"

"Noel!"

"Okay, well Emily said Ruby was telling Celeste she could hear and see men being hanged in the yard and it was making her ill. Now this place did used to be a prison, Becky, and maybe Ruby knew that and was trying it on? Or maybe she's trying to spook the other patients, I don't know."

"Or she could really be clairvoyant? I knew she was suffering with something!"

"Well, I can't see Dr Hardy swallowing that one, can you? Anyway, Ruby's calmed down a bit now she's seen Celeste, so whatever Celeste did was all good."

"Yes, I think Celeste should be allowed to visit again. We don't have to tell Isaac she's a medium or he'll be the one to freak. I just think we should do whatever helps her, don't you? Claire will agree with me, I know she will. Anyway, apparently it's quite common for people with DID to be psychic. Did you know that?"

Uncomfortably aware that the other people on the bus had gone quiet; Becky dropped her voice to a whisper. "I can't really talk. Was there anything else?"

"Yes. Emily said Ruby had mentioned a satanic baptism, that 'she' would be thirteen soon; and that 'he' knows but they've paralysed him – although she didn't say who."

"Pardon? Do you think she means Callum? Oh my God! Paralysed?"

"Don't go freaking on me! We're talking Ruby here!"

"Sorry Noel, but I'm afraid I believe in Ruby. She's not been wrong yet."

"Oh, I wish I hadn't told you now, I really do. I'm up to my neck in it here."

"Is everything else okay?" she asked, trying to keep her voice steady.

"Only just – we're hanging by a thread. So how is he? Callum?"

"Still unconscious. He was talking when he was picked up but now he's just out for the count and he's not even sedated."

"He'll come round. It's only been a couple of days and he was missing for a week! He's in the best place. Try to keep calm, Becks. What are you doing now?"

"I'm on my way to Woodsend," she hissed, with her hand partly over her mouth. "They've stopped the investigation and I want to see what I'm up against."

"Oh my good God! Do you really think that's wise? What do you think you'll achieve doing that? Look at what's happened to everyone who's been there and one of them a big hairy-arsed detective! I don't believe I'm hearing this, Becky."

"I'm just going to return Celeste's call, and then have a look round while I'm out that way. I want the case re-opened and I want to find Alice."

"Closed the case? I didn't know that. Are you serious?"

"Listen, Noel, I'll call you later. I promise I won't do anything other than have a walk around. I want to be back here before it gets dark anyway. I'm not leaving Callum overnight."

"I'm not happy about this."

"No, neither am I. But there really is only me left and if I don't do something this will go on and on. Anyway, I really can't talk here so I'll ring you when I'm on the bus back, okay? Then you'll know I'm safe."

She ended the call, then rang Celeste.

"No!" Celeste shrieked. "You mustn't go on your own." She sounded out of breath. "Just a minute, love, I'm walking up to the front door. I've been to see Ruby like you said. Look, Becky, listen to me – don't go on your own. Don't go near that old mill in Bridesmoor, and do you hear me, don't go talking to the Deans either. You don't know what you're dealing with. "

"Actually, I think I do."

"Who's the pretty lady in hospital? White skin? Blonde hair? Kay?"

"Erm…blimey…it could be Kristy Silver. Why?"

"She needs your help. Badly. Urgently. There's a link here, I'm sure. The nurse in charge there – I think you know her?"

Taken aback, Becky nodded. "Um, Nora, yes."

"Where are you now?"

"On the bus. I'm getting off at The Druid Inn. Why?"

"Oh no, you mustn't. Look Becky, I live in Cloudside. You'll pass it on your way. Please, trust me – get off a stop early and come to see me instead. At least hear me out first, because there are things you need to know – I'm piecing things together, you see; and you must never go there alone. There has to be someone you can trust who would go with you!"

Becky sighed. The bus was already climbing up The Old Coach Road towards Bridesmoor. A peevish rain spattered across the windows, the moors stretching out for mile after sodden mile on either side. It might not be a bad idea to be armed with more information, but who on earth could go with her? Celeste wasn't young or fit enough by the sound of it, although she'd never met her. Who then? Noel wouldn't get the same days off. Ideally a level headed male – someone to square up to the Deans if they appeared...and then a name popped into her head. What about Toby Harbour? Question was though, would he go against his superiors and keep the visit to himself?

"Well yours would be the next stop," Becky found herself saying as she reached for her bag. "Bit of a hike from up here but—"

"Good, I'll put the kettle on. See you in ten."

***

Becky stepped off the bus at the highest point on Bridgestone Moor. Ahead the pithead wheel dominated the landscape like a blackened scarecrow, and to the left lay a barren expanse of moorland between the mine and Cloudside Village. If she'd taken the bus directly there she wouldn't have to do this, but it was only a mile or so out of her way and Celeste had been pretty adamant. Resigned to a blustery walk, she put her head down against the prevailing wind and began to tramp down the muddy lane. There wasn't another soul in sight.

The pit had been dead now for about twenty years or so, being one of the last South Yorkshire mines to close. There were mixed feelings. Some were angry at the loss of a good income, others relieved because Bridesmoor had an unusually high mortality rate. The stories went along the lines that you could hear the souls of dead miners trapped underground, howling in the wind. And some people had seen, usually when falling out of The Highwayman or The Druids Inn, grey figures covered in soot, stumbling across the moorland with hands outstretched. Becky smiled. Everyone loved a good ghost story. Sadly though, the mortality figures were not borne out of imagination but were

60

weighted in fact. There had been more men electrocuted or trapped following gas explosions here than anywhere else in the country, along with the highest rate of widowhood and fatherless children.

On a whim she turned to look down over Bridesmoor village, and with the wind behind her stood for a moment imagining what it might be like to live there. It looked like the end of the earth. You could see the whole village from up here – a sprawling estate of bungalows, a few rows of terraces, and a small church at the end just as the houses petered out and the woods began. Was that it? She screwed up her eyes, trying to work out where the old mill might be, concluding that as a water mill it must be somewhere in the trees at the bottom of the village near the river. Hmm…there were woods to the east and the west of it too. Well concealed.

A sudden sharp gust almost lifted her off her feet and she gasped, bending double in the face of it as she whirled around. A belt of sleety rain slashed into her face and with cold, wet fingers it was a struggle to get her umbrella up. *Flaming hell!*

Then out of nowhere, with the wind blasting in her ears as she wrestled with an inside out umbrella, a black Nissan truck suddenly roared down the lane and almost knocked her down. In an effort to save herself she toppled into the dry stone wall, ripping her coat and skinning her elbow. *What the…?*

She looked up just in time to see the vehicle vanish over the horizon.

Charming - fancy not even stopping to see if she was okay!

Slightly tearful at the pain now searing through her ankle, and hobbling a little, her mind flitted back to the second the truck had passed. *Now that was odd. No, really odd.* A shiver crept up her spine.

Splattered in mud, it either had blackened windows or no driver.

***

Chapter Eight

Bridesmoor, October 1972

Rosella's eyes slowly adjusted to the light. She blinked repeatedly, turning her head very slowly to face the window. *Oh, back here again then…with the sound of rushing water…had she given birth? Why wasn't she in the cave anymore?*

It looked like the kind of late afternoon you'd light bonfires and rake leaves: darkly golden with fog coiling around copper-tinged tree tops. The air smelled smoky and damp, like autumn was setting in. It could be October, she thought, or even early November? That would be at least four months, then. And no one had come for her.

The mattress underneath was itchy and stank of body odour – or was that herself? And her hair crawled with what felt like thousands of lice. She scratched furiously at her scalp, drawing blood until the pain negated the torment, before sinking once more into dreams. When she opened her eyes again it was night.

God, what the hell was in those evil potions?

An owl's hoot was echoing around the woods, and a full moon illuminated what was a crisp, clear night studded with stars. She tried to shift onto her side in order to ease the throbbing, smarting pain of bed sores, grimacing as sickeningly familiar stomach cramps gripped her body yet again. Each one shook her in a hot wave of colic, leaving her wrung out and panting, tears streaming, bile burning her throat. What in hell's name did the bastards give her to make her feel like this? *No point in calling out. It would be better if she died. No one was going to find her, anyway.*

The next time she woke, the indigo sky had misted into an ethereal grey, enveloping the room in a tomb of shadows. This was the worst time - between three and four in the morning – and she immediately closed her eyes again, praying for an escape that wouldn't come – it never did. The huge wooden wardrobe in the corner loomed over where she lay staring at it, fixated on its lock and key. Any moment now and that key would turn and the door would creak open just like it always did. And there she'd be – that wild-eyed woman in the apron cowering amongst the coats with half of her face bashed in, claw hands snatching at the air in an effort to get out of her prison. It was just a dream, a drug-induced nightmare, of that she was sure. All the same... She kept her eyes fixed on it.

Please God no more...

Gradually, insidiously, moonlight permeated the veil of fog, glinting on the wardrobe mirror as it held Rosella's full attention, her eyes firmly fixed on the lock - waiting for the click. The key turned by an invisible hand.

'*Rosella...Rosella*'... Something brushed against her hair.

She flinched, nervously scanning the room. *Who or what was there?* Suddenly a giant spider the size of tumbleweed scuttled up the wall and then fell onto her head. She swiped it off, scrambling this way and that on the mattress to get away from it. *It wasn't really there. It wasn't real...*

"Go away, go away," she said out loud. Pulling her legs up to her chest, she backed up as far as possible to the wall. "Go away!"

There had been no footsteps. There was no other person in the room. Wild-eyed she scrutinised the walls, the floor, and the doorway: no one. These were hallucinations. She was not mad, not mad, not mad...

She stopped dead. Withdrawal? Drug withdrawal? The thought struck her suddenly and with huge impact. *Not a single person had been to her this evening. At all.*

Why?

She lay listening intently. Apart from the rushing of water there were no sounds. Her legs were heavy and stiff but she found she could now move them. She wiggled her toes and flexed the muscles, then shuffled over to the window. A cool waft of air hit her face through the cracked pane. *Air. God, fresh air!* Her head throbbed but was clearer than normal too; more like a bad hangover than fighting the usual anaesthetic. Perhaps they had simply forgotten her tonight?

Peering into the darkness, the scene below was one of heavy woods pretty much on all sides, with just a small expanse of grass directly to the front of the building. It was like some kind of fortress. And so quiet; the trees shrouded in a white mist that seeped onto the lawn in a ghostly effluvium. And it was then, as she watched, that a file of darkly robed figures carrying torches emerged from the forest to glide across the grass and around the side of the building.

She jumped back. *That was 'them'!*

Crumpling onto the mattress into the smallest, tightest ball, she lay waiting and listening for footsteps to clunk up the stairs. Maybe they wanted her partly awake this time? Or someone would come up in a minute with a horrible cocktail. *Oh no, not again, please, please no…*

But no one came.

Time hissed on until eventually she unfurled herself and strained to hear over the rushing water. How odd. There was nothing.

Her hands felt again at the raised, lumpy scar on her tummy. Maybe she was pregnant again? What if she had given birth after all and a year had passed, and this was another one? That would explain it – if they weren't coming for her? Desperately she tried to focus: if she was pregnant again they wouldn't want to risk losing it, which meant the latest ritual could be done without her.

The impact hit her drugged brain with full force.

This was the time to get the hell out of here then! They were busy, weren't they?

She forced herself into a sitting position. Every bone in her emaciated body craved collapse: she could barely move let alone walk. And what about clothes? She looked over at the wardrobe. There were coats in there. *Oh God, no, not the damn wardrobe…*

She sat for a moment with her head between her knees, waiting for a wave of dizziness to wear off. The walls were collapsing inwards and the floorboards rising up to meet her. It would go in just a minute – the thing was to stay awake. *Just stay awake*…Once the feeling subsided she needed to try and stand.

She could do this…had to…there wouldn't be another chance.

Clasping the old rug around her, she pushed herself up to standing position and stumbled towards the ancient wardrobe, momentarily caught off guard by the sight of her reflection in its trio of mirrors: huge blackened eye sockets dominated a cadaverous white face that stared back in horror. She recoiled, legs trembling so violently they threatened to give way. Then with a deep breath she lifted her hand to turn the key…

Hesitated.

The woman in the apron might be there and grab you, pull you inside with her.

Don't look…just get on with it…

What if someone hears? If it creaks?

She held her breath, motionless for several long seconds, swaying to the sound of her own pulse and the endless rush of fresh water. There *was* something else too but a long way off…very faint and getting fainter, probably from below in that dungeon they took her to…a low murmur...chanting!

A spark of rage ignited deep inside: *They'd be high on it, the fuckers*. So there *was* a ceremony then! Just without her. Probably tonight some other poor, miserable victim would be strapped to a table writhing in agony while that horrible man twisted and turned a knife inside them. That face, when the goat's head mask had been removed, would be etched onto her brain for all eternity – those thin, bloodless lips and hooded yellow eyes that glittered with excitement the more she screamed; the lisping voice telling her she was a whore who enjoyed it.

Lunging for the key she opened up the wardrobe and flung back the doors, fighting down the rising panic. *Just grab a coat…don't look…just grab something and go…*

That was it. She had it. *Go….*

It was an old gabardine that stank of mothballs, but it would do. Still staring wide-eyed at the contents of the wardrobe, she quickly retreated, pulling the belt tightly around her waist as she backed away. Every step was like treading on a knife's blade as she turned around for the exit with arms outstretched. What if they had a look-out – someone posted downstairs to sound the alarm if intruders showed up?

The door to the landing creaked open, showing the faint outline of a stairwell – silvery shadows flickering across the walls, branches from trees scraping at the grimy windows. With her breath held tightly in her chest, she padded towards it, ignoring the ghostly whispers and hair-stroking from invisible hands.

'Rosella…Rosella…don't leave us…'

The tumbling brook was much louder now, each step of descent bringing freedom tantalisingly nearer. *Please God, please God.* All she had to do was get outside and then run like the wind. *Please…*

Every creak of the staircase sent fear shooting round her bloodstream, there being just enough moonlight to show cracks and missing boards as she picked her way down. Then finally she was downstairs, wild-eyed and frantic for an escape exit.

She glanced around, spying a door immediately to the right. The cellar, she thought, probably leading to the underground chamber where they held their disgusting ceremonies. Chanting echoed on the chill of a draught floating through the cracks in the walls – along with what sounded like wild dog grunting noises. Skirting past it she darted through the kitchen towards a side door and tried the handle.

Shit, it was locked. Of course it would be. Stepping back she searched for another way out. Later, much later, she would always wonder if there had been some kind of spiritual help in that moment and her prayers were answered, because her eye happened on a diamond glint, like sunlight on steel – a splintered window pane to the right of the door.

It was her best chance. Reaching up she pulled away the remaining panels of glass section by section, trying not to rip her skin and snag blood vessels as she worked. Blood streamed down her forearms but she kept on going until there was enough of a hole to climb through; and then scrambled out to freedom.

She landed awkwardly, but the ground was soft. High over the moor top, a full moon slipped in and out of the mist, illuminating a solid bank of trees to the rear. Clutching her stomach she half hobbled and half ran towards it; and only when protected by a cloak of darkness did she pause to get her bearings. Breathing was agonising, her senses swam and fatigue burned into her limbs. Shivering uncontrollably she looked for options: there were several dirt tracks and she picked one at random, racing down it as fast as possible, branches snapping into her face, until eventually it petered out. Which way now?

To the left and right was a steep lane. Ahead a soft haze lay over fields.

Which to take?

***

Chapter Nine

Sunday 27th December 2015
Cloudside Village

Celeste watched Becky half-walking, half-hobbling down the cul-de-sac towards her bungalow. She had her head down against the sharp wind and by the look of it there was mud splattered all over the side of her coat. On a summer's day it was a nice walk down the lane towards Cloudside across the moors, and even on a day like this it could be bracing with a stunning view on all sides; but Becky looked mithered, wet and irritable as she shouted into her mobile phone.

At the entrance to the driveway she stopped, clearly frustrated she couldn't hear whoever she was trying to talk to, and leaned against the garden wall to rub her leg. Celeste stood at the window watching. *Hmmm...interesting...* A murky black cloud had formed around Becky. Frowning, her head on one side, Celeste focused on the dark shape as it expanded before her eyes and deepened in intensity.

The whole scene developed over a couple of seconds and already Becky was hurrying down the drive with the black shape akin to a hunchback or a sack of coal attached to her. It was far too late, Celeste realised as she went to open the door - the phantom thing was going to sail straight into her house.

"I am so sorry, Celeste," Becky said, wiping her feet on the welcome mat. "I had a bit of an accident on the way over and..."

Celeste watched her porch dim several shades as if a hail storm was looming, followed by the shadow seemingly detaching itself from the host to sweep across the floor and into the hall – where it remained like a cloak laid down for a lady.

"What's the matter?" said Becky. "You look like you've seen a ghost, or perhaps I shouldn't say that, knowing what you do for a living?"

Celeste tried to smile, to pretend as she did so often, that she couldn't see what she could see. "Yes, love. And you look like you've been in the wars?"

Becky nodded, acknowledging her dirty coat. "Yes, this car came out of nowhere and knocked me into the verge. I'm okay, I just hurt my ankle and grazed my leg, but the driver didn't stop – I couldn't believe it! You'd think if you'd knocked someone down…. Anyway, there's no signal on my mobile either and I just wanted to call the hospital and ask if Callum was alright. I wanted to let him know I might be back a bit later than planned and not to worry. I'm daft really," she continued, as Celeste ushered her into the living room, "it's not like he's on planet earth yet, and here I am expecting him to worry what time I'll be back. He doesn't even know what day it is at the moment, bless him."

"Sit yourself down, love. Cup of tea?"

"Oh yes please, that would be really lovely."

"Just in case you're wondering – Gerry, my husband's in the bedroom at the back. He's on oxygen a lot of the time – chronic emphysema – so if you hear a hissing noise that's what it'll be. Did you get through on your mobile only…?" She indicated her landline.

"Yes, I think so. Thanks, though."

Celeste frowned. The whole room, normally bright and airy, had been tipped into a sepia half-light.

"Is everything all right, Celeste? Only I get the feeling…" She shivered.

The older lady shook her head. "Actually, Becky, I think you've unwittingly brought something unsavoury in with you. I'll get us that tea and we can talk. To be honest I don't think we've got much time."

Poor Becky had blanched visibly. That she'd once had a brush with the dark side was all too evident because she was obviously petrified it would happen again. You had to be brave to risk it again, she'd give her that; although what choice did either of them have? And herself an old lady with an invalid husband! 'They' – because it was 'they' – would probably see her off this time too, no doubt making sure her final hours would be spent alone and in terror just for the hell of it. Which left just Becky.

Becky took a sip of hot tea. "It's gone dark early." She glanced at her watch. "It's only half past two and we need the lights on. Is it rain coming, do you think? I'd best not leave it too late to get the bus back. At least I don't have to walk back across the moors – there's a bus route from the High Street, isn't there?"

Celeste listened to the non-stop nervous chatter as the light bulbs failed to light the room properly, and despite the cranking central heating pipes it wasn't warm either.

She pulled a cardigan on and turned up the gas fire. "Yes you can get a bus from outside the pub – it's two minutes' walk."

Silence sat between them for a moment.

Then she plunged in. "Becky, I'm sorry but we can't hang about. Look, the reason I asked you to come and see me is – and I know this sounds dramatic but I think you'll understand – well, time's running out, and you and I are the only ones left who know what's going on in Woodsend. We're very vulnerable. Your young man isn't going to wake up; that blonde lady will not survive; and a little girl is going to suffer immeasurably if we don't do something. Ruby mentioned a satanic baptism and I am pretty sure she was talking about Alice. But you know, or I assume you know, that *they* dabble with the black arts and that's what we're up against?"

Becky nodded. "Yes I do. I would never have believed any of it if I hadn't seen what happened to Jack McGowan, and experienced something similar myself. The problem is we've hit a brick wall – the investigation's been closed down. So what can we do?"

Celeste stirred her tea, frowning at the gas fire, which had remained blue and ineffective. "There are links, Becky, I'm sure of it but we'll have to work fast to put it together. Did you know Martha Kind came to see me before she died?"

Becky nodded. "Our lovely social worker? Yes."

"Well, I told her about a diary her predecessor kept and she went to ask the lady's husband for it and he gave it to her, which I had a feeling he would. Well, a day or so later Martha was dead. Now, I kept being shown that book and I think it's important. So… well," she leaned forwards, "someone's got it, you see? And I'm guessing because I keep getting an image of her, that it's the lady lying in hospital – with bars at the window. That's why I asked you who she might be."

Becky eyed her intently. "Well it does sound like Kristy, I have to say. But why would she have it? Do you think Martha sent it to her not knowing she was ill? Why do you think it's with Kristy?"

"I don't know. I just keep being shown the book. I have a spirit guide I trust implicitly and that's how I know. Like I said, I really need you to trust me on this."

"Hmm…well, I suppose Martha may have sent it to her because Kristy had called a meeting about all of this…" Becky shook her head. "Sorry, let me explain – Kristy's a lead psychiatrist specialising in Dissociative Identity Disorder. She had a patient with a very similar history to Ruby and that's how we all linked up. She tried to help Jack too…oh, and she'd been asking questions in Woodsend."

Celeste nodded. "She was stopped. They stopped her. Are you going to go and see Kristy? Were you close?"

"Not close no, but I was going to go. I think she's on her own in the world."

"Yes, go and see her. But hurry. They're protecting her."

"How? I don't understand! How do they do it? I mean, I understand someone trying to mow me down because they think I'm onto them, and I even understand people conducting cruel ceremonies because they get off on it. Horribly, I even get the child abuse part because there are some lousy, evil people in the world. But what I don't understand one bit is this dark madness inflicted on us from a distance. I don't get the power over someone lying in a hospital bed, or how the shape shifting out of shadows happens? How do they infect your dreams and send you mad?"

"A lot of what they do will be very human and very culpable. They'll use drugs, both herbal and illegal, and inflict pain and suffering as you say – to release energy. But the rest? Well, some people believe you can raise the inhuman – dark, negative entities – through black masses, group chanting and sacrificial blood release. What these people do to gain power over others, exact revenge, or satisfy their perversions is to invert everything to do with the church. They even take items from churches in order to defile them for ceremonies. They use black bibles and recite prayers backwards; extract fat from graveyard corpses or use foetuses to make candles; torture and debase other living creatures, notably children and animals, babies even... They'll conduct these rites at particular times of the year. There will be thirteen of them and a mediumistic person to channel the entity is particularly useful – someone like Ruby for example. And of course it is all executed with a specific target in mind."

The room was now positively icy and the lights dimmed further.

"To anyone who doesn't think it's real it can be an exciting game, an excuse to live a certain way, a thrill...but black magic has existed throughout centuries and there are some highly disturbing and inexplicable examples of things going badly wrong. Personally, even though I am a medium and believe in spirit, I didn't believe anyone could really raise evil; but after my experience in Woodsend, I now think that they can. In fact I know they can."

"From a distance?"

"Yes. Sometimes they will use a keepsake or item taken from the person they want to harm – like hair or nails or clothing – to personalise the demand. Or it might be a doll or poppet, so that's what you'd look for..." Her voice trailed away.

"Are you alright, Celeste?"

"Oh my dear, they don't know what they're dealing with, you see? The idiots think they can put the genie back in the bottle whenever they please, but they can't. They've made themselves instruments for channelling intelligent evil into our world, and as soon as they've served their purpose they'll be thrown away. He who sups with the devil should use a long spoon and all that… "

Becky glanced over her shoulder and then swung round to look at the doorway. "I've got a weird feeling – like we're being watched. I'm scared."

"Yes. So am I."

"Oh God, I thought you of all people would tell me not to be. That you can shut these things down and —"

"We're not talking about the ghosts of humans," Celeste's voice had spiked with panic and frustration. "We're talking about the demonic! And 'they' have let it in. It's here. That's why I told you – time's running out. Very soon you and I will be stopped because it knows we're on to them. There is an intelligence."

"I'm scared of possession, Celeste – is that what they'll do?"

"Demonic entities don't have a human body of their own – in fact they despise humans – but one of the ways they can destroy us is either by manifesting, often as a child or an animal, or possessing a person. They will find a way once they've been given a gateway by these self-serving fools. You must stay strong – extremely strong – and protect yourself. Some people are naturally more at risk from possession than others, of course. In my opinion they are the lonely and disenfranchised, the mentally ill, and of course, those who dabble with the occult…wherever there is heightened vulnerability or a vacuum of faith, I suppose. But we can and must protect ourselves."

They sat in contemplative silence for a moment or two, while the wind buffeted the windows and a low moan whistled down the chimney.

Becky took a deep breath. "A vacuum of faith? That seems terrible."

"It's just my opinion."

"Okay, I'm frightened out of my wits but I'm going to try and think positively – take control of what I actually *can* do!

Supposing I find the diary, and supposing between us we can coax some more information out of Ruby? Even supposing I find Alice and manage to persuade her to come with me…who do we go to with the information? The thing is, and I have to tell you because this just gets worse, I was tipped off recently about a very senior police officer – the one who closed the case as it happens. So how is this thing going to end? Do you see? Frankly, I'm terrified Callum will never wake up and that I'll be attacked again and this time I might not survive. Celeste, what do we do and who do we confide in?"

Celeste shook her head. "I've been thinking about that too, and there is someone else who might be able to help: he's not in a good position and certainly has his own demons, but there's Ruby's boyfriend, Jes. It's just something Ruby mentioned when I saw her earlier, and now the feeling we need to contact him is growing. I met him once and he's a rough man, operates in the underworld for sure…but I think he might hold a key."

"God, I wish Callum was with us."

"So do I. Look, Becky, don't question me on this one, okay, because I'm going to ask you to do something? We've got to be exceptionally resilient spiritually for all the reasons I've outlined, and I'm glad you take it seriously because without this protection they will win! They've got some pretty nasty stuff on their side."

Becky nodded.

"You need psychic protection at all times even when you're sleeping – especially when you're sleeping."

"Yes, I'll go with that."

"Right. Imagine you're filled with light – from the solar plexus to the top of your head. A brilliant tube of white light that expands to fill your whole body until there is a huge bubble with you cocooned inside it. Have you done that?"

Becky nodded.

"Do you believe in God? It doesn't have to be Christianity or any particular religion – but a divine spirit – everything that's good, positive, pure and whole... kindness, benevolence and truth."

"I'm a humanist but, yes, I believe in spirit too. Well, I do now!"

"That's fine. Light over darkness is all I ask, because you need to visit Kristy and you're going to need a shield of armour when you go."

"She's possessed, isn't she – like Jack was?" Becky's gaze once more flitted around the room. "I'm scared, Celeste. Really scared of going because of what I might see, and, well, do you know if just being with someone who's possessed means it will latch onto you? My biggest fear is to lose my mind, to lose who I am."

"Do you mean, 'is it contagious'? I don't think so. During exorcisms it has been known for an evil entity to attach itself onto anther's aura if it isn't conducted properly, but I don't think a demonic possession will come out of the host unless it's exorcised, no."

"Okay."

"How did Dr McGowan come to be possessed, do you know?"

"He hypnotised Ruby. I was there but I didn't really see what happened because I passed out."

"Whatever was inside her must have recognised the chance of a more influential and powerful host? Interesting."

"I'll be honest – I'm really frightened of even seeing Kristy. She was so sober and so 'together'. It's going to be a shock because if it can happen to somebody like her it could happen to anyone. And all she'd done was *visit* Jack, you see? She hadn't hypnotised him or been present at an exorcism!"

"She wouldn't have been protected. Just don't look into her eyes or recognise what is inside her or it will hypnotise you and draw you in. Don't converse with it and be prepared for it to imitate her very adeptly. I'm guessing she conversed with what she would have thought was Jack. Now, remember your main objective is to get the diary – search her room and ask your nurse friend. Keep your eye on the prize."

Becky laughed drily. "What choice do I have?"

"We all have choices. You can run away and never come back, of course you can, and you'd be safe."

"I'm not sure I could live with myself, though."

"Quite. And my belief is that if we fail in this life we'll be brought right back in the next one faced with an even harder task."

"I'm glad I don't believe what you believe!"

"Now listen – one more thing – I want you to promise me on your life that you will not go to Woodsend on your own looking for Alice. I have a bad feeling about that. It's a far more dangerous place than you can ever imagine. I see windows and doors in every house blackened and closed. Locked and barred. There is fear imprisoning those in every household there and with good reason. Don't go."

"Okay but at some point I'm going to have to. Is there anyone I could trust? I mean, if I get this diary for example, what's our next step? Because it seems to me that whoever gets involved in this is almost immediately put in harm's way. We need someone who can take action quickly and who has contacts. I wondered about a young police officer I met - Toby Harbour?"

"How well do you know him?"

"He sat with me the night Callum was admitted to hospital. He's young and naïve but I'd trust him."

"He has to know what he's up against then or he can't do it. He'll be overpowered very quickly. They always overpower the naïve and unsuspecting, like taking candy from a baby."

"Yes."

"Make sure you put him fully in the picture and that he has psychic protection. Tell him it is not a joke. We wouldn't go into a physical battle without armour and weapons, yet most folk are quite happy to take on the dark side totally unarmed. All of which makes it very easy for 'them'. "

"I promise. And I'll ring you to let you know how I get on."

"Yes please. Oh and I would like to visit Ruby again very soon if that's okay? I'll need someone with me though because of that switching – I think it could be very dangerous instructing her in mediumship if she's not... you know..."

"Yes, I'll make sure I'm there."

"Good. Meanwhile I have some work to do on another level."

A light rain spattered against the window and another heavy gust of wind buffeted the walls. A velvety dusk descended on the room and Celeste seemed to slump in her chair.

"Celeste? Will you be okay?"

The slow hiss of Gerry's oxygen cylinder seemed to fill the house, reminding them both of his invalid status and vulnerability. "And your husband?"

"I feel a bit sick and woozy, dear, that's all. I've had a long day going over to Drummersgate and then coming back to see to Gerry."

"Shall I turn the heating up for you? Draw the curtains?"

"The heating's on full. But yes – do draw the curtains. Thank you. Actually I'm ever so tired."

Becky reached for a travel rug from a nearby chair and put it across the older lady's knees. "I'll have to get a shimmy on but I'll ring tomorrow and hopefully I'll have that diary with me. Then we can decide what to do next. Is there anyone you want me to ring to come and help with Gerry?"

"I feel as though I've the flu coming on and that's all we need, isn't it? I mean I'm no good to anyone if I'm poorly, and you can't do this on your own. Becky love, you must get some help." Her voice trailed off somewhat and Becky strained to hear. "Would you pass my address book? I think I'll ring Gerry's brother in Scarborough and ask if he'll have him stay for a while. I want to do it now. Right away."

"And be here on your own?"

"Yes. It's for the best."

***

Chapter Ten

Laurel Lawns Private Medical Home

Kristy Silver was not at all well.

After a phone call to check on Callum, Becky took a taxi straight up to Laurel Lawns. The phrase 'having the devil at your back' seemed apt, she thought, flying into Reception amid a swirl of leaves. Celeste had given her the heebie-jeebies. Still, hopefully the diary and whatever was in it would be here.

After signing the visitor's book she took the lift, frowning in concentration as it cranked through the floors to the top. What was so important about this diary? Martha's predecessor, Linda Hedges, had been the social worker covering Woodsend during the 1990s while Martha was off sick. *Bet she'd found something out and written it down*! The question was, had Martha read it and in doing so, put herself in the firing line? And had she really then sent it to Kristy? It was a distinct possibility. And of course, Celeste seemed to have a hunch that it was here. And Celeste, she was coming to realise, did seem to have an uncanny knack of knowing things others didn't. The lift bumped to a halt and the doors juddered open.

Although it was only four in the afternoon, the short December day had cast the clinic's corridors into gloom, and through the elegant Georgian windows, rectangles of lamplight extended over immaculate lawns. Becky walked smartly towards the ward and straight up to the nurses' station. Her old friend, Nora, looked up and shook her head gravely when she saw her coming. "Are you sure you want to do this, Becky?"

"That bad?"

Nora nodded. Although the same age as herself, Nora seemed drawn and somehow weighed down as she led the way to Kristy's room. They'd moved her further down the hall, she explained, because of the noises unsettling the others.

"What noises?"

Nora turned to face her when they reached Kristy's door. "I shouldn't say this but you and I go way back and, oh God, Becky, you'll see for yourself in a minute. Frankly, I've never known anything like it but no one's doing a thing to help this woman – they're just leaving her here! A lot of the nurses have gone off sick, you know? We can't cope with it. She needs Solitary and expert psychiatry...but Dr Morrow won't listen and the trustees insist it's all kept hushed up. Like I said, are you sure you want to do this? I mean, her colleagues and friends have had to be kept away..."

Becky nodded and so Nora took the keys out of her pocket. "Okay, well she's heavily under and you've got a panic button. I'll be here in a flash if you need me. Just don't make eye contact. I'm serious – it's worse if you do."

Becky nodded and a second later she was in. Behind her the door clicked shut and she took a moment to adjust to the scene, keeping her back to the wall. Inside she said a prayer and pictured white light around herself in the way Celeste had taught.

Kristy's breathing was rattling in her chest as if there were ten emphysemic men in there. Her wrists and ankles were in tight restraints and her pale, normally silky blonde hair lay matted in clumps on the pillow; her alabaster skin a roadmap of broken veins.

In stark contrast to the fresh cool air outside, a strong sulphurous odour filled the hot, suffocating room; and inside her coat over several layers of woollens, Becky broke into a sickly sweat.

Part of her wanted so badly to help Kristy in the same way Kristy had done her best to help Jack. Another part of her wanted out of here right here and right now. She stared at the virtually unrecognisable creature in the bed. How could this have happened? How?

The diary...keep your eye on the prize...this is why you're here...

Against all her instincts Becky inched slowly towards the bed. As she drew closer, the overpowering smell of rotten eggs became ever stronger and she tried to inhale only through her mouth, as the sound of increasingly heavy, wheezy breathing filled the room, pulling her into its rhythm.

Finally she was level with the bottom of the bed. Although Kristy's eyes were shut there was a feeling she, or something within her, was aware of Becky's presence. Clutching the sheets, Kristy's fingernails were blackened and bitten to the quick, and blood streaked her arms and chest as if she'd been clawed by a wild animal. Her skin was corpse-white, glazed with feverish sweat, and the carotid pulse throbbed visibly in her neck. The grotesque image was hypnotic though, and Becky had to force herself to stop staring.

A few feet away from the bed was a small cabinet, seemingly empty, but it was worth a look. As quietly as possible she tiptoed over, keeping a nervous eye on Kristy before scanning inside it. No sooner had she bent down though, when a loud chuckle made her stand up again sharply. It seemed to be emanating from deep within Kristy's chest and sounded like several drunken men laughing raucously at a dirty joke. She had maybe one or two seconds at best to get this diary. Bobbing down she frantically felt around inside the cabinet – no, there was nothing – before backing rapidly towards the door – her focus still fixed on Kristy.

She was almost there, about to reach for the panic button, when Kristy's eyes flicked open.

OhmyGod!

Becky stared open mouthed. Kristy's eyes were no longer blue. Rather they were alien pits of oil-black. The lips were beginning to stretch and horrified, Becky couldn't look away, as a clown smile cracked open to reveal a long, forked tongue that flicked in and out like a viper between rotting teeth.

There was nothing she could do for Kristy; she had to save herself and leave right away. Sod the diary.

"Yes," came a choral hiss from Kristy's body. "Fuck off, bitch!"

Becky fleetingly scanned the rest of the room as she banged furiously on the door for release. The rest of the furniture had clearly been removed because there wasn't so much as a chest of drawers to look in. Kristy had been left here in a spartan cell until she suffered an undignified and terrifying death, hadn't she?

In blind panic now she pounded on the door repeatedly, shouting to Nora; while behind her Kristy's body began to thrash around violently. Involuntarily Becky watched out of the corner of her eye as the sheets worked their way down to reveal a shockingly skeletal torso: every rib jutted out like a blade with the hollow abdomen dipping so far back as to almost touch the spine. The bed was now rattling on the floor with the power of the creature's fury and the restraints were tearing into Kristy's skin as her neck jutted back almost at right angles and a scream roared from her throat.

Finally remembering she had been given a panic alarm, Becky pressed it over and over and over just as a key turned from the other side. But it was then, just as she was about to dash through to the safety of the corridor outside, and she almost missed it, that a small, soft voice stopped her in her tracks. She cocked her head to one side.

The look in Nora's eyes told her she'd heard it too: Kristy's real voice, tiny and faint as it was, coming from what sounded like the end of a very long tunnel, "In the locker."

"You have to get her a priest if only for the last rites," Becky said as they walked back down the corridor. "She's Roman Catholic and she'd want it, I know she would. We have to do something for her – it's terrible, shocking. "

"I know and I've tried but the last priest we had – for Jack – went off sick immediately afterwards. I tried to contact him a week ago but the church official I spoke to said he'd gone on indefinite leave."

"Relatives then? She must have someone?"

Nora shook her head. "She was married but her ex doesn't want anything to do with her. I'm not sure what she did in the past but it seriously pissed him off. Sometimes, whatever voice is inside her describes something pretty bad, but not bad enough to merit being left like this. Poor woman. I knew her, you know? She was a really good psychiatric registrar when I was working in Leeds."

Becky suddenly burst into tears.

"Were you good friends?" Nora put an arm round her shoulders and they stopped by one of the long sash windows overlooking the gardens. "Oh Becky, it's terrible, I know. It was bad enough with Jack but his mother put pressure on the doctor and got him to agree to a priest. He was sacked, by the way, that doctor! The official line is that we had a hell of a lot of suicides on his watch and he was incompetent, but it wasn't that – it was getting an exorcist in! I suppose it's all about reputation in the end and we've got quite a few of the rich and famous in here. If you want to know my opinion, I'd say Jack owes his life to us getting him that priest." She indicated her head towards Kristy's room. ""I'm afraid she hasn't got a chance."

Becky dabbed at her eyes. "I'm really sorry. It was just such a shock seeing her like that. You know all of us who've tried to help this patient of ours, Ruby, well we've all come under this kind of attack; and I'm tired as well, I suppose."

"People don't realise the strain we're under in this profession. But I've never seen anything like Jack or Kristy – ever." She glanced at the clock on the wall. "Oh Becky, I haven't much time. Dr Morrow will be in any minute and between you and me he's a right bastard – you know – the sort who dresses you down in front of visitors and other members of staff – enjoys threatening you and seeing you humiliated? I've got to be one step ahead all the time, particularly with Kristy's medication and I can hear her screaming from here!"

"Sorry, yes, and I won't keep you a moment longer, but before I go Nora, I have to ask you just one more thing – please can I just take a quick peek in Kristy's locker? There's a diary that belonged to a social worker from our department and we really need it. It isn't Kristy's personal diary or anything like that, I promise, and it's really important or I wouldn't ask. I'll explain later but it's to do with child abuse and there's another child at risk. I haven't time to say anymore, just please trust me. I'll return it, I swear."

Nora nodded, already bustling towards the nurses' station. "Okay then, but we'll have to be really quick."

"Thank you so, so much."

Becky followed Nora past the main desk and down the corridor towards the lockers with her heart pumping wildly. She was going to get the diary! It would be there, she knew it would. Nora fiddled around with a ring of keys and she waited, fighting down the increasing and inexplicable sense of urgency rising inside her, just as a man burst through the double doors. Conspicuous in a suit, she knew at once he was Dr Morrow even before he stopped short and swung round on his heels. Hooded yellow-tinged eyes took in her appearance with one evanescent glance.

With a slight lisp he asked, "Who's this?"

"An old friend," Nora answered brightly, handing Becky the diary. "She's just borrowing a book."

Nora's entire demeanour had changed and Becky took her cue to leave promptly.

His name badge, she noted as she left, read, 'Dr Crispin Morrow."

She'd look him up.

***

<u>Chapter Eleven</u>

Woodsend, Autumn 2002
Ruby Dean, age 14

I lost a day again. Maybe more. It's like I wake up and think, 'What day or time is it?' The thing is, it's happening more and more and it's getting confusing because I don't know why and I'm thinking, like, what happened during the time I was asleep or whatever…

Maybe it's a lot worse at the moment because of the medicine? Our mother's giving me stuff for the pain: she knows a lot about herbs – she's always making up pastes and vials of liquid. She'd never call the doctor unless it's really bad, which is fine by me because I hate the bastard.

When I was little I followed her to the ruins once to watch what she did. There were all these huge, shiny black berries ripening in the sun by the old abbey walls; bumblebees were droning and a purple butterfly landed on my shoulder; then suddenly my mother winged round like she knew I was there all the time and just crammed one of the berries into my mouth and made me swallow it. When I woke up the tree tops were swishing round and round the moon. I tried to stand up but kept bending over double with this thumping headache and sweat breaking out all over. It was awful, scary – I thought I was going to die. I suppose it was her way of warning me off.

She puts those belladonna berries in pies too, depending on who's coming. I used to hide behind the kitchen door and this one time she was singing, 'Four and twenty blackbirds…' and tipping fresh blackberries and late autumn raspberries into a pie, having a high old time, then she went off to get the big ripe black ones from her laundry room. Half a dozen or more had gone in before she turned on me and flashed the knife. It glinted in the sun and I backed away and ran into the woods. I could hear her laugh spiralling round the valley and all the crows were screeching out of the trees. It's not like I'd tell on her or anything, cos me and my sister would be put into care and that's where even worse stuff happens and I'd never see my sister again.

Belladonna can kill you if you take too much: you have to take just the right amount and then it's the best drug ever and at the moment I'm glad of it. It's nice. She mixes it with hemlock – the same stuff she takes to put herself into a trance.

Well, I wish I was in a trance now. I can hear that pig clomping up the narrow staircase and my flesh creeps. I suppose this means my time must have come.

Ahead of him a black shadow stretches out along the corridor even though it's a sunny day, slipping round the doorway long before he does. He looks more like a funeral director than a doctor, always dressed in a black suit, curly grey hair springing out in wiry tufts from his ears and nose. Something about him is so fucking repugnant – there's a fanatical gleam in those horrible yellow eyes like he gets off on your pain. The more embarrassed or uncomfortable you are the more he drools. One time when I was about four and had the chicken pox my mother left me alone with him and even though I was crying and shouting for her she never came... *and no, I can't...I can't...No, Eve, no...*

"Get out of my room. What the fuck are you doing here?"

His hooded eyes glint delightedly. "Hello, Ruby! Feisty little thing, aren't we?" he lisps. "So who are we today then? Alice in wonderland? Micky Mouse?" He snaps open his black bag and brings out a syringe.

Vaguely I'm aware of my own voice, only it isn't my voice anymore. "Fuck off. She wants a proper doctor."

"Ida!" He says, turning to our mother, who's standing in the doorway. "We're going to need...oh good you've got them."

She starts spreading out towels and hands him a pair of rubber gloves.

What the fuck?

"Hummmmmmmm..."

"Ruby, stop that infernal humming. Shut up now, the doctor's here and you've got to get this baby out."

Looking down at the bed there's this writhing girl with thin arms being tied to the bedstead by her mother. She shoves another rag into the girl's mouth to muffle the screaming; then a needle is pushed into a vein and her legs are thrust apart. Blood pools onto the sheets as the man in the black suit thrusts his hand inside of her and starts to pull out the baby that was stuck…by its legs."

'Four and twenty blackbirds…'.

But I'm lucky, I'm the good girl not the bad one – the punishment happens to her and she deserves it because of what she does with *him*…because she likes it…

Where I am, though, oh it's so nice here - late afternoon and just going dark in the fairground. The sky's a deep indigo blue dotted with a few stars, and underfoot you can feel the vibration of the rides. The smell of hotdogs and sizzling onions is in the air, and my skin still feels warm from sunbathing all afternoon by the river. Money burns in my pocket as I stand looking at the Waltzer and the handsome gypsy boy with dark flashing eyes staring just at me. He holds the pole in the centre of the carousel, his loose, white shirt undone to the waist, a cigarette balanced on his lower lip. 'Come on', he says, reaching out with strong, brown hands…'Come on, angel girl. Come and have some fun!'

Have I seen him before?

***

Days later or hours later

The harvest moon has painted the forest silver and sprinkled the river with a million crystals. The water is fresh and cold as I wade in washing off caked blood; falling into it, letting the exquisite iciness rinse over my face, smoothing back my hair. There is nothing now except me and the rippling, gurgling river. *Heaven take me.*

That aching, dragging feeling in my tummy is finally floating away as I sink down and down and down, the moon swilling and swaying overhead, my lungs filling with glorious freezing oblivion.

"What in fuck's name are you doing?"

A man's voice registers from outer space and suddenly all the pain surges back into screaming, gasping reality. My elbow's half wrenched out of its socket and my face is in the mud, then my hair's being pulled back and his mouth is clamped hard on mine. Back over into the mud.

"Puke it up now. Make yourself sick!"

The man swimming into vision has the darkest hair and huge brown eyes. His jeans are torn and he looks a lot like the gypsy boy in my dreams – only instead of swinging me around the fairground he's examining my forearms, staring at all the scratches and needle marks. "Are you a druggie? What the fuck happened to you? Aren't you a bit young?"

A voice, not my own, says, "I'm sixteen."

I don't know what happens after this. Maybe I lose more days? This one's already fading.

***

Chapter Twelve

Sunday 27th December 2015
Laurel Lawns

Becky walked down the driveway towards the gothic wrought-iron gates. No rumble of traffic disturbed the brooding silence of the gardens either side, and her heels echoed on the wet tarmac.

With a bit of luck there should be a bus along in around ten minutes, she thought, hurrying along – the wind was whipping up again and snow threatened. Pushing through the pedestrian exit at the side of the gates, she emerged on the other side into the quiet darkness of a country lane and squinted into the dusk. There wasn't a soul in sight.

From somewhere out in the fields a sheep bleated and the first spots of sleet stung her cheeks. Honestly, she should have called a taxi – it was ridiculous trying to save a few quid like this, but old habits die hard as they say. Still, at least the long bus journey meant there would be enough time to read the diary. How incredible she'd managed to get hold of it; what a coup! Itching to tell Celeste, she started to call her on the mobile, then quickly realised there wasn't a signal. Oh well...she dropped the phone back into her bag...no worries, she'd text her later.

The bus shelter was empty and she sat down, hugging herself to keep warm. A cold draft whined underneath the glass panels, blowing in a rustle of dead leaves. How dark it was, like night already. She looked at her watch. Fifteen minutes had passed, the horizon already merged in heavy cloud.

I assume you know they use the black arts...

The diary...would 'they' know she now had it? They'd known Martha had...Somehow. What could happen to her out here, though? Seriously? Would a car skid off the lane from out of nowhere? Would the bus crash? Would Chester's voice suddenly shout into her ear while she was out here alone? Yes, that was the most likely option – when it came to herself it seemed they liked to target her deep-rooted fear of madness. Kristy's deformed face flashed before her unbidden, and Becky stood up. Where the hell was the bus?

Some people are more at risk of possession than others…like the lonely…

Well that was just it – she was one of the lonely! Those shrieking, drunken nights out in Leeds were a thing of the long distant past. All those girls now women with families while she was facing divorce, had few relatives and no children. All there was in life now was work. Oh yes, she was cut-off and lonely all right.

Just don't look into her eyes…

Had she? Had she, though?

Yes! The moment had caught her off guard but she had, definitely, and now every time she tried to sleep and every single time she woke up in the early hours alone in the dark those eyes would be staring straight into her soul. Oh how crazy was this? Tears prickled her eyes. However had all this happened? Again she said a prayer and again pictured a brilliant divine light surrounding her body. She must believe, had to believe…but how did you know if the belief was strong enough to protect you? It was blind faith yet still she inhaled the imaginary white light as if it was steam, envisaging it enveloping every part of her until she sat safely inside a shimmering bubble of protection.

Pacing up and down, constantly checking over her shoulder, Becky prayed and prayed that the bus would come. Why was it so black dark out here, and so quickly? Inside her bag the diary sat waiting to be read and soon she would be the only person outside of Woodsend who knew its terrible secrets. Would those secrets die with her? Or be lost with her insanity?

In the distance headlights now bobbed into view, the bus driver crunching down a gear as the vehicle reached a slight incline, blue smoke billowing from the exhaust.

90

Becky stepped out of the shelter and into the sleety wind to flag it down. At the exact moment a glass panel at the back of the shelter blew out and shattered.

Hundreds of glass crystals showered the floor, peppering the seat she'd been sitting on just moments before. She was still staring in shock when the bus drew level and the doors hissed open.

"That were a near miss, love," said the driver, laughing. You alright?"

It was just a coincidence…

She struggled to raise a weak smile, fumbling for change before stumbling down the aisle on legs that had turned to jelly. He was still chuckling, nodding to her in his rear-view mirror, his shoulders juddering with mirth – probably the most amusement he'd had all day. It was enviable really, to be that blissfully ignorant. Why couldn't she be a normal person too? What had she done to deserve this and who the hell could she turn to? Her life was in danger – it was – it definitely was…and there wasn't a single person to put their arms around her and say it was all going to be okay. Not one.

She sat at the back of the bus looking straight ahead. *Gale force winds and a stress fracture, that's all it was…coincidence…no it wasn't, you know it wasn't…*

Buttoning down rising panic she tried to recall the Lord's Prayer but could not. Instead her mind leapt down a myriad of different alleyways, chattering incessantly, frantically busy with questions but no answers.

Come on, Becky, you've got forty minutes stuck on this bus – read the bloody diary…come on.

It seemed the bus was entirely empty except herself. Looking out of the mud-spattered window all that was visible was her own bloodless face; and occasionally a powerful gust of wind buffeted the bus, the smell of diesel overpowering as the bus lurched up and down gears in effort to keep moving. She'd be sick if she tried to read the diary now. But read it she must and the sooner the better.

The first few pages she scanned.

Linda Hedges had harboured suspicions about Woodsend after being asked to visit highly disturbed teenager, Bella – Derek and Kathleen Dean's daughter...*Yes, she knew about Bella*...The GP had not followed up and in the end her grandma had called out the police. Then came Thomas Blackmore...*Kristy's patient*...and both children had duly been incarcerated into psychiatric care. Linda's job should have been done at that point, except she'd been that little bit too curious it seemed, because the woman was clearly talking about keeping private notes in case anything happened to her. Why would she think that? Becky's stomach clenched into a knot as she forced herself to read to the conclusion: Martha and Kristy would have been the last two people to read this and look what had happened to them!

She rested the book on her lap for a moment, quelling an increasing travel sickness from looking down. Bridesmoor Colliery had loomed into view, the pithead wheel partly obscured by rolling cloud. What if the driver lost concentration or a phantom appeared in the road to make him swerve? An image of the bus lying on its side in the bog, wheels spinning, formed in her mind's eye and seemed so real, so likely, that it played out in front of her and now there were people she knew being told; announcements in the news.....*Stop it, stop it*....Forcing herself to re-focus on the diary she quickly read to the end. Too quickly, she realised later, because she'd been totally unprepared for its contents.

Linda Hedges had found unmarked, shallow children's graves in Five Sisters Cemetery. The graves appeared to be relatively new; yet when she checked it out there were no records of any correlating births or deaths in the area.

The information sank and sank and sank...*OhmyGod... How many years? Who knew? Whose children?*

They had now reached Bridesmoor's highest point and the wind was pummelling the bus so alarmingly it rocked and swayed. Becky stared at her reflection: the fluorescent interior of the bus served only to make the darkness outside seem even darker, with herself illuminated as if on a fairground carousel. She slid the notebook back into her bag, and as she did so, caught on the edge of her vision, a man in a black hat and coat on the back seat. *How come she hadn't noticed him?* She whirled round. But there was absolutely no one there.

Her heart thumped so hard in her chest it made the blood surge painfully through the radial and carotid pulses and she gripped the seat in front of her. *What in fuck's name was that?*

She hadn't eaten all day and light-headedness was making her sick and faint. Inside her chest, her lungs were as tight as an asthmatic's and she fought for breath. It was an illusion. A trick, that was all. Celeste was right, though – time was running out – she would be stopped for sure if action wasn't taken very, very soon. There had to be someone she could trust…*think, think*…someone who would help and believe all this before it was too late.

She closed her eyes and began to pray for help and guidance with all the force she could muster. The prayer came easily and fluently this time, and shortly afterwards the bus eased into top gear and began its descent.

When she next looked out of the window there were street lights and rows of terraces, a boarded up pub and a queue of people waiting outside a chip shop. Tears stabbed at her eyelids. Lord knows she wasn't a crier, but never had loneliness shrouded her more.

She looked at her watch: ten minutes before the stop for the Infirmary – she'd better send Celeste that text and phone Noel. Someone else had to know what she now knew. The more people the better.

***

Noel sounded harassed. "Sorry, Becks. We've had a lockdown. Are you alright? You're not in Woodsend are you? Please God, tell me you're not out there on your own?"

She clutched the mobile, trying to keep her voice strong and steady. "No. Celeste persuaded me to visit her instead and I'm glad she did. Listen, I've just been to see Kristy at Laurel Lawns."

"Oh my God, you didn't? How is she? What's happened?"

"Terrible. Shocking. Like Jack was. There's a whole load of stuff I need to tell you urgently, Noel, and it's really important. In fact, it wouldn't be an exaggeration to say my life's at stake as well as…"

"What?"

"But before that, listen – do you remember the priest who helped me just before Christmas? Did you get his name?"

There was a slight lull while Noel flailed around. "Err…No…oh hang on wait…yes, yes I do actually – it was Michael!"

"And that was at St Mark's Church, wasn't it?"

"I went back to thank him but no one there had heard of him; in fact the Rev was a bit snappy with me – said I must have imagined it. What's this about your life…?"

"Well, someone must know him. I want to get in touch with him as soon as possible for Kristy or she's going to die. It's a bad situation – really bad. The doctor there is blocking any chance of her getting help from the church but she's got to have it. The thing is I saw him face to face and he looked like a nasty piece of work. Nora was out and out scared of him."

"What was his name? What happened to the last one?"

"The last one got fired. Anyway, his name badge said, 'Crispin Morrow'. I'm going to look him up on google now I've got data on my phone."

"Where are you?"

"Five minutes from the Infirmary…"

"Becky, tell me why you're in danger? Is it the same thing as before?"

"Kind of. Noel, I'm okay but I've read the diary that Linda Hedges kept – it was in Kristy's locker – and there's stuff that has to be got to the police but I don't know who to trust. I have to show you…"

"I'll come to the DRI."

"Yes, please. Look, I'll have to have a bite to eat or I'll pass out, but while I'm in the canteen I'll google this Dr Morrow –

see what I can find. Then I'll go and sit with Callum while I think what to do next. I'll need to tell Celeste and I need to tell you because we have to do something and soon. I'll be here all night."

"You're going to be exhausted."

"I know but I can't leave him. I think he knows what's in this diary too, and I think 'they' know he knows, which is why he's not getting better."

"Pardon? I don't follow."

"I know…I need to explain it to you in person."

"I'm up to my neck at the minute, Becks, but you know I'll be there as soon as I can."

"Thanks Noel. I'll see you soon then?"

***

Dr Crispin Morrow. *Good grief, he should surely have retired by now!*

It looked like he'd acquired his medical degree back in 1963 and subsequently qualified to practice as a GP in 1967.

Funny, she thought, he didn't look as old as seventy-three. He'd seemed middle aged, sixty at the most; only his yellow hooded eyes, as leathery lidded as a chameleon's, had indicated he might be older. For sure there had been something creepy about him, although nothing she could quite put a finger on.

On further research it seemed there was very little about him in the public domain. He'd practiced medicine in Bridesmoor village for over forty years and still did, albeit part time. She tapped away on her iPhone while stabbing at chips and wolfing down a cheese sandwich, trying to find evidence of his psychiatric work. It seemed he'd had various staffing psychiatry positions, including one at an adolescent unit and several at private clinics. There really wasn't much more to go on. So he was fully authorised to work as a psychiatrist and a general practitioner, then? Alas, that was all the information on him. There was no home address and no family links

Googling his surname alone revealed nothing further. The facts were stark though – he'd been the village GP when both Bella and Tommy were committed to psychiatric care in the nineties. *Had he been the one to block Bella's referral?* Her heart skipped a beat as she made the connection. Oh but to try and verify that – these people were always well protected legally and medical notes were highly confidential as she knew only too well. But that was one hell of a coincidence, was it not?

And wouldn't he have been the one to issue birth and death certificates in the area? What about those unmarked graves? Her hands began to shake as the new information hit her. Putting down the phone next to her plate she stared into space. *OhmyGod!* And when her mobile rang a second later she almost jumped clean off the chair.

"Becky, it's me," said Noel. "I've just done a bit of digging around. Your Dr Crispin is about as popular as the bubonic plague. Worse – he specialises in adolescents and most particularly in anorexia, which is usually girls, or has been to date."

"Noel, he was the GP in Bridesmoor – has been for over forty years!"

"You're kidding?"

"No, and it gets worse – you have to read Linda Hedges' diary. I don't want to be the only one who knows what's in it. Oh God, Noel, it's just so bad you can't imagine." She lowered her voice as a couple on an adjoining table had stopped talking and weren't doing much to hide the fact they were eavesdropping. "The coincidences are glaring but unless the police get involved I can't see what to do for the best, and to be honest I'm not confident in that direction."

"Why?"

"I had a tip off. Look, Noel, our best hope is finding Alice and I think I'm going to have to just go and get her out of there myself. And we have to find Michael for Kristy or she's going to die a horrible death. We'll have to smuggle him in behind Cripsin Morrow's back. And if I can just get Alice…"

"I vote for the police."

"No. I'm scared of them, Noel. They can stop me."

"What? The police can stop you? Becky, I don't get this."

"No, I know. Look, I'll tell you everything tonight when you come over and then we can make a decision as to what to do." A sudden vision of Callum lying in his side ward bed shot into her mind's eye. "I have to go – I need to check on Callum. Anyway, it doesn't matter what time you get here but please take care, Noel. Watch your back. I'm serious."

***

Chapter Thirteen

Bridesmoor, November 1972

5am and freezing. Cora speedily picked her way home through the woods. An early morning mist mingled with wood smoke had coiled around the trees and an owl hooted in the distance. Still, now at least she had a much fuller picture of what was going on in her marriage. And she owed her husband nothing.

Since she had seen for herself exactly what Lucas and his coven got up to at Tanners Dell, and having protected him from gossip all these years, a quiet rage now rooted itself inside of her. He'd stolen her life and locked her in, and for that she would never forgive him. Pieces of the puzzle previously dismissed as coincidence or bad luck now slotted together to form a shocking and diabolical picture – one which dominated her every waking thought. Her husband was not only a Satanist but a mass murderer. And worse – she almost laughed with hysterical disbelief at this bit – some of the sworn-in coven members were senior police officers.

And as if that wasn't bad enough – she glanced over her shoulder into the gloom of the forest– they used dark arts that seemed to work. How all those untimely deaths and accidents made sense to her now: fear entombed the two villages like fog over a stinking swamp, and if anyone still dared to gossip it was from behind net curtains and locked doors. Women took their children to school by the hand and waited for them at the gates in nervous huddles. Not a single child played out after dark, and no one ever went for a walk down by the river or through the woods unless they had a Rottweiler, and even then they hurried back.

Meanwhile, Lucas went to the pit each day as the newly appointed Deputy. and the men who worked under his watch were stoical and silent. The Druids Inn opposite the colliery now hosted but a handful of old men making a pint last all day; and The Highwayman entertained a few teens playing pool, with the occasional thirsty traveller dropping in. It was a ghost town with the inhabitants stuck in a time warp they could never escape.

If she wasn't his wife, of course, she'd be dead. Instead he had her trapped in misery and fear. With five children and no income it was always going to be tough, but there wouldn't be a single person around here willing or even able to help – she was Lucas Dean's wife! And even if she did try to leave he would hunt her down and haul her back for punishment. And then of course, there was Paul. She sighed. If ever there was a boy born in the mould of his father it was him.

As she hurried along, her thoughts fired one after the other. Could she go to a solicitor with this? But what if he contacted the police, which he undoubtedly would, and she was left in an interrogation room with Ernest Scutts? What if the solicitor himself was in on it? What would the coven do to her then?

The GP then? *God no*! Crispin Morrow ran his practice from the front room of a terrace on the main road, and she recoiled just thinking about him, recalling with disgust the way those yellow eyes gleamed when her children had been exposed for various inoculations, not to mention the time he'd examined her following a miscarriage: the memory, the revulsion of it - still so humiliating - made her feel sick.

He's one of them…

She swallowed down the shocking thought that almost everyone in a position of power in the area could be involved. The Reverend Gordon…how could he step inside a church and preach from the pulpit about praying for people less fortunate? How could the man hand out what he claimed was the blood and the body of Christ? How could he? No wonder hardly anyone went to church here. Did they know what she knew? They couldn't, though. People guessed, they were afraid, but they couldn't know just what a terrible thing was happening on their own doorstep.

So she was isolated then, with only one thing left to save her skin – the second key to that ancient cellar door. He knew she had it. He'd ransacked the house, not caring if the kids were asleep when he upturned their mattresses, rolling them out of bed onto a cold floor. Barging into the bedroom they shared he'd yanked her up by the arm and roared into her face, "You were seen, you stupid bitch. Now give me the fucking key or I'll beat you to hide."

He'd left her so badly thrashed she could barely walk, stopping just short of putting her in hospital. But he wouldn't find that key. Not ever. And she was alive because of it – because he didn't know who she'd given it to – and because of the thin veneer of respectability she provided should anyone official come calling.

He rarely came home these days anyway; leaving his family with just enough money to pay the bills while he spent the rest however he pleased – a new Cortina, bottles of whisky, whatever he snorted up his nose, and smart clothes.

Carrion's Wood was at its deepest now and Cora picked up pace towards the lane. The small terrace would be freezing when she got back, with condensation running down the windows, and as usual the kids would have to get dressed underneath the covers without washing because they'd no hot water. That she'd been left in a position like this! A nerve tightened in her jaw and inside her pockets her fists clenched around fingers numb with cold. The trip had been worth it though – a few more pieces had at last slotted into place – and she was more than justified in never having him in the house again.

Ida! That fucking gypsy reject! Rumour had it she'd been kicked out by some Irish travellers and then ingratiated herself with the Romas. The Romany gypsies were the ones who had colourful caravans and glossy horses, who parked on the Common. The women wore bright headscarves and full skirts and the men mucked in with local work. They had always been welcome and their kids played with the local kids. Or they did until this summer when one of their girls had gone missing.

Cries of, "Rosella!" had echoed through the woods from dawn to dusk as men, women and children, with numerous dogs in tow, had trawled through the fields and combed the woods day after day. Suspicion about the old mill had sparked arguments and a group of the men had broken in and ransacked the place. They'd found nothing but a damp old building with hazardous floor boards, but still Lucas' name was rumoured on the air, until fights broke out and previously amiable, laid-back gypsies lay in wait for innocent men coming home from their shifts. For several weeks chaos and disturbance reigned, but then the mood suddenly changed.

Cora thought back. In the space of a couple of days one of the gypsy women had a stillbirth, and another a miscarriage quite late on in her term. It was a rainy weekend in late July – and the warm ground had soaked up the excess water, turning the Common into a bog. Drenched and muddy, the woman who'd had the stillbirth had walked over to the woods in the early hours, dressed only in a cotton nightdress, and then hanged herself.

After that a dark cloud of unease hung over the camp. With all the fight drained out of them they stopped looking for Rosella, and although for a while they holed up on Drovers Common discussing what to do, it wasn't long before they decamped and moved on. A month of searching had produced nothing – it seemed as if Rosella had simply vanished into thin air – and the police had called off their investigation. One at a time, local people came over to pay their respects and offer condolences. And as the nights drew in, fear stretched into the shadows, flitting back under doorways only when the sun came up.

At the sight of the departing merrily painted wagons, anger brewed behind closed doors once more, the gossip shifting to Lucas Dean and just what the hell went on in that old mill. And shortly after that came one of the worst mining accidents in modern history, and then the gossip stopped.

Cora's mind raced as she hurried along the path. Those gypsies, how they'd suffered – and yet if only they'd known it was they who'd brought the darkness. They'd taken that nasty bloody witch in, hadn't they? Out of kindness, no doubt, although you'd have thought one of them at least would have sussed her out? Because it was definitely Ida who dished out the drugs and worked the hexes – he couldn't do that sort of stuff before he took up with her. Miscarriages and premature death? Paralysis and blindness? That was her bit.

Did you suss her? Be honest…

She pushed down the unpalatable truth. No, she hadn't seen Ida for what she was but nor, in fairness, had anyone else. The woman was a shapeshifting genius. She knew now alright, though. Her thoughts deepened. So when had Ida met Lucas exactly? Before or after Rosella had gone missing?

Out of breath now, she looked up – the edge of the woods was in sight and dawn was beginning to streak the sky with fuchsia, wood smoke scenting the air. *Before or after? Before or after?* And did it matter? How secretive they'd been, the two of them! Since she'd been rumbled spying on them they'd moved the coven yet further underground, only meeting during the hours others slept. The thing was, when you watched a place for long enough and quietly enough, you found out what you needed to know. You saw who came and went at 3am while your children were sleeping. Which was how she'd come by information that the gypsies and the village gossips hadn't.

They were good at slinking around in the shadows were these demon worshippers – always cloaked in black, travelling alone and as swiftly as cats. If you didn't know where to hide, when to wait, and what to look for, you'd never notice a thing. And unless you were inside that mill you wouldn't hear anything either – with tens of thousands of tons of water roaring past from the surrounding moors.

A twig snapped not too far away and Cora's heart jolted. She upped her pace for the last few yards. No one would be walking a dog in here. The darkness seemed to amass behind her as she broke into a near run, emerging a few minutes later onto the high-hedged lane. Dewy cobwebs laced the brambles and an autumn mist hung silent and low. Panting with the exertion she hurried up the hill.

That bloody woman wasn't a gypsy she was a fucking, demon witch. Oh, how Lucas would have loved discovering that – what a match made in hell. Just think what he could do now he had

Ida's tricks to heighten his power and increase his perversions. But how did he get those child victims? How did he get babies? It was sickening and disgusting, but what could she do? The pair of them would make sure she died in agony.

It was then an eerie grey shape caught her eye.

Oh God, there was a ghost on the Common and it was coming towards her.

She stopped dead and almost cried out. The apparition was dressed in a long dark garment, its skin pearl white, luminescent in the dawn. The eyes were scooped-out hollows, blood dripped from its mouth and its hands were reaching out to her.

Cora stood riveted to the spot.

"Help me," said the ghost.

Cora's eyes widened and kept on widening.

"Please. I beg you. My family have gone."

The words hit her head on. This was the lost gypsy girl. This was Rosella.

She had to think fast. The child was little more than a walking skeleton and with a shock she realised the girl's legs were bare and bleeding. Cora looked her up and down: apart from the obviously emaciated appearance there was an overpowering stench of vomit and human filth. *This was Lucas' doing. It was... it was....*

There was no way she could take her back home for a bath or call the doctor or police! And those little snitches Paul and Derek would tell Lucas for sure – if she did that she'd be signing not just Rosella's death warrant but her own too. No one could see them. No one. The village was in lockdown against her and not a soul could be trusted.

The girl lurched forwards and Cora tried not to gag.

"Where did they go? My family?"

"You were with the gypsy camp?"

Rosella nodded.

"Are you Rosella? Oh my God. Have you come from the old mill? Were you being kept there?"

She knew before the girl nodded. Oh dear God, what *had* he done? She had to get this child away from here and make damn sure she never came back. "Listen. Wait here for me. I will get you some clothes and some stuff to clean you up a bit, and I'll get you some money – but you have to get out of here and you cannot be seen. Trust no one, do you understand?"

Neither woman needed to question the other further; and Rosella let herself be led over to an old shed behind one of the houses. Cora took off her overcoat and wrapped it around her. "Don't move and don't make a sound. I'll be back as quick as I can."

With her heart leaping about wildly, Cora then hurried home keeping close to the shadows. Letting herself in through the back door she quickly checked the children were still asleep then grabbed what little money she had, a carrier bag of old clothes she could no longer fit into, some soap, a towel and a few slices of bread no-one would miss. Then she topped up a plastic bottle with orange cordial and tap water before rushing back.

Rosella was barely conscious, her skin mortuary cold, but she couldn't stay with her. "Drink this. Now listen to me. Wash as soon as you can – put these clothes on. I'll have to take my coat back. Get out of here, love, and don't ever come back. Don't bring your family back here for revenge either. I'm *his* wife! I know you've been abused but you're lucky to be alive and they're all in it here, do you understand? Be quick and be silent."

"They'll want revenge when they know what he's done to me," the girl croaked, gulping down the juice and trying not to retch it back.

Cora winced at the sight of the huge, jagged scars running down the girl's abdomen as she helped her take off the coat and try to dress. Dark purple bruises covered most of her body and fresh wounds seeped down her legs.

"No they won't. They were on the rough end of some nasty stuff while they were here – that's why they had to go. They searched for you for weeks and weeks but they didn't know what they were up against and some of them got sick."

Rosella pulled on a sweater, groaning with the pain of raising her twig thin arms, one of which had bent at an unnatural angle as if it had been broken and set badly. "But where would they be? Did you hear anything?"

"I heard they'd gone south, that's all I know. Maybe you can guess where they're likely to camp? I'm sorry I've no more money…but it should get you on your way…" She stopped mid-sentence as if she'd heard something on the wind. "You'd best get out of here now, kid – go on – go now! There'll be a bus outside The Druids Inn about six. Keep out of sight but make damn sure you get on it."

***

Chapter Fourteen

Cloudside, Sunday evening

Celeste waved off her brother-in-law, Trevor, having persuaded Gerry he needed a holiday. He liked watching waves crash over the sea wall from his brother's guesthouse window in Scarborough, and the two of them enjoyed playing cards and telling jokes, making Trevor's wife giggle. Not that he'd wanted to leave and certainly not in such a hurry, but she'd told him she didn't feel too good: if she was going to get the flu she couldn't look after him, and with lungs like his a flu virus could prove fatal. She wouldn't want that on her conscience. Reluctantly he agreed, and so she packed his suitcase and helped him dress while his brother drove over.

"You're up to something," he said, while she kneeled to tie up his shoelaces.

Smiling – he knew her so well – she held his questioning stare. "Trust me, Gerry. It's best you're not here."

His chest heaved wheezily with the effort of breathing. "Oh God, love, I thought all that business was over?"

"If it was I'd be very happy – very happy indeed – but it isn't and I've a job to do. I'm sorry, love. You always knew mine wasn't an easy road to travel."

"Will you be alright? Have I to worry?"

"I'll be a lot better when I know you're well away from here, let's put it like that. I'll ring every day."

He nodded, reaching for his oxygen mask again. "I wish I weren't so bloody ill."

Putting her arms round him, they rested foreheads together for a moment. "I love you, Gerry."

His arms, once so iron-powerful from hewing at the coalface every day, held her gently. He kissed her hair. "I love you too, you crazy old witch."

Two hours later his brother's car accelerated away into the night. She stared after the vanishing tail lights, citing a prayer for his safe travel. Then, when there was no longer a sound of the engine and the close was in darkness once more, she turned and walked back up the drive towards the empty bungalow.

This day had been a long time coming and the thought was a deeply sobering one. She'd been sent to Woodsend to help innocent children and allowed herself to be hounded out of the village instead. In a desperate state, Ruby had come to her for help years later, but once again she had let her down. In fact, she had failed so utterly in her task that people were continuing to die horribly and now the situation was about to deteriorate still further. No, it wasn't her fault, but she had the gift of seeing what was happening and must face up to what she had to do. Fear must not hold her back this time.

Right, well at least Gerry was out of the way.

Steeling herself, she stepped inside.

The house was much colder in than out; the rooms bathed in a sepia light.

'Celeste…Celeste…Celeste'…

She locked the door behind her, standing in the hallway as the dim lights flickered and the shadows whispered her name.

The dark entity that had followed Becky was here in this house and must be confronted. Oh she could run, for a while, but the price would fall heavily on others – possibly children and yet more innocent medical staff, or the young police officer who was about to be roped into all this – and for that she would pay. Eventually.

Fear breeds fear…

Have courage. Have faith.

What she had to do was connect with this thing. 'See' what it wanted and who was at the heart of it. And in order to do that she would have to use some tricks of her own.

Setting to work, Celeste drew all the curtains and blinds, before lighting a candle and placing it on the kitchen table along with the other things she needed in order to scry. Scrying could be extremely dangerous and normally she wouldn't meddle or try to contact spirit in this way; but if there was any hope of getting an upper hand before both herself and Becky were stopped, she would have to be shown the true picture. The dark entity, she was positive, would not be able to resist showing off by parading its power and challenging her to step up to the plate. There was no place left to run to and no one but herself to see this out. Without doubt this was her life's task, and she braced herself for what was coming.

As was the usual practice, she recited the Lord's Prayer before asking for spiritual protection. "Dear Lord, please protect me. I only use this method for the greater good. Dear Lord please safe guard my soul from all negative forces. Thank you and Amen."

Then she opened her eyes, focusing intently on the flame in front of her. Silence hissed in the void, before being quickly filled by the reassuring appearance of her spirit guides – as familiar to her now as flesh and blood; lifelong friends. First there was Sage, who had been a childhood babysitter – only appearing as a guide a few years after she'd passed. Sage was a kindly, rotund lady who always brought sweets with her and a yappy little Jack Russell called Cindy. Sage's hair was permed into lilac perfection with a double quiff at the front in a similar fashion to the present day Queen Elizabeth's, and it had been a pleasant surprise to see her again. The other spirit guide she had was a much more ancient and powerful one, a Buddhist Monk who never gave his name or any information about himself, and appeared only as a brilliantly orange sphere. In her mind she called him Buddy, although he only communicated with imagery and appeared when there was a deeply significant problem. Normally Sage took care of tarot readings, messages to others, and warnings. But the last time she'd seen Buddy was back in Woodsend after Gerry had been taken to hospital.

He was here now.

After meditating for a while Celeste picked up the black mirror she rarely used to scry with and peered into its depths. Staring into the mirror in the candle-lit darkness should connect her with whatever or whoever was in the house and fear instinctively swelled inside her chest. Her hands shook. Any second now a face would appear either instead of, or behind, her own.

Who would come?

The black mirror reflected the vague outline of her face and a crown of backcombed hair. She continued to stare into it.

Show yourself...

Now the black glass began to waver; very slightly at first like staring into a millpond at night. Fear stuck fast in her throat but she swallowed it down.

Something's coming.

Stay with it.

All at once the image altered and the eyes reflected were no longer her own.

Who are you? Who's there?

In response the half-formed face quickly vanished as if down a drain.

Show yourself, you coward...

Someone laughed with a long low chuckle that echoed around the kitchen, but she held steady, watching and waiting. A landscape was now being shown to her: swaying silvery treetops and a twilight sky...rooks flying in and out of the canopy... The picture steadily grew as if painted by an imaginary artist, eventually zooming in on a woman hanging out washing in the dark. Rain dripped steadily from the trees and her boots were mired in mud. Zooming in further, the washing appeared to be dirty and saturated in something dark and oozing, yet still the woman's hands worked, methodically dipping into deep pockets and pulling out more pegs. The mirror crept up like a camera lens behind the woman's head and a pungent wave of nicotine and wood smoke wafted from the scene, along with the faint sound of ethereal humming… *'Four and twenty blackbirds baked in a pie…'* Suddenly, as if sensing an intruder the woman stopped humming. Her back stiffened and slowly, oh so slowly, she inclined her head as if to turn around.

*Now she would see…*Celeste clung onto the mirror with shaking hands, sickness hotly working its way up from her stomach as the woman began to turn… *Something bad was coming… God give me strength… God give me strength…*

Then out of nowhere a bat flew directly at her face with lightning speed, and the mirror was smashed from her grip by an invisible hand.

As the glass shattered into millions of tiny glinting shards, the candle was snuffed out and the kitchen plunged into coalface blackness. The sound of frantically fluttering wings filled her senses and a vice-like clamp of pain suddenly gripped her chest, squeezing her heart and shooting deep, throbbing pulses down her left arm and into her neck.

God protect me… please Dear Lord protect me…I'm not done yet. I have work to do… I have to do it… Please…

Clutching her chest she calmed her breathing as best she could and hobbled towards the door. In Gerry's bedside cabinet there were some spare angina tablets. Taking it step by careful step, she felt her way along the corridor towards the back bedroom, almost tripping onto the bed where less than an hour ago she'd tied Gerry's shoelaces. Blindly rummaging in the drawer her fingers found the box he kept them in and she took one, sitting in the darkness until it took effect. A few seconds later her face flushed hotly and her heart relaxed its spasmodic grip.

Thank you, God.

She wasn't beaten yet. But the dark power was extremely strong and it would do its level best to kill her.

Back in the kitchen, Celeste put the kettle on and forced a plain biscuit down before cleaning up the glass on her hands and knees. The atmosphere was thick and oppressive as if someone was breathing down her neck, and more than once came the sound of little claws scurrying invisibly across the floor. As a child she would lie in bed and hear cockroaches scuttling around on the lino floor of her parents' old cottage and that's what it sounded like – her own very personal phobia. As she stood up, still with the dustpan and brush in hand, a door in the corridor slammed shut as if caught in a breeze, and the curtains in the lounge swished open and shut, casting a silvery arrow of moonlight on the hall carpet.

She ignored the tricks and with renewed determination summoned all her strength before once more sitting down at the kitchen table. This time she would scry using a bowl of water tinted with black ink. After lighting a candle, Celeste closed her eyes and prayed for protection. Again an orange sphere appeared in the corner of her vision – her Buddhist monk. That meant the job must be done.

The trance came quickly and she peered into the ink as it began to undulate and ripple. The scene unfolding was exactly as before, with a woman in a headscarf pegging out filthy washing in the woods. The rain was torrential and the ground a quagmire. Reeling back from the stench of smoking herbs and rotting leaves, Celeste forced her attention away from the woman, and scanned the rest of the picture for information. A tiny white dot on the perimeter was now expanding and she leaned forwards to see more clearly. *Show me…* Standing at the doorway to a stone cottage was a wiry man of middle years, with a shock of white hair and a widow's peak. He seemed to be acknowledging her and raised his hand just as a glint of light caught her eye, causing her to glance upwards. A small pale face was looking out of an upstairs window; but the second she tried to focus the image faded and the camera panned out once more to the washerwoman. Then suddenly the lens rushed up to the back of the woman's head.

The bowl of ink started to vibrate wildly and the infernal humming amplified to screaming pitch. Celeste's head was pounding, sweat breaking all over her body, every arthritic joint screaming in pain.

Still she held on, staring into the ink.

Show yourself…Come on then, show me…

111

In a flash of fury the woman whirled around and glared directly at her with eyeballs that were completely white, at the same time as charging forwards with the very obvious intention of stepping right out of the picture.

Celeste reared back, tipping over the bowl of ink just as a monumental crash sounded from the front room. It sounded just as if the Welsh dresser had fallen over with all its crockery and on instinct she dashed down the corridor, fully expecting to see a mountain of broken china. Instead, the room, bathed in silvery moonlight, was calm and still, the dresser unscathed and still loaded with dinner plates. However, in the centre of the room, suspended like balloons in the air, were four or five separate balls of mist. Entranced, she stood in the doorway as each of the life-sized suspensions then began to morph into a face. Some of them appeared to be silently screaming, others twisted in pain.

She backed out immediately and slammed the door shut behind her before running blindly to the bathroom, tears streaming down her powdery cheeks. God, she was too old for all this – it took it out of you. She sat on the toilet seat, leaning forwards with her hands over her face. This was way too dangerous now, and a decision must be made before something happened to her she would not recover from. Enough had been done for tonight – she had no fight left in her and this thing was going to finish her off. An overwhelming fatigue weighed down her limbs and the urge to slump onto the floor like a rag doll was overwhelming.

Don't or you'll die.

The bright orange sphere she so rarely saw was huge now, filling the room, and she smiled faintly. *Buddy. Thank you, dear Lord.* It was all part of the plan, part of her journey, and she must overcome this physical weakness. God, how her head was banging. She put fingers to her temples and waited for the dull thumping to abate so she could see clearly what was being shown to her. The vision was weak like through an old black and white television set with a poor signal, and came loaded with a sickly wave of migraine, but it was there. Becky. Had she got the diary from

Kristy? Had she read it? This job was not finished until she saw her. *Oh God, the pain in her head…*

Forcing herself to stand up, she managed to get to the landline in the hall and speed dial the local taxi. She must see Becky, after which she'd check into a hotel for the night. She would not be coming back to this house again. Not ever. Then she slipped her coat on and grabbed the overnight bag she kept in the cloakroom in case Gerry was urgently rushed to hospital, closed the front door behind her and locked it.

Despite the freezing night air, the second she stepped outside the oppressive sickness lifted and her head cleared. She stamped her feet to keep warm until the taxi arrived, hoping it wouldn't take too long; while all around, on the periphery of her vision, brightly coloured orbs danced and flickered in the garden and along the driveway. He heart swelled. She had not been forsaken.

***

113

Chapter Fifteen

Drummersgate Forensic Unit
Sunday Evening

After handing over to the night staff, Noel decided to make one final check on Ruby before going off duty. Taking the stairs two at a time he bounded up to the first floor. The corridor was fully lit and all the consultation rooms empty. Apart from Ruby, who was in the isolation room, there was no one else up here and his footsteps clicked smartly on the tiled floor.

It would be nice if she could come back to her own room: the upset had been violent but fleeting, and she'd switched out of her aggressive teenage boy character, Dylan, pretty quickly. The poor girl had been through enough without being left up here on her own all night.

He looked through the viewing panel into the padded room. She was sitting quietly on the mattress, staring absently into the middle distance. He tapped the door and her gaze shot hungrily towards him as he walked in amid a jangle of keys.

"How are you feeling, Rubes?"

She nodded, smiling shyly.

"Do you remember anything?" he asked, leaning against the wall, hands casually in his pockets. "Do you know why you're here and not in your room?"

"No."

"Do you remember being in the dayroom watching television this afternoon?"

A cloud passed behind her eyes. "Yes, I think so."

"What was on? Anything interesting?"

Her pale blue eyes stilled to a vacant expression. She was going to switch again.

"Ruby?" His hand hovered over the panic alarm. When Ruby switched to the Dylan character she had no problem overpowering either him or any other grown man; but he hesitated for a moment, waiting to see which of her alters would appear.

As usual, her face registered mild surprise as if she was falling backwards, before she eventually focused on him once more – only this time with different eyes. The whole personality switching concept never failed to unnerve him. It really was like talking to an entirely different person but in the same body.

The woman looking at him now had the same features, which wasn't always the case, but this time wore a much harder, more challenging expression, the eyes glittering from within; and she seemed younger - more self-assured. "It was love. I loved him."

Noel shook his head. "Who am I talking to?"

"Eve."

"Eve, where's Ruby?"

"It doesn't matter. She's had a rough day. You've got me. Anyway, we work together now – you know that."

He nodded. "That's good, I'm glad you talk."

In truth, Ruby was only skirting the surface of her condition when she said her alters talked to each other. The woman had hundreds of them. Mostly though, it was the cocky teenager, Eve, who presented herself; occasionally it would be Marie or one of the younger children. Before Amanda, her psychologist, had resigned, Ruby had drawn a picture of her 'inner system'. Where most people had one personality they referred to as their true self, usually containing memories and information, Ruby had a network of corridors with compartments for each person within her mind. Each corridor and each room had a different colour and a different name. Some of the compartments were locked and the alter could not get out without a key; others lived in vaults which were never to be opened; many roamed the corridors as ghost children, and then there were those in the control room, and of course there was a gatekeeper in charge.

The main characters were Eve, Dylan, and Marie. Ruby now maintained that the previous gatekeeper had kept them all terrified; the children had bars and bolts on their bedroom doors and no one dared come out. Since he'd gone, though, they'd gradually emerged and begun to talk to each other. Marie was the new gatekeeper and she held the keys, deciding who could speak and who couldn't, although there were some children who would never be able to communicate and some best left, she said, in the vaults.

Mostly Ruby would switch to Eve. Eve said she was sixteen and Eve was borderline feckless. Eve was the one who dreamed of riding pillion on a Harley to Paris, or going to all night raves and snorting cocaine. And Eve had absolutely no fear of authority.

Noel looked into the laughing eyes. "Loved who?"

"That's for me to know and you to find out. Have you got a fag on you, Noel?"

"Don't smoke, Eve. Now listen, it's late so why don't you do us all a favour and let Ruby speak to me, eh? I'm off work now. I'm knackered and I want to go home, but what I thought I'd do – out of the kindness of my poor old heart – was give you the chance to go back to your own room tonight."

Eve pulled her bottom lip out. "Aww, poor you."

He stood up. "All right, I tried. Tell me something though, so we can avoid a repeat performance. What made Dylan appear like that? Was it something on the television?"

Eve shrugged but looked down, pretending to examine her bitten fingernails.

"Eve?"

"Okay, I'll do you a deal. If I tell you what upset us can we get into our own bed cos we hate it up here and Chantelle gave us a book we wanna read?"

He nodded. "A book? What kind of book?"

She grinned. "*Jane Eyre*."

"Really? That's brilliant – you'll love it. Okay then Eve, your turn!"

"Right, well it was that programme on holidays. They were showing caravans and that's one of our things – we can't..."

Noel crouched down so he was level with her. "Okay, okay. Stay with me. What kind of caravans?" he asked softly. "Something to do with the gypsies where you grew up?"

Eve turned her head to one side so he couldn't see into her eyes. "No. They weren't gypsies."

"Well…?"

"The park at the back of the woods. That's where they took us. To the men."

She turned back to face him, her features blank as if she'd fallen asleep with her eyes open. "Eve? Ruby?"

A few minutes elapsed. He couldn't leave her. Overhead the fluorescent lights buzzed and he looked into the camera high up on the wall. He really should be halfway home by now, flying over the moors on his motorbike to freedom. He sighed with fatigue.

"Ruby? Come back, Ruby. It's okay. You're in hospital now and you're safe."

Her eyelashes flickered slightly and her lower lip trembled. One of her youngest alters had surfaced, little more than a terrified toddler. The child's persona would not lift her head and her body began to tighten into a ball. A single tear dripped down her cheek and she brushed it away. Then another and another.

He soothed her with his honey voice. "Come back Ruby. It's all right. You are safe now. Come back, Ruby."

She would lose time now – this was one of her worst ones: the toddler was very badly traumatised and would lie in a foetus position sucking her thumb for four hours or more at any one time. He stood up and made a call. A few minutes passed and then one of the night staff appeared. "Help me get her into the bed and wrapped up, would you?" Noel said. The two male nurses lifted her onto the mattress and pulled the covers over her slight childlike form. "She's going to wake up and wonder where she is. You'll need to check on her every hour at least."

Unexpectedly, Ruby suddenly started to kick at the sheets, her feet lifting up repeatedly as if she was dancing on hot coals. And then a high-pitched voice none of them had heard before cried out, "Not my feet, no, no, not my feet. No, please…" And then the screaming started like it would never stop.

**

In the end Noel stayed on for another hour. Ruby had to be sedated for her own safety and the on-duty psychiatrist called from another hospital. By which time she'd divulged quite a lot of information. Or the latest alter to start talking had. Seven year old Tara.

What a day! It was a relief to get outside into the fresh December night air. The car park was floodlit and his Kawasaki ZZR stood alone, bright red and gleaming, at the far end. The 'Mean Machine' he called it, enjoying the familiar surge of pleasure as he walked towards it. Age thirty he'd now kind of got the life he'd been after for a while – a stylish loft apartment in Leeds Docklands; the powerful bike; spare time spent in the gym or out walking in the Yorkshire Dales – stopping for a pub lunch in one of the many beer gardens in summer or by a log fire in winter. The only thing missing was someone to share it with. The gay scene in Leeds wasn't for him after a couple of encounters had left him disillusioned. And of course, working shifts didn't help. Still…maybe one day. Right here though, and right now, with fatigue setting in and the day behind him, it was good to be young and fit and free.

At ten o'clock in the evening there was no one else around, and once out on the open road the Kawasaki roared across the moors. The wilderness held a strange beauty at any time of year but in the winter when the ebony sky was studded with a galaxy of stars, it was breath-taking, and already the stale heat and stifling mental anguish was way back there in a time capsule. What a God-given pleasure it was to be speeding home after a hard day's work. Already the sensation of falling into crisp, white sheets after a long hot shower was reeling him in, when he suddenly remembered – damn - he was supposed to call in to see Becky.

A little bit of his joy ebbed away at the required effort that would involve. Surely he could go tomorrow afternoon after the early shift? He was only going to manage about six hours sleep tonight as it was. Whatever it was about the diary could surely wait until then? He'd phone when he got home. Yes, that was a plan. He'd do that – she'd understand. She knew what it was like to be totally done in.

At that moment and out of nowhere, a large black car showed up in his rear view mirror, inches from the tail yet making no effort to overtake. He put his foot down, expecting to leave it standing but several seconds later it was still there, practically welded to his bumper. His heart skipped a beat. *Hey, this is fucking dangerous, man!*

Glancing into the wing mirror he frowned, puzzled. The bike was clocking up 90mph now and he'd be damned if he'd go faster than that on a public road. He slackened off on the throttle – the road was dry and the other side moonlit clear. "Overtake me then, you bastard!" he shouted inside his helmet. But the car surged forwards with what sounded like a V8 engine, closing the gap further – so close the rear guard was now being shunted.

"Fucking hell – do you want to kill me?"

Opening it up, Noel accelerated rapidly to over 100mph and then 110 mph, hoping to leave the car well behind, but fast approaching that hair's breadth borderline between top speed and loss of control. If he came off now he'd die instantly.

Still the tailgater matched his speed, shunting the rear guard in several second intervals. The Kawasaki could top 180mph but this was a public highway and it was dark; there were blind bends and humpback bridges. Even more alarming and confusing was that the car didn't seem to have a problem gaining on him, no matter how fast the bike accelerated.

He was going to die. Any second now it would all be over.

Perhaps, he thought later, he had a guardian angel? Or maybe it was pure adrenalin that made him go for it, but when a sharp, right fork appeared he didn't think twice. Decelerating rapidly he veered off the road at a crazy speed, almost losing the bike to the boggy moorland in the process, before quickly recovering and accelerating hard down a single track lane. *Surely*

119

the sedan couldn't follow? Surely? Either side were dry-stone walls and he tore through the night at break-neck speed not daring to even check the mirrors until some house lights came into view.

There was a village ahead and he realised it must be Cloudside. Easing off the gas slightly he risked a fleeting glance in the wing mirror and did a double-take. All was black dark. He checked again. No, there really was nothing there. Slowing down rapidly now, the bike juddered to a halt at the T-junction to the village and Noel checked the mirrors once more, just to be sure. Nothing.

Fuck, did that really happen?

Every bone, every muscle, every sinew was shaking as he rode along the quiet high street to the main square, where he parked on the cobbles. Taking off his helmet he sat and stared at the empty street for a full minute. If he didn't know better he'd say that was attempted murder. Either that or he'd just had the misfortune to lock horns with a psychopath.

A door opened from somewhere and the sound of pub chatter burst into the evening air; the warm lights of 'The Hare and Hounds' beckoning with a siren call. God, he needed a drink.

***

Chapter Sixteen

Doncaster Royal Infirmary
Sunday Evening

Becky found Callum alone in the side ward where she'd left him earlier that day. Fury swept through her as she walked into the unlit room. His drip had run dry – clamped off but un-replaced; his lips were parched and flaky, and his catheter was full to bursting point. Clearly he hadn't been washed or shaved, and there wasn't a nasogastric tube in situ to feed him either. Worse still, his skin was shiny with sweat, his respirations were rapid and shallow, and the cardiac monitor showed he had tachycardia. Where was everyone? This was way not good enough!

She marched to the nurses' station. "Who's in charge here, please?"

A hard-faced woman of indeterminate origin took her time looking up from the notes she was reading, and said in staccato English, "I am Sister in Charge. Is there problem?" Her name badge stated 'Anna' and her expression was unreadable.

Something about her lit Becky's fuse. "Oh yes, you bet there is!" Listing all the tasks needing immediate attention she found herself raising her voice and blinking away tears of frustration. "He's a man in his prime and he's not waking up. His pulse is ninety-eight, he's sweating and dehydrated and no way should he be abandoned in a side ward. Doesn't anyone care?"

Anna registered zero emotion at the outpouring before replying, "We can move Mr Ross into the main ward. I will see the drip and catheter are changed. What else?"

"I think he's in pain and he needs a wash."

Anna nodded. "Okay."

It was the best she was going to get for now, so Becky bit her lip. "I'll expect someone in his room in the next ten minutes then?" she said to Anna's back, as the other woman began to unlock the drug trolley with a self-important rattle of keys.

Back in the side ward, she did her best to calm down. What if no one had complained? Would he have been left here in discomfort all night? And why hadn't his family arrived? And what if he was reliving a horrible nightmare but couldn't call out or ask for help? It didn't bear thinking about. She took hold of one of his clammy hands. God, she was so tired she could weep. *Please don't let him die.*

Before, when he was missing, she'd resigned herself to the possibility that he might be lying somewhere in the undergrowth or left for dead in the woods. But at least it would have been a hero's death whilst doing the job he loved. Dying here in a flowery hospital gown, with a catheter in full view was hardly the same. He was a dignified man. Always had been. She wiped away the tears as they welled and dripped down her cheeks, remembering the moment he'd first approached her in front of all his jeering mates at a sixth form dance with an awkward, 'All right, Becky?" The way he'd insist on walking her home, gently pushing her against the front wall of her parents' 1930s semi, running his hands up and down her spine, seeking out her lips with his. Oh, and daft things, an earworm... *Still Waters...* Suddenly she was sobbing hard – huge racking sobs that started in her solar plexus and choked in her throat.

Please don't let him die. Please, God, please don't let him die.

The world would be so bleak and so empty without the shape of Callum in it. A person she had loved with all her heart and sorely missed all these years – and she'd had him back so briefly – a good man! *Those bastards.*

She looked up to find a student nurse staring at her in dismay.

"Was I talking out loud?"

She shook her head. "No, but you're dead upset. Can I get you anything?"

"No thanks, honestly I'm fine. I'd just like Callum to have what he needs, please." She pointed to the drip and the catheter.

"I'll sort it. Sister will do the drip in a minute. We've been short-staffed and the nurse assigned to him was suddenly taken ill and had to go home."

She raised her eyebrows. "Really? I didn't' know that."

"Yes. She had three patients needing hourly care but she'd only been with Mr Ross for about ten minutes when she started with nausea and vomiting. She looked awful – really ill. Anyway, Miss Brent – you know, our nursing officer from hell – sent her home so she must've been bad; and then we had a couple of emergency admissions." She looked at Callum. "I'll make a start, I've got half an hour before the end of my shift. Sorry."

As she fussed around, Anna came in to change the IV infusion. Silently and without looking at either Becky or the student, she walked over to the cardiac monitor and then took his temperature. "I'll call the doctor."

"Why? Do you think it's an infection? Or another internal bleed? What?"

Anna fixed her with a stare. "I will call the doctor."

The student nurse shook her head as Anna swiftly left the room. "She's actually really efficient. It's just her manner that's, you know, not what we're used to."

Sure enough events did now happen quickly: a house officer arrived to write up more painkillers and antibiotics, after which Anna administered them and a porter came to whiz Callum away for another scan.

"Can I come with you?" she asked the nurse taking him down to the X-Ray department.

She nodded. "Course you can, love. Stick with me. He'll be all right. Don't you worry – they're just thinking it's a little bleed. He might have to go to theatre but it's been spotted so that's the main thing."

Becky nodded, gathering together her belongings. It was going to be a long night but at least she'd got a friendly face and someone who talked to her now.

***

In the end the scan showed nothing untoward. Three hours later and still there didn't appear to be a logical reason for his sudden decline.

On return to the ward a space had been prepared for his bed to be positioned close to the nurses' station, and fifteen minute observations had been instructed. Becky drew up a chair so she could sit with him through the night. At least she would be here to make sure he was comfortable and not left alone again. Not ever.

The other patients had settled down to sleep, and the ward was dark apart from a few night lights. The only other soul awake was a terminally ill man in the opposite bed; emaciated and deeply jaundiced, the skin hung in folds from his bones where he lay propped up against a stack of pillows. The sour smell of decay oozed from his pores as he gasped wheezily into an oxygen mask for each breath. She'd been a nurse for long enough to know he probably wouldn't last much longer.

Things happened in hospitals at night and one of them was death. Often it came in the early hours between sleeping and waking, stealing a corpse from behind drawn curtains with one last moaning sigh, before being silently wheeled away in a metal coffin. In the morning there would be an empty bed and the distinctive reek of disinfectant. Or a new face. The missing patient would not be mentioned, and a new day would begin.

Callum had been propped up too. An oxygen mask covered his face as he continued to breathe well enough for himself, although there was now a slight rattle in his chest. Becky frowned. Hopefully the antibiotics would take care of any chest infection. Thankfully his colour was good and his temperature had dropped back to normal, as had his pulse. Perhaps it had been pain that caused the alarm? Or was it fear? She stroked his forehead. Hopefully it wasn't fear – she wouldn't wish that on anyone. Fear was the worst thing of all because no one else could see it and nothing could be done

With a sudden jolt she remembered… *Noel – where on earth was he?* Good grief, it was nearly midnight. She felt for her bag and checked the diary was still there; her thoughts had been so distracted she'd temporarily forgotten the traumatic events of the day and now they came flooding back. She was the only person who now knew about those secret graves in Woodsend, and it really would be better if he and Celeste had the information too - as soon as possible. Oh dear, she should have called Celeste, but it was far too late at night now and would have to wait until morning.

Her thoughts churned. Had Noel made any enquiries about Michael, the priest? Would there be anyone else if they couldn't find him? Kristy had to be helped urgently. But she couldn't leave Callum again even for a few hours – if something happened to her, who would look after him then? Like herself, he had no one really. There was an ageing mother with full-blown dementia; his sister had emigrated but was being kept informed, and then there were his two teenaged children who were supposed to be on their way – and that was something else that was odd. Where were they?

She held his hand tightly. *Oh why wouldn't he wake up?*

"You know why, sweet cheeks!"

The shock of his voice hit her with a sickening punch to the gut. Loud and nasty it had spoken directly into her right ear. *Oh no, no, no, no…*

Whirling round she couldn't see the little man in the black hat called Chester. *They* were attacking her again, that was all – but she knew what it was this time and anger surged through her veins. *Go away!*

"Aww…that's no way to talk to an old friend. We met right in this hospital too! Aww…come on for old time's sake, Becky, won't you? I told you thing's would get worse for ya if you messed with the boss!"

Fuck off! Fuck right off.

"Well I can see you're in some kind of mood there, Becky, I really can. But you know what you godda do…and…"

Becky swung round this way and that. *Where was he, the little…?*

125

In the bed bay the other patients lay sleeping soundly. A tinkle of music escaped from someone's headphones and the nurses were murmuring to each other over the clack of knitting needles at their desk. All was as it should be with the exception of the dying man opposite. And her frantic, wild-eyed search stopped there. She did a double take. *What the…?* Almost as if there was an invisible thread, her attention was pulled towards him and couldn't be pulled away again no matter how hard she tried.

The man's face had cranked sideways at an unnatural angle, and glossy black worms were crawling out of his empty eye sockets. Suddenly one of his claw hands swiped the oxygen mask away and the skull shot round to face her. "Hi!" said a velvety toned bass voice. "You look all done in, sweetie."

This was not the poor man who was dying in his bed. This was black witchcraft playing with her mind. Reject it, reject it – none of this is real. And how disgusting to desecrate the old man like this when he should be leaving the world with dignity!

With violently trembling legs she forced herself to stand up and walk over to the window, keeping her back to him and her mind closed to both the images and the voices. No she was not going mad and no it was not real. Celeste had taught her a thing or two about self-protection and once again she had let her guard down. She must stay strong.

The view from the ward was of a mind-numbingly ordinary multi-storey car park, and she focused on that whilst repeating a prayer of protection over and over again, blocking out the mocking laughter from the hideous creature in the bed opposite Callum. No, he was not climbing out of the bed, and no it was not him breathing into her neck. She was tired and weakened and she was not going to be ill again just when Callum needed her most. Not to mention Alice and poor Kristy. *Oh God, please help me, I have to be strong.*

"Hello, Becky! I hope you don't mind—"

She nearly jumped clean out of her skin.

"Oh my God! Celeste! What are you doing here?"

"Looking at your face I'm glad I came, love. I had a feeling you were going to need me." She inclined her head towards Callum. "I have to protect him first but then we need to talk urgently. Why don't you go down to the day room and ask those nurses if we can have some tea?"

Becky swayed with fatigue and relief.

"Go on – you need to sit down before you fall down."

"Celeste," she whispered. "The man in the bed opposite Callum. What do you see?"

Celeste looked over while Becky kept her eyes averted. "I see a man about to meet his maker."

"Does he look normal to you? I mean for a dying old man struggling for his last breath?"

"Yes."

Becky sighed heavily. "Good. Thank God."

***

Chapter Seventeen

Doncaster Royal Infirmary. Midnight

When Noel finally joined them, Becky and Celeste were in the staff canteen having a midnight meal of chicken casserole. He'd never enjoyed working nights: being unable to sleep during the day meant feeling jet lagged on shifts. But tonight he was wired, with sleep an alien concept.

Becky glanced up as he walked over. "Oh thank God! I've been so worried about you. Your mobile wouldn't work. You look terrible."

He gestured towards the serving hatch. "Thanks – back atcha! I'm just going to get something to eat before they finish serving. Won't be a minute."

After he'd bolted down a mountain of cottage pie, he leaned back and stretched before appearing to notice Celeste for the first time. "Hello again!"

"Bet you're surprised to see me again so soon, love?"

"After tonight I don't think I'll ever be surprised about anything ever again. If I'd walked into a room full of white rabbits eating pickled eggs with chopsticks I wouldn't have looked twice." He shook his head, smiling to himself. "Funny, isn't it, how we start to accept weird things as being normal? I mean really – what's sane and what's not? What keeps us out here and others locked up with a lunatic label slapped on their heads? Thin line…thin line…"

"What's happened, Noel?" Becky asked.

He related the motorbike incident and the impossibility of the car gaining on him on the straight; and the feeling that whoever was driving was not messing around or trying to scare him but really did want him dead.

"I don't think that car was real," said Becky.

"Oh, for fuck's sake."

"No, honestly – hear me out – this is why I desperately needed you to come over tonight. If we don't share this stuff and face up to it we really are in deep shit. I've got Linda Hedges' diary with me and you need to read it right now!" She took it out of her bag and slid it across the table.

Noel picked it up. "I can't believe you managed to get this!"

Becky inclined her head towards Celeste. "Let's just say I had a bit of help. Anyway, read it. Noel, there are satanic rituals and human sacrifices going on in Woodsend – children being born and used purely for that purpose! Linda found a plot of relatively recent, unmarked graves in the cemetery, which means that for years and years, births and deaths were not being registered. The day after she discovered this and made enquiries she collapsed and died."

As Noel scanned the notebook, the other two waited.

"I'll get more coffees to keep us awake," said Becky.

Eventually he closed the book and put it back on the table. "Shit!"

Becky stared at him. "Now do you see what I'm on about? And Alice is *still with* Paul Dean! Ruby told Celeste today that they'll baptise her when she's thirteen – that's baptise her in the name of Satan! And she'll be thirteen any day now."

Celeste interrupted, "Once Alice has been baptised in the name of the Antichrist she will be taking part in satanic rites, the dark arts and sacrifices! I am not party to the rituals but I have been shown enough by spirit to know that pain, torture and fear feed their energy. They want power over others, or revenge on an enemy, and of course some just want personal perversions satisfied, which will include murder, rape and paedophilia. Anyone who joins will have to commit some horrible act that will bind them to the coven forever. Stupidly they believe the evil invoked is controllable and not the other way round. In reality they themselves become vessels for the inhuman; and to cut a long story

129

short any hope of Alice living a normal life will effectively be over. If she doesn't die she will go mad."

"I can't believe this is real," said Noel. "No way. It's fucking medieval."

"Oh yes," said Celeste. "This is the diseased mentality of hags and warlocks dating back to the beginning of time. And much as we like to think we're all modern and sophisticated and have all the answers, I'm afraid this kind of thing still exists and in fact, is more potent than ever because the rest of us refuse to accept its very existence. In our book evil is in our imagination and possession is madness. We make it easy for them."

Becky leaned forwards. "If ever proof were needed that this threat is real, just look at Jack and Kristy! They were two of the most level-headed, intelligent people I've ever met, not to mention humanists with big hearts, and look what happened to them! Only Kristy isn't getting the help Jack had and if you'd seen what I saw today you wouldn't need any more convincing; especially if you add in the fact that she *coincidentally* has the same doctor who presided over Woodsend for forty years. So how did that happen?"

He held up his hands.

"Exactly. And even though Callum was conscious and talking when he was found, he certainly isn't now; and I only just learned from the night staff that his kids haven't arrived yet because they had a car accident en-route. Oh and his nurse went off sick this morning within minutes of being in his room, leaving him alone all day with a soaring temperature and tachycardia; and tonight I had one of the most horrific experiences I've ever had. On top of that Celeste has some pretty shocking information too, but you've got to keep an open mind, Noel."

"Sorry. I had the scare of my life tonight and stupidly had a couple of pints to steady my nerves. I've been persuading myself for the last two hours that nothing sinister happened apart from having the bad luck to be chased by a nasty driver."

"Only you know that it couldn't have happened like that."

"Yes. It actually wasn't physically possible."

"'They' can throw all sorts of obstacles in our paths..." said Celeste. "...banks of fog, a bat flying into your face, a snake in the car – anything to cause you to go off the road or have an accident of some kind."

They sat in silence for a few moments.

"I think we stay sane precisely because we don't really believe any of this," Noel said eventually.

"And now?"

"Now we're insane."

Becky laughed. "No we're not. We just have to accept that this is real. It is! There are some pretty nasty people out there who're meddling with the dark arts."

Noel nodded. "I suppose I just don't get how that actually works. But somehow it does..." His voice trailed off for a moment before he snapped back. "Oh, I didn't tell you earlier when we spoke, Becky, because you'd got enough on your plate, but Ruby had a bit of a set-back today."

"What happened?"

"She was watching TV when a holiday programme came on about caravans. She switched to Dylan and attacked some of the other patients. We got her into the isolation room and left her to calm down, but when I went to see her at the end of my shift she switched back into Eve; started telling me about something being love, about 'loving him', but stupidly I lost the thread and asked what had happened earlier instead – you know, what had set her off? Anyway, that's when I got Tara."

"The seven year old?"

"Yes." He looked across at Celeste. "This is confidential and..."

Celeste nodded. "I can go if you want, but Becky has asked me to work with Ruby to help her control her clairvoyance. I can't avoid her alter personalities and I'll be supervised at all times. Anyway, I've no interest in her medical condition, only to try and help. It's up to you if I stay or go."

"Stay," said Becky. "We need you. Please stay."

She nodded, and folded her hands in her lap.

Noel continued. "Okay, well I think this might help...Tara described a caravan in the woods at night. She says her father took her and her sister from their beds one night, and her sister was then locked in one of the caravans while she was taken to another bigger one. Her sister was told to stay quiet and they would come back for her, but she could hear her crying as they left. Tara described a table covered in a purple cloth with a broken black cross hanging on the wall. There was a strong 'horrible smell' and there were candles burning. 'Huge, big fat men' were getting drunk, and it was all smoky. After that she blanked out and started screaming about her feet being on fire. They'd burned upside down crosses on the soles, can you believe?"

"Evil pigs."

"I'm assuming the 'good sister' was kept safely in the 'other' caravan while it all happened? Nevertheless, the seven year old did recall being taken there by her father and she does have the scars on her feet to prove it!"

"Was she able to relate any other detail that could help?"

He shook his head. "No, she was extremely traumatised. I don't think, to my knowledge that seven year old Tara has spoken to us like that before."

Celeste frowned. "Who is Ruby's mother?"

"Natalie," said Becky. "She was brought up by Ida, though – Paul Dean's wife, or partner anyway – but her natural mother was Natalie Dean."

"Paul Dean's first wife?"

Becky shook her head. "No, sorry – she's Paul's sister."

"Now I feel sick," said Noel. "Did Ruby tell you this?"

"Yes, well Marie did! Ruby's got a grandma called Cora who still lives in Bridesmoor. Cora and Lucas Dean, who lived at Tanners Dell in the old mill, had five children together – Paul, Derek and Rick, and the two girls, Natalie and Kathleen. Natalie's dead now but she was Ruby's real mother."

"Where did Ida come from, then?" Noel asked.

Celeste spoke softly and rapidly. "Her name isn't Ida, it's Lilith."

132

"You've lost me," said Becky, turning to look at her.

"Me too," said Noel.

"That's what I've come to tell you urgently. She's on to me now. I can feel her around me, using my eyes…" Celeste started to shake all over and Becky put an arm around her.

"It's okay, Celeste. Just tell us what we need to know if you can."

"Earlier this evening, I was shown a short, wizened woman with black hair wound into a headscarf – this is how Ida presents herself, I believe – but the thing is, she has shown herself to me now. I see her as the demon she really is and she knows that and doesn't like it. Normally she'd only show herself to hypnotise someone or scare them out of the wits. Most people will only see the human packaging. You must understand, this is not Ida or Ruby's step mother – this woman's eyes are totally white – no irises and no pupils – all white! This is not a human soul. I'm going to be sick. Her name isn't Ida. It's Lilith." Celeste fell back against her chair, her eyelids fluttering as if she was having a small fit.

"Are you okay, Celeste?"

Celeste nodded but she'd lost all her colour, fumbling in her bag for paracetamol. "Find out about Lilith! You'll see…it's all making sense. I'm sorry, I've got the most excruciating headache and it's getting worse."

The other two waited while she took a gulp of water and swallowed the tablets. "I'll be alright in a minute, I'm sure."

Frowning, Noel said, "Becky, do you know if the other sister, Kathleen, is still alive?"

Becky nodded. "I would think so. She's Derek's wife. They had Bella, who's now in psychiatric care, of course."

"What about Rick?"

Celeste shook her head, "No."

"Well, Cora should have a few answers, I suppose!" said Becky. "If she's mother to them all?"

"Don't be tempted to go and see her," said Celeste, pressed her fingers to her temples. "I'm being told you must not – it's too dangerous."

"We've got to get Alice out of there, though. We've got to blow this apart – there are children involved and it should be headline news. Oh God, who can help us?"

"Jes," said Celeste. By now she was looking drugged and haggard, struggling to keep her eyes open.

"Are we talking about Ruby's dealer boyfriend in Leeds?"

Celeste half-smiled. "He wasn't always that way."

"I don't understand something," said Noel. "What happened between Ruby giving birth to Alice at the age of fourteen, and then turning up in Leeds years later in her twenties. Did she live with Jes at that old mill the whole time, do you think?"

"He looks like her," said Celeste.

The other two shook their heads in confusion. "Who? What?"

"I've got the name *Rosella*…I've got her as quite a strong presence now. Find Jes, one of you before…before…I…"

"Celeste, are you always like this when you go into a trance or should we be worried? You don't look at all well," said Becky.

Celeste was ashen.

Noel said, "We need to find Jes then, and we need to speak to the grandmother, Cora."

"And we need police help," said Becky. "I think I'm going to trust Toby Harbour, after all."

Celeste murmured. "Yes."

"Well, I'm not going to sleep tonight," said Noel. "Actually I doubt I'll ever sleep again. So if you call Toby I'll try St Mark's to see if I can find Michael for Kristy. Is that a plan?"

Celeste's voice cut in. "I feel horribly faint."

"Put your head between your knees," said Becky, putting an arm across her shoulders again. "Noel, would you get her some more cold water?"

Celeste let herself be pushed forwards. "Do you know, I just don't feel myself? It's the weirdest thing – like I'm out of my body."

Becky frowned. "Celeste, are you going to be okay?"

The older lady looked poorly, with bruised half-moon shapes under her eyes. She nodded slightly. "I think it's passed. I desperately need to sleep – it's been an extremely taxing day and all my energy's gone."

"Shall we get you a taxi home?"

"Just to the Moat House. I don't want to go back to the bungalow."

"Why can't you go home?" Becky asked.

"Trust me, love. I'm better in a hotel tonight." She glanced at the clock on the refectory wall. "Well, what's left of it. I'll ring you in the morning, Becky, but I want you to both promise me that you'll watch your backs. Don't let your guard down for a minute. Not now I know just what we're up against. Do you know, I'm so tired I don't know that I can even stand up?"

"I'd offer you a pillion ride but I think a taxi might be better," Noel said, trying to make light of it.

Celeste clung to the edge of the table as if she was about to fall, her colour grey.

"Do you have a heart condition?" Becky asked.

She nodded and then shook her head. "No. Yes. Well, I had angina this afternoon for the first time but I've no pain. I just feel odd."

"You probably just need a good night's sleep then." Becky quickly dialled a local taxi firm on her mobile, waiting for it to be answered. "Ring me anytime, Celeste, if you feel worried… Oh, hello – yes taxi to the DRI as soon as possible please… Moat House… Mrs Frost. Yes, ten minutes is fine, thanks."

The chattering night staff seemed to suddenly disperse and the canteen lights dimmed. Each stared at their reflection – just the three of them sitting hunched over a table with their empty coffee cups; as if marooned in a tiny boat on a tar-black ocean.

***

Chapter Eighteen

2002, Tanners Dell

Ruby, Aged 14

He is the gypsy boy from my dreams with his golden skin and glossy, dark hair. He kisses my neck where it tingles and runs gentle hands around my waist. "I love you, angel girl…" Above us sunlight dapples between the shimmering leaves and his touch sends little shivers down my spine as he unfastens my blouse button by button, then covers my mouth with his. He smells of fresh air and tastes of tobacco; and shame washes through me…because I like it so much.

Afterwards we lie on the warm earth listening to the water burbling over the rocks.

"Where did you come from?" he asks, tracing fingers up and down my arm. "You're like some kind of water nymph with your fairy hair and your fairy nose."

I feel a stupid half-smile on my lips because how the hell should I know?

"I've seen you before in another life, did you know that? I came here looking for something else but then there you were – floating in the water."

"I saw you in a dream."

"Did you? Did you now?" He rolls onto his stomach, searching my face with his twinkly brown eyes. "You must have had a life up to now though, angel girl. Did you lose your memory or something?"

Again I shrug and nestle in close to make him stop asking me stuff. "I don't know."

He kisses my forehead, strokes my hair back. "But you're from round here, right?"

"Mmm."

Ah, but that's just shard of memory now: a brilliant electrical flash in the dark bowl of my head – and now it's gone. I think another day must have disappeared since then, but I don't know for sure. I'm waking up now, you see, and it's black dark, so like, what happened in the middle? For a moment all I can do is try to breathe calmly because this happens all the time, except right now I just don't know where the hell I am.

There's a slight draft as the bedroom door nudges open and in comes a short, stout man who walks around the edge of the bed and stands at the bottom staring straight at me. Who is he? He seems to want me to do something and I struggle to sit up. Sleeping soundly next to me is a stranger – a handsome man with swarthy skin stark against the pillow – if only I could catch the fragment of my dream I might know him – but the knowledge skitters around on the edge of my mind like a butterfly evading a net. A sliver of moonlight glints in the wardrobe mirror and branches scratch against the window. Still the portly figure at the end of the bed stares at me. What does he want? Am I supposed to be doing something?

The pull of his stare intensifies and his eyes are scary, boring into mine, pale and hard like glass. Fear stirs in my stomach. He seems to be moving towards me. How can that be unless he's floating with no legs? No, this isn't right. It must be a nightmare and I have to wake up. This isn't safe, it isn't normal. *Wake up, wake up, wake up!* I close my eyes and open them again. Only to find the man's face is an inch from mine and someone is screaming the house down.

"What the fucking hell…?"

The man beside me is shaking me and slaps my face. "Snap out of it, Ruby. It's just a dream."

"Ruby?"

"That's your frigging name isn't it?"

"Oh."

His anger dissipates in a heartbeat and he reaches for me. "Aw, I'm sorry. You're a strange little thing, aren't you, angel girl?

Come on, now." He strokes my hair, holds me close "You've had a bad dream, that's all."

I still don't know who the hell he is.

"I'm here now. I'm gonna take care you of you, alright?"

He reaches over to rummage in a bag, then gives me something – a small pill – and I take it. And soon everything is alright just like he said.

"I'm gonna find out who you are," he says as I drift away.

"Why?"

"But first I need to find out who I am."

"Don't you know?"

The name 'Rosella' skirts around the edge of my mind on a cloud of scent, like she lives in a summer meadow. And then she's gone.

***

Chapter Nineteen

Doncaster

Monday 28th December, 2015

Noel cut the bike's engine and parked outside St Marks Church. At three in the morning it was glacially silent as he walked around to the porch door. Locked. Of course.

Stepping back he looked up at the spire reaching into the starlit night, taking in the vast stained glass windows and the gargoyle-adorned stonework. Built on the site of an original Anglo-Saxon church, which had burnt to the ground in Victorian times, it had subsequently been lovingly restored in all its gothic splendour and he marvelled at the hard work and dedication that must have gone into it. All around the building lay graves – Celtic crosses, marble headstones and toppling slabs – now shrouded in celestial mist; and it was to the oldest part of the graveyard that he now walked.

Most of the headstones had sunk along with the vestiges of their occupants, the epitaphs barely decipherable, yet the place exuded a peace and comfort quite like no other; as if time had paused from the rush and chaos of modern life. How many had died as children, he thought, from disease or 'sudden illness' and not really that long ago either? Life expectancy had changed beyond all recognition. There was probably more of an acceptance of death back then, although the lack of medical or scientific knowledge must have presented a strange kind of terror. Little wonder people both turned to and feared the supernatural in equal measure.

Before he'd come here for the first time, with Becky just before Christmas, he must have passed this place a thousand times and never given it a second glance, partially hidden as it was behind wrought iron railings, posters and great swaying oaks. With his hands deep in his pockets and his jacket collar pulled up, he walked back to the church porch and slumped onto a wooden bench to wait for dawn. *Dear Lord, what on earth was going on? If only he could make sense of it all.*

He'd never believed in the after-life or ghosts or even God – all of it, to his mind, was based on myths and superstition. Although brought up in a traditionally Christian household from where he had gone to Christmas carol services and various weddings and funerals, there had never been much in the way of religious contemplation; in fact one of two of his elderly relatives had even gone so far as to turn him off Christianity with their out-and-out condemnation of homosexuality. But now the questions were forced on him: whatever had happened to Ruby had been pure evil inflicted on an innocent child and her subsequent mental illness he could understand; but the strange events since her hypnosis had unlocked something else altogether – a darkness hell-bent on wiping out any investigation into her past. *How could that happen and why? Did something else exist? Really?*

He leaned forwards, head in hands.

Way too many inexplicable events had happened now. Way too many. That black sedan inches behind him taking bends at over 100 mph and still shunting the rear guard with ease… His thoughts tracked down a labyrinth of routes with a dead end at every turn. Nothing made sense. *The demonic Lilith? Oh for goodness sake…* Keep to the facts… Becky needed to find someone she could trust in the police force who would break the whole thing open once and for all. And here he was trying to help Kristy. Kristy with a classic case of mental breakdown because of the strain. *If you'd seen what I saw…*

The tombstones appeared luminescent, sparkling with crystal glints where the moonlight caught the frost; and on the periphery of the graveyard a wall of yews bowed darkly. All was silent and utterly still.

At that moment a cloud floated across the surface of the moon and he looked up. *Was there ever such a haunting sight?* A breeze sighed into the back of his neck and a flurry of leaves rustled around the porch door.

He frowned, his attention suddenly drawn to the line of yews at the far end of the graveyard. Was there someone there or was it his imagination? *A lit cigarette? A spark of red?* He narrowed his eyes, peering harder into the gloom. No, it was just his wild imagination. He blinked and shook his head. He was spooked, that was all – how silly – imagining a dark shape standing there; a man in a long black coat with a black dog on a chain, the dog with red eyes. How silly. How very *Rosemary's Baby*…Those films – *The Exorcist* and *The Omen* – they'd scared him witless as a boy and they scared him bloody witless now.

He looked at the ground and stamped his feet. *Hours to go yet. Was this a crap idea or what?*

He almost smiled at the thought of recounting this to Becky – far better that he'd gone home for some rest if not sleep, like she said. He kicked a small piece of gravel, letting it rattle across the tarmac… just as an audible sigh breathed into his neck.

He swung round.

There was nothing there but the stone wall of the church; and his own breath steaming on the air.

God, he really was spooked…ridiculous…totally ridiculous…

He turned back to face the graveyard.

Holy shit there was someone there…

Standing under the yew trees there was absolutely definitely and without any room for doubt, the figure of a man holding a large, black dog on a chain. Transfixed, Noel squinted into the dark, realising with a thump to the chest that both man and beast had eyes of pinprick red. He sat riveted to the spot for what seemed like an eternity, as the figures appeared to lift off the ground and float towards him.

Adrenalin kick-started his flight but it was like wading through deep water with his movements in slow motion. His energy had drained away, and the surreal atmosphere crackled with static as, grabbing for the bench, he managed to propel himself upright and n stumble as if drunk onto the path towards the lich gate. *Don't look round…don't look round…*

There was an all-night café up the road. He'd wait in there.

***

Running on bleary-eyed, caffeine-fuelled fatigue, Noel caught up with the vicar of St Mark's at just before seven. The last four hours had been spent staring into one coffee after the next trying to think of anything other than what he'd just witnessed. It wasn't real, that's what he kept telling himself. *It was not fucking real.*

It was still dark when he returned but there were cars and people around. Apparently he was lucky because normally the vicar wouldn't arrive until eight but he had a busy day ahead with two funerals before lunch, and wanted time to prepare.

"What can I do for you?" he asked, bustling inside amid a rattling of keys and flicking of switches for the overhead heaters.

Noel's tongue seemed to stick to the roof of his mouth as he tried to find the words. "We really need help."

"Come through," said the vicar. "Come into the vestry – I'll put the kettle on."

Never had there been a conversation more awkward, Noel told Becky later. But somehow he'd managed to relay what had happened to the medical team since they'd treated Ruby, and how everyone who had tried to investigate Woodsend had either died or become extremely ill. Finally he related what had happened to Becky at this very church and described the priest who had helped her.

"Priest?"

"He said he was a priest... Roman Catholic, yes I know."

"Well he wouldn't have been employed here at the C of E, would he? No, I don't know him at all."

"We need help, we really do. Our lady doctor is seriously ill and..."

The vicar frowned. "Would you like me to see her?"

"Yes."

"I would need permission from the doctor supervising her, and from my superiors."

143

"But that would take time. And her doctor's a problem." He explained why.

The vicar raised his eyebrows. "Are you telling me what I think you're telling me?"

The information sat between them.

Noel leaned forwards. "Look, just like you I'm a professional person who's come across something terrible and inexplicable. I have to get this doctor some help because she has no one else, and time is running out. My colleague and I are at our wits' end. We know the doctor looking after her care is blocking any kind of spiritual help but she needs it, she really does."

"Have you been to the police about this village?"

Noel shook his head. "Yes, and the officer who investigated it is now in hospital in a coma. Meanwhile, I have to get this lady some spiritual assistance, and that's all I'm asking for."

"I see. Yes, well no doubt she's in a state of mental and spiritual collapse with the stress of it all and needs…"

"She's possessed."

The vicar stared at him. "Ah now, come on—"

"Didn't Jesus cast out demons?"

The vicar smiled tightly. "I think that was written before mental illness was understood."

"Hmm…you lot quote from the bible when it suits you though, don't you?"

There hadn't been an intended insult but a cloud passed behind the other man's eyes.

"I will see this lady if you obtain her doctor's permission as well as her next of kin's, and then I will have to approach—"

"Then if you'll excuse my language – she's fucked because that isn't going to happen." Noel stood up to leave. What was the point? No wonder that nasty little gang in Woodsend had got away with this for so long – everyone was letting them! He got as far as the porch door when the vicar's voice called out behind him, "You could try St Mary's in York Close."

Noel stood stock still for a second, then raised his hand in acknowledgement and carried on walking.

***

By the time he bounded into work less than an hour later, he had a name and number in his back pocket. It would have to keep for a few hours yet, but how the hell was he going to get through today when the information was burning a hole in his head? Whatever had appeared in the graveyard a few hours ago, if it had been to frighten him off, had served only to heighten the urgency. Poor, poor Kristy. It could be himself next and he'd hope that someone would help him if that time came.

Upstairs, next to the staff room there was a shower and he stripped off and stepped in, letting scalding water bring his mottled, cold skin back to life. What a weird twenty four hours it had been! Dog tired with scratchy eyes and a rumbling stomach – what a way to start the working day too. Still, his mind chattered like it would never stop and his nerves were jumping like they'd been electrocuted. He'd take Handover from the night staff and then try and make a call to this guy, Michael, and fix up an appointment. How brilliant he'd been able to track him down. Becky would be so relieved.

The priest at St Mary's had been pretty coy but when Noel described Michael in meticulous detail and related just what kind of trouble a lady doctor was in, he'd finally relented and given him Michael's telephone number. Michael worked privately and was not part of any religious order. Now a retired professor in theology he lived alone on the outskirts of Leeds. Apparently he was not at all well – recently diagnosed with terminal cancer of the prostate – and would only see someone by appointment and if it was urgent. Noel had grimaced at the information, but time was of the essence and Michael was very likely Kristy's only chance. It seemed odd though, when just a couple of weeks ago the man had been a tall, broad-shouldered picture of health.

After showering he threw on yesterday's clothes and used the emergency stopover supplies he kept in his locker to freshen up. It never felt good without the usual routine of scented soap,

145

essential oils and good cologne, not to mention a good night's sleep and clean underwear. Oh well, doubtless he wouldn't be running into David Beckham today.

Just as he was slamming the locker shut his mobile bleeped. Becky's name flashed on the screen: 'URGENT. CALL NOW!'

He rang her back while running downstairs to the ward, "What is it Becks? Night staff are waiting to knock off."

"It's Celeste. I needed to talk to her urgently because of something that happened about an hour ago. I kept calling and calling her room. In the end I asked the hotel staff to check on her... Noel, she's dead!"

***

<u>Chapter Twenty</u>

Earlier that morning

At seven o'clock Becky had finally reached DC Toby Harbour on his mobile.

"Hi Toby! It's Becky – Callum's partner over at the DRI? I need to speak to you and it's really important. Is there any chance you could call in?"

He sounded as if he was running. "Where? Up at the hospital?"

"Yes. I've been here all night. Look, I just need to quickly freshen up, so could we say half an hour from now in the canteen? I'll buy you breakfast."

"Aye, alright."

"You okay – you sound out of breath?"

"Just doing t' morning run. Got football practice tonight and I'm well unfit. Anyway, yeah, I'll be straight over. Can I ask what it's about, though? I've got a right busy day on."

She took a deep breath. "Yes, but Toby, I need you to keep this one hundred percent to yourself – the whole thing! Please, please do not tell a single soul, especially not any of your colleagues or superiors – no-one. There is a little girl's life at stake and there may be several other people's too. I need you for half an hour at most while you have breakfast and I promise I'll explain. But please promise me you won't tell anyone you're coming?"

"Yeah okay, I'm on me way, Becky."

She clicked off the phone. *Please God he could be trusted.*

Last night had been one of the worst nights she could ever remember. After Celeste and Noel had left she'd returned to the ward, still with the memory fresh in her mind of the dying man in the bed opposite Callum. Frankly it had been something of a selfish relief to find the curtains had been drawn around the old man's bed, and with some trepidation she sat down next to Callum

147

and took hold of his hand, her focus firmly fixed on the man she loved. The night would be a long one.

From within the curtained area came the distinctive Cheyne-stokes respirations of a human being about to die, with the gap between each rattling lunge for breath often as long as several minutes. The stench of fear and death hung in the air, and she thought about the other patients who might wake up listening to a life slipping away in the bed next to theirs. How many people had died in the bed they were now sleeping in? Whose turn would it be next? As a nurse who had often worked a night shift, she knew it was usual for a dying patient to be removed to a side ward and wondered why that was not the case here.

Aged eighteen, one of her first tasks on nights had been to lay out a dead body. It had been during the grey hours of pre-dawn; and she had been left alone in a side ward with a fresh corpse. No matter how many times she told herself the man was now an empty vessel and the soul had departed, it had still spooked her beyond measure: the orifices had to be plugged and the body washed, which involved turning it on its side. Invariably an audible sigh would escape during the process as air was forced from the deepest part of the lungs, but she hadn't been prepared for that and so when it happened she dropped the dead weight on its face. After standing by the far wall whimpering for a while, it had then taken a superhuman effort of mind over matter to persuade herself to heave the poor deceased person back around and put on the shroud. Up to that point she'd though of herself as a pretty practical kind of girl, and the episode had shocked her. Just what was it about corpses that freaked us out so much, she wondered?

Another desperate, rasping inhalation emanated from behind the curtain and Becky forced herself to think about other things. Being awake all night could really get you down, she thought, gripping Callum's hand. Leaning in close to him, she whispered, "What did you see, Callum? What do you know? Something's stopping you from waking up and I honestly believe it's black magic! How crazy is that?" She bowed her forehead to his. "Oh please, please wake up. I'm so alone."

A tremendous fatigue overcame her, dragging her like a weighted body further and further down into the depths of what rapidly became a highly disturbing dream; one in which she was still very much awake. Initially it was akin to having had too much to drink and being unable to stay awake for another second: the ceiling was spinning and the floor started to roll queasily, but then the edges of the ward began to blur and Callum's bed was swaying like a boat on the swell. Holding on to the metal frame her face burned hotly and nausea lurched greasily from the pit of her stomach. *Oh God, I'm going to be sick… right here on the floor…*

Briefly she blacked out, before emerging into a dreamlike state where the air had turned strangely blue as if lit by an electric storm and all the other beds had vanished, revealing a different kind of room altogether – a pre-war hospital ward which stretched at least three times the length of this one. But empty. Entirely empty. It was then that a line of figures shrouded in domino robes and masks began to file in through the double doors at the far end, silently gliding into the middle of the room.

It's just a dream. Just a damn dream. It's your subconscious playing tricks. Wake up…wake up…

She tried to stand, shouting for help while repeatedly pressing the emergency buzzer, but nothing happened and no sounds came.

After that she must have lost consciousness again because when she came to, she was frozen to the bone, lying on the floor next to the hydraulics underneath Callum's bed. The back of her skull was sore to the touch and her lungs were rigid making it difficult to inhale. Clutching at the bedclothes they slipped onto the floor and she flopped down again.

How long had she been here?

Eternity was the only way she could describe it later. Eternity and yet perhaps only a few hours because outside it was still dark, although the bed opposite was now a scrubbed, shiny mattress smelling of disinfectant.

"Goodness," said one of the nurses. "What on earth are you doing down there?"

Her neck and limbs were stiff, her skin icily numb as she struggled to sit up. "I fell. I must have fallen."

"You've been here every night since he came in, haven't you? You know you really ought to go home and get some sleep. We can take care of Callum."

The clock showed it was just after six and the first medicines were being given out with cups of tea. "I don't suppose I could have some hot tea, could I please? I just..." She rubbed the back of her neck and wrapped one of Callum's blankets round her shoulders. *It would be ridiculous to cry.*

"Of course," said the kindly nurse, reaching over to the tea trolley. "Here you go, love. Oh you poor thing – are you sure you're alright?"

She nodded, gulping the hot liquid down her parched throat. "Oh God, that's good."

With one last look at Callum, she finally agreed to go and lie down in one of the visitors' rooms that had become available, and on the way, before she could rest, decided to call Celeste in order to help her understand what the hell was going on.

But Celeste, it transpired, was dead.

***

Toby was already halfway through a cooked breakfast by the time Becky burst into the canteen. Signalling to him she'd be two minutes, she joined the queue for tea and toast, relieved to have a couple of minutes to compose herself.

Celeste is dead. OhmyGod... OhmyGod... And then there were two...

Toby Harbour was fresh faced and clean-shaven – an overgrown teenager wolfing down bacon, eggs, sausages, tomatoes and mushrooms like his life depended on it. A tiny part of her regretted involving him, but what choice was there? If she went to the police desk she could be routed through to someone who'd report straight to Ernest Scutts and that was far too much of a risk. Toby was the only person she knew on Callum's team who might be able to discretely do some fact-finding. That was all she'd ask for – just some fact-finding to see where it led.

He stared at his empty plate as if he couldn't believe it had all gone.

"I wish I could eat like that and not put weight on," Becky said.

"There's nowt to you."

No one had said that in a long while, Becky thought, although to be fair her clothes did hang off her these days. When this was all over – if it ever was – she'd buy herself a whole new wardrobe; see what was in fashion these days for a girl at least two sizes smaller than she had been. And when the divorce was through and the house sold, she'd buy a little one-bedroom flat in Leeds Docklands like Noel had, with polished floorboards and high white ceilings and sash windows. Everyone needed a dream and that would be hers. Unless Callum…Well, best not think about that.

"I have lost a bit recently," she said, taking a gulp of tea. "Do you want anything else to eat?"

"Are you not eating that toast?"

She pushed it over to him. "Toby, you remember that odd incident the night Callum was brought in – you know when…?"

He grimaced. "Yeah, well I'm hardly gonna bloody forget, am I? Spooky or what?"

"Hmm. Well, I hope you've got an open mind."

"Oh God, what's coming?"

She grimaced. "Okay, look, I have to tell you some stuff and I need you to listen. And then I'm going to ask for a bit of help, that's all."

"Shoot."

She shot. And when she was done she passed him Linda Hedges' diary, which he scanned through.

"And on top of all that, Celeste passed away a few hours ago in her hotel room."

"You're joking? What did she die of?"

Becky shrugged. "I don't know but it was sure as hell sudden. So do you see – there's something extremely frightening going on that no one believes unless it happens to them, by which time it's far too late. And I think, well my theory is, that it stems from a satanic coven in Woodsend." She held up her hands. "Yes I know, a lot of these things have been proved rubbish over the years and they don't exist and if they do it's a bunch of mad people or a paedophile ring that needs to be infiltrated... but ..."

Toby nodded.

"...but in this case there really is something horrific going on, and people are dying and getting hurt. There have been way too many for it to be a string of coincidences, and now only me and my colleague, Noel, are left. But who's going to believe us without evidence? And what about our own safety? There was an attempt to drive Noel off the road yesterday, for example. We're both in danger and time is of the essence before we're stopped from exposing this. Long story short, Toby, we need enough proof to take to another police force outside the area: so we have to find Ruby's boyfriend, Jes, and we need to speak to Cora Dean. With Callum spark out and Kristy sectioned under the mental health act, there is no other testimony apart from Ruby's. And Ruby is, of course, clinically insane."

Indecision hovered in the young officer's eyes. Gung-ho combined with the desire to help clearly jostled with a deeper level of caution and disbelief. Fear, Becky thought, governed us all.

"Alice is twelve!" she re-iterated.

Finally he levelled with her. "I work really closely with Sid Hall, Becky. He'd know if I were up to summat. But I'm off duty later so I'll try and track down this Jes for you. I used to work in the Chapeltown area and I've an idea where I might find him. With regard to the woman, Cora, I'm a lot more cautious – if she hot-wired it back to her son you'd been asking questions they could come looking for you. And if Scutts hears about it when the case is officially closed he'll have my balls tied round a lamp post. I've not crossed him but I've 'eard he's a nasty bastard. One or two officers have disappeared off the force under his watch, but I

152

always thought it was for a good reason. Anyhow, not to digress, I'll have to think on that one."

He stood up.

"So, what? You'll try to find Jes tonight?"

Toby nodded, reaching for his parka. "Yes, it'll have to be later on, though. I'll ring you on your mobile, shall I?"

"Yes please. Look, if for any reason you can't get hold of me then here's Noel's number." She scribbled it down and handed it over. "Or I'll be here on the ward with Callum."

He smiled tightly as he transferred the number into his phone. "Yeah, well Callum was always good to me – kept me protected from the politics. I owe him a lot. I can't say I believe any of this stuff about dark forces, Becky, but I'll keep an open mind, and I get that a lot of people are getting hurt whenever they get close to that place. I hope Callum picks up soon, I really do. For what it's worth, neither me nor Sid think it was a car crash, and the photos on his mobile were all deleted by someone. That phone's empty now – Sid told me. Odd that, innit?"

"Really?"

He nodded.

"Be careful, Toby," she said as he walked away.

She watched him wind his way in between tables full of nursing staff hungry after an early start. The day was brightening with all the immediacy of blinds being shot up, and she pictured a white ball of light around him. He was sure going to need it.

***

Chapter Twenty-One

Drummersgate Forensic Unit

Understaffed as they were, Noel had to take paracetamol and lie down on the staff room sofa. It was like having the flu and a hangover combined – impossible to think straight let alone take care of patients and give out medication.

Celeste was supposed to have been coming in later to see Ruby, and Ruby was looking forward to it. She wanted to know more, she said, about her clairvoyance and what it all meant. Apparently, last night she'd tried talking to the ghost drummer boy and helped him pass over. It was exciting but also scary because other spirits had started shouting in her ear – always the left one – and some of them were angry because they said she'd promised them things she couldn't remember and were going to 'get' her. Not all of the spirits, she said, were dead people from the prison, either – some were demons.

He rubbed his hand over and over his face as if that would breathe life into it, but his reflection still stared back at him from the blank TV screen like an exhausted Bassett Hound. No, there really was little choice because he was neither use nor ornament today, as his mother used to say – shameful seeing as how it was his own fault – but he'd have to pull a sicky. Ruby didn't need to be told about Celeste's death just yet – only that she was unable to come in today. God only knew how the poor girl was going to react, and Emily couldn't be expected to cope with the aftermath.

It was never a nice job ringing management to say you were too ill to work, but they'd have to lump it. Anyway he'd been working flat out for months now without a break, and covering extra shifts; he was bloody exhausted. You could only run on empty for so long, but with constant fear draining your system as well, the body simply wasn't designed to cope and this old engine, he thought dryly, was stalling.

The startlingly bright day outside highlighted his groggy lethargy. Oh for a darkened room and a soft, warm duvet. Except that wasn't going to happen, was it? Tempting, yes. Massively. But there was way too much at stake to cop out like that. So, after making the cringe-worthy phone call, he grabbed his jacket, jumped onto the motorbike and snapped his helmet down. *Right, let's get the job done.*

***

This time he constantly checked the mirrors and scanned the road ahead in a state of heightened awareness. The second a black sedan with a strangely powerful engine showed up he'd pull over immediately, set the phone to video and speed dial the police. *Come on then, you bastards…I'm ready…*

Every couple of seconds he looked into the wing mirror, keeping his speed down. Thankfully, normality appeared to be the case this morning, with only a smattering of white vans and delivery lorries in sight. Very few people took this particular road since they would either be visiting Drummersgate or taking the long, scenic route towards Chesterfield or the Peak District beyond; and all was quiet. Eventually he came to the junction for the A1 and, relaxing a little, was soon heading for Leeds and in particular the village of Guiseley.

Guiseley sits to the north of the city and is, in estate agent terms, a desirable location; with well-built stone houses close enough to commute to Leeds whilst also bordering the north Yorkshire countryside. A short drive and you could be in Harrogate or even over to the coast. There was, Noel thought, as his bike purred throatily into the leafy suburbs, a feeling of quiet money here: that this was perhaps where a retired professor and his family might live very comfortably. He pictured Michael opening the door – a tall, well-built gentleman of mature years who was no doubt going to look thinner and more tired than when he'd seen him last. Nothing, however, not all of the years he'd spent in nursing put together, prepared him for the shock of the other man's appearance. It caught him so off guard that the words of introduction he'd prepared came out in an incoherent jumble.

Michael's flesh had withered from his facial bones to such an extent that his head now resembled little more than a skull. Jaundiced eyes stared out from cavernous sockets, and the man's clothes draped from a rail thin body, his trousers belted double over a sweater to keep them from falling down. As Noel attempted to recover himself, there came a waft of staleness from the house interior and a stench of decay from the man himself.

Noel held out his hand. "I really am terribly sorry to intrude, but we met in St Mark's church not so long ago – you prayed all night with myself and a friend who was in a bit of a state – and well, I'm afraid we desperately needed some help, and… Look, I'm a nurse and I can see you aren't well enough for this. I'm so sorry, please forgive me." He turned to go.

"How did you find me?"

Noel turned back.

There was a glint of recognition in the other man's eyes.

"Well it wasn't easy. I'd been looking for a while. In the end I waited all night until someone at St Mary's pointed me in the right direction. We're desperate, you see? There's something terrible going on – it came to our door at the psychiatric hospital where myself and the friend I mentioned, work. Long story. Suffice to say that several members of the medical team involved will never practice again and some have died. It started after a patient from one of the mining villages near here was hypnotised."

Michael stood back from the door and motioned for Noel to enter. "I can't stand for long, you'd best come in. I'm in a bit of a mess – you'll have to excuse me."

Noel saw immediately what he meant. Dirty dishes were piled up on the drainer, the remains of a long-ago meal were congealing on the kitchen table and the curtains were still drawn. Michael had obviously been sleeping downstairs on the couch for some time too. The air was rancid; at a guess the bins hadn't been emptied for a while and the mewing cat's litter tray was full.

"Is no one helping you?"

Michael shrugged. "A nurse comes in with painkillers but there's little she can do about all this. I don't want anyone in, really."

Noel nodded. That was so often the case. Many people who were either elderly or infirm didn't want strangers in their home even though they were struggling. It was understandable though, when the last thing you had left was your dignity. "Shall I put the kettle on? Make us a cup of tea?"

The other man nodded, slumping into an armchair by the cold, empty fireplace.

Once in the kitchen Noel switched onto automatic pilot, unable to curb his natural caring and cleaning tendencies, and zoomed around emptying the litter tray, feeding the cat, putting dishes into the dishwasher and opening a window. Flying around, multi-tasking as he related to Becky later, he wiped surfaces, rinsed out a couple of cups and flicked the kettle on. It was ridiculous really as Michael would not be hard up for money. Still, even if he didn't find help for Kristy today, maybe he could make this man's last few weeks a bit easier by arranging private help.

Back in the living room, Michael accepted the tea gratefully while Noel brought him rapidly up to speed. "So now Kristy, we believe, is in a state of possession too. And what's worse is that the doctor in charge of her care is Crispin Morrow. So you see, Becky and I are the only two people left now? She's supposed to be contacting a junior police officer this morning and he's our last hope. Everyone who tries or gets involved in this ends up hurt, you see?"

Michael nodded thoughtfully.

Noel frowned. "Do you mind me asking when you were diagnosed?"

"Two weeks ago. The day after I started with symptoms I had a diagnosis of stage four – too late already! How about that?"

"Good grief."

"Yes, I know. In fact my decline has been so rapid I haven't even told my family yet. I'm a widower but I have a daughter and two grandchildren, a brother and a nephew who I'm close to." He put his head in his hands.

"Michael, please would you let me help you?"

Michael nodded. "Thank you. Bless you, thank you."

The day did not pan out as Noel expected it to, with himself making dozens of phone calls and cleaning up; but by the end of it private domestic help had been arranged as well as a private nurse; and Michael's daughter, brother and nephew had all been informed and would be arriving as soon as they could.

"It took me by total surprise," said Michael. "One day I was fine and the next I was in agony... I can remember the exact moment – I was standing in the queue at our local newsagents when I felt this huge crushing pain in my lower back. I broke a sweat – I'm not joking I was bent double and barely made it to the car. Since then I've been stuck here in this... how can I describe it? It's rather like being on the ocean floor with my speech and movements all in slow motion and the real world miles away – as if it's all a dream. And sometimes I'm not sure if I'm awake or sleeping because the visions come either way – creatures speaking in tongues and someone poking or pinching me; and although I've been desperate to urinate I've been unable to rise from the bed." He hung his head. "I'm afraid the mattress..."

Noel's heart squeezed with compassion for this gentle, well-educated man.

"That can all be sorted out," he said, patting the other man's shoulder.

As the day died in a fuchsia-streaked sky, he went to make more tea and toast, drew the curtains and turned on the lamps, then attempted something he'd never done before. From rolled-up newspaper, twigs and logs he built a real fire, and when it finally crackled into a blaze he almost cheered.

"Nothing like it, is there?" said Michael, leaning forwards with outstretched hands. "I've got central heating but this place has been colder than a morgue even with the thermostat turned up full. It just wouldn't get warm."

Noel frowned. "Michael, what's your take? What's happening? Give me the truth as you see it because we haven't got much time left."

"Well, my take is simple really – whatever was attacking Becky has attached itself to me, except somehow she resisted where I was perhaps an empty vessel."

Noel frowned and shook his head, not understanding. "You know more about this sort of thing than I ever could, but how is that possible?"

"The transfer of an evil entity into another's aura is entirely possible, absolutely. As for the darkness being intelligent enough to identify people, sniff them out and psychically or physically attack them, I don't know. I've been an atheist for most of my adult life, arguing theologically on the non-existence of any kind of superpower and frankly, winning! I was ordained originally but later I lost my faith. Then a friend of mine had a bizarre and inexplicable experience and I re-discovered it. That was about ten years ago now but who knows how these things work?"

"Did you go back into the Church of England?"

"Yes, well Methodist actually. I've tried many religions but frankly I go wherever I'm needed; mostly to those of any religious persuasion who've lost their faith or are undergoing some kind of crisis. Or I did."

"Was your friend in a similar situation to Kristy's, do you mind me asking?"

Michael's eyes welled with sadness. He shrugged. "Suicide. He hanged himself."

"I'm so sorry."

"It's a long story, Noel. Suffice to say he dabbled in things he thought were good fun but were, in fact, far more dangerous than either he or anyone else, including myself, could ever have imagined. He lost his mind first."

They sat in contemplative silence for a few minutes, gazing into the fire.

"Eventually, Michael said, "From your description of what might be going on in Woodsend, it seems perfectly possible those people have summoned a demonic force. And now it's spreading pain, terror, disease and debauchery – everything that defiles humanity. Recruiting too, with promises of power and revenge."

"What can we do about Kristy? Can we save her, do you think? Is there anyone else in your opinion, who we could ask to help?"

"What happened to the other psychiatrist? To Dr McGowan?"

"He was exorcised by a priest and he's now back with his family in Ireland, albeit struck off the register and facing divorce. They had a different medical officer at Laurel Lawns then, and his mother got the agreement."

Michael frowned deeply.

"That priest is no longer available, apparently," Noel added. "On long term sick leave."

"Hmmm…How would we get past this Dr Morrow, do you think? He must have time off?"

"Surely you can't..? I mean, you're not well enough…"

"Find out when he's off. Ring Becky and ask her to fix it up, and I will bring a friend of mine to do the actual exorcism – he owes me a few favours and he's studied possession for years. It's against the rules but he'll do it off the record – he's a good man, a special person."

"Oh my God, thank you, thank you."

"I'm going to die, Noel and there's no getting away from that. My family will be here tomorrow and I'll say my good-byes. Then I'll be ready."

***

By the time Noel left it was dark. Although Michael had protested, he fetched a bag of groceries for him and put them away so he'd got ready-made meals and fruit drinks in the fridge. It would tide him over until his family and the paid help arrived next day. Meanwhile, fighting leaden exhaustion, he picked up his mobile and scrolled down the list of missed calls. No, he wouldn't be well

160

enough to work tomorrow and no, he couldn't go to the opening of a new bar in Leeds, and no, he wasn't interested in solar panels. Finally there was Becky's number with a message to call.

She picked up straight away.

"I've got stuff to tell you," she blurted out.

"Stop! Becky listen – I've got help for Kristy but you need to find out from Nora when Crispin Morrow's off duty. Do it right now, will you? Michael is terminally ill and it's urgent we go in as soon as possible. He's got just days. I've never seen such a rapid decline and—"

"What – terminally ill, did you say?"

"Stage four prostate cancer as of two weeks ago!"

"Two weeks," she said bleakly.

"Exactly."

"Oh my good God."

"Yes. So we need to act fast. His family are coming tomorrow so let's see if we can fix it up for the day after? Do you have Nora's private number? Keep her out of the loop as much as you can by the way, just give her the bare bones – that Kristy deserves some religious support and as Crispin Morrow won't allow it then it will have to be when he's not there – and that's the extent of her involvement. We don't want any harm coming to her."

"I'm on it. Doing it now. I'll ring you back in a bit."

***

161

Chapter Twenty-Two

Chapeltown, Leeds

Monday night

In the end it hadn't been too big a job tracking him down. Toby rubbed his hands together in the freezing night air as he queued for fish and chips on the street corner. On a night like this only the most hardy and desperate of prostitutes stood out on the pavements waiting for kerb crawlers. Scantily dressed in pelmet skirts, their bare legs were mottled from the cold and they huddled together smoking and chatting – most of them just teenagers - with scraped back hair and dead eyes.

Whilst wolfing down greasy chips with a plastic fork, he surreptitiously observed the kind of punters cruising by. Middle aged men most of them. 'Pathetic bastards,' he thought. 'Imagine being that sad you had to pay for it!'

Ruby would have been one of these girls not so long ago. From what Becky told him, she'd been a user from the age of fourteen but her memories were addled to say the least. Had she been a prostitute then too? And did Jes bring her here at such a young age or was it after she left the mill when she'd have been around twenty? He shook his head. The girl could have been anywhere and done anything – off the radar like so many other lost kids. In many ways she was lucky to be alive because this was the underworld, and once you crossed the line you could easily vanish into thin air and not be missed. *There but for the grace of God...*

He finished off the chips and looked around for a bin. Right, now his stomach was full he could start looking for Jes.

"Hi, gorgeous! You want good time, yes?"

He swung round to face a young girl with slanting eyes and a deadpan expression. The accent was eastern European and she flashed open a faux fur coat to reveal black PVC hot pants and a bra top with holes cut out of it. Her skin was pearl white, her body that of an emaciated twelve year old.

"No, love. Just looking for a mate." He indicated she should fasten her coat up. "It's freezing. Maybe you could help me find him?" He gave her his can of coke, which she immediately cracked open and knocked back. "Name of Jes? Dark hair, forties…"

Passing headlights caught the girl's stoned expression. "Ah yes, Jes. Everyone they know him."

Toby blinked, his heart racing. Had he found him already – with the first girl he asked on the first street corner in Chapel? "Really? That's amazing. I haven't seen Jes in ages."

"You want come with me?" she said, moving closer. Her face was devoid of all the hope and animation a young girl should have as her God-given right. "Twenty pound - is good, yes?"

"I'm not looking for that, love. Honest. Just me mate – if you could tell me where he lives?"

She shrugged and held out her hand. "Five pound. You are his friend. I take you."

Okay, well she might be taking him to a couple of thieving thugs and leave him for dead but he handed her the money and took that chance. He could run faster than anyone else he knew if the worst came to the worst.

The girl snatched the note and stuffed it down her bra top, then led the way to a row of boarded-up shops a few blocks down. Here the yards were strewn with discarded take-away cartons and litter lay decomposing in the drains. He followed her down a gennel and through an alleyway to the back of one of the terraces, then up a wrought iron fire escape and eventually through a heavily scuffed door covered in graffiti. Once inside the word, 'seedy' sprung to mind as the distinctive aroma of marijuana lingered in the air, along with ingrained tobacco and the stench of human sweat. "You follow," she said, scooting down the dimly lit hallway past several rooms pumping with heavy base music. Right at the end of the corridor she stopped and knocked sharply on one of the doors.

"Fuck off!"

She turned and shrugged. "He is in."

She knocked again and pushed it open. A swarthy bloke, handsome in an uncut kind of way, lay on a pock-marked sofa smoking weed. Springing to his feet he glared at her. "Who the fuck's this?"

Toby stepped forwards. "Go on now, leave us." he said to the girl, pushing her gently out of the door before closing it behind him. The two men stood facing each other. "I'm Toby – a friend of Ruby's."

The flash of recognition in the other man's eyes told him he'd got the right guy but he'd probably get thrown out in seconds if he didn't play this carefully. Holding out his hands in an appeasement gesture, he blurted out, "We need help. You are Jes, aren't you? What a relief! Ruby said I'd find you here. Look mate, she's in trouble and so is her daughter. Can we talk?"

Jes stared for a moment longer before sitting down again, his arm along the back of the couch. Casually gesturing towards the fridge in the corner, he said, "Help yourself to a beer. Toby, did you say your name was?"

Good. He'd bought himself some time. "Thanks, yeah."

Jes watched and waited until Toby pulled open the can and sat down. "So…friend of Ruby's, are you? I didn't think she had any friends. Isn't she banged up?"

Toby nodded. "Can't say I blame her having a go at that bastard, Paul Dean though, can you?"

Jes shook his head, eyes narrowing. "How come you know Ruby? They haven't let her out, have they? You're not, you know, like in a relationship with her or anything?"

"Nah, nothing like that! It's more that I know Becky, the nurse looking after her. Ruby's still in the nutcracker suite if you know what I mean? Probably forever now. I can't say it's surprising really, what with her background."

Jes never took his eyes off him. "Interesting. A friend of her nurse. So what's all this about her being in trouble then? And a daughter, you say?"

Toby nodded and took a gulp of lager. The guy was both shrewd and wired. No doubt he had some heavies working for him too: on this side of the line you came up against all kinds of psychos the police wouldn't even be able to find let alone touch. You could be dumped in a skip before you knew it. "Aye. Like I said, Becky's asked me to help because Ruby's worried about her daughter." He related what he knew about Woodsend, aware that Jes was scrutinising him intently; unnervingly. "I don't mean to be rude but you're a last ditch attempt at trying to get some information."

Jes leapt up. "You're a copper!"

Fuck. "Off duty." He remained sitting but held his arms out wide. "Jes, I'm not interested in you, I swear. None of my colleagues know I'm even here – I'm off patch and off duty. I really am asking just as a friend. We need a lead – anything you can tell me for Becky and Ruby's sake, not to mention this young lass, Alice. I won't mention your name and I won't quote you – I just need something that might help - anything. You've got my word."

Jes towered over him. "I don't need this shit."

"No one does, but it's desperate now. Really…" As fast as he could, Toby related all that Becky had told him, leaving nothing out and including what was in Linda Hedges' diary. "So you see – everyone who's tried to help is either dead or seriously ill?"

Finally, Jes conceded Toby's sincerity and sat down again. "Right. Okay. Well it's worse than I thought then. I honestly thought, hoped, the whole thing would die out – that maybe it was just something me and Ruby would have to live with and try to forget."

"Tell me," Toby insisted, less urgently now. "Tell me what happened there – right from the start. I want to do something about it but I can't if I don't know owt."

"Well there was no point in people like me and Ruby coming to you lot, was there? Even now it's a dead loss from what you're saying."

Toby waited.

"Okay, well what I suspected was all in bits and pieces anyway – none of it could be proved. And every time I got close I got burned – very, very badly burned like you wouldn't believe. But I tried."

"How do you mean, burned?"

"Ill. Don't ask me how the bloody witch did it, but man you'd get so sick you couldn't fucking move. If you've ever tried to detox from smack you might have some idea what it was like. It stopped you in your tracks – you had to get the hell out to save your own skin – then sneak in through the back door again and hope they didn't sniff you out… It was like that demon witch could smell your blood."

"Witch? Would this be Ida Dean? Not that anything can be done about alleged witchcraft."

He nodded. "Exactly. She's Ruby's mother, the poor little cow. No wonder she was fucked up and suicidal when I met her. We holed up in Tanners Dell, down in the mill for a while, but she'd wake up screaming the walls down, saying she didn't know who I was and there were ghosts floating into her face and stuff. Drugs calmed her down. In the end though, we left and I took her to the family camp in Devon. That's where we found out we had the same genes – my mother was good with her, got her talking, see? Anyway, when she knew we'd the same blood she upped and left. I still would've taken care of her but she legged it all the same."

"So how—"

"Yeah, well she had no place else to go, did she? I found her in the mill again a few weeks later – it was the only place she knew to hole up in. And she was in a really bad way by that time – seriously bad, totally loopy, like she was possessed by the fucking devil or something – so I brought her here to Leeds, to an old mate's as it was then. We were both addicts and she was desperate for a fix. It was my way of looking after her, I suppose – to take away her pain. It hurt like hell to watch. After that she might disappear for a few days, but she always came back. And sometimes she seemed to know who she was; but most of the time she didn't. The last time she went AWOL I went looking for her as usual but I didn't get to her in time. She'd already knifed Paul Dean in his bed."

"Hang on, I just need to understand something - could we rewind a bit? So you met her when she'd had this child already? She was fourteen, yeah?"

"No, sixteen."

"Apparently not, no – she must have been fourteen, mate. She's twenty-seven now and her daughter will be thirteen this year. That's another reason we've got to act fast - because this child is going to get a satanic baptism for her birthday."

"Fourteen? And she'd already had a baby?"

Toby nodded.

"Jesus wept! So hasn't this nurse friend of yours reported the child as 'at risk' or something? Got child protection involved?"

"Yes but the entire case was closed down yesterday by my senior commanding officer. He says the girl isn't in any danger from her parents, Ida and Paul Dean, so you—"

"Ernest Scutts?"

Toby blanched. "Er…yeah, but how did—"

"Don't tell me you don't know? Oh for fuck's sake, what chance have we got with you fucking amateurs? I spent years tracking these bastards and so did Ruby, and we were neither of us in a fit state! Yeah, Scutts is in the nasty little coven, as is the friendly local GP, and the Reverend Gordon who preaches sermons every Sunday in Bridesmoor. They've got it all sewn up and no one can touch them because of what that witch does to people who try."

What? Scutts? Holy crap… "And you've known about this for how long?"

"Years. Since before you were born, that's for sure."

"How? I mean, how come you've got such an obsessive interest?"

Jes strode over to the fridge, handed Toby another can and snapped open one for himself. "My family are gypsies and I was born in Devon. My mother's dead now but one summer when the camp was in Woodsend she went missing for several months and was never found. Meanwhile some of our women had miscarriages and still births – one of them committed suicide in the woods there. There was other bad stuff too and in the end they didn't have much choice but to leave. All except Ida – she stayed because she'd got in with Lucas Dean." He let the information sink into Toby's brain for a moment. "Paul Dean's disgusting old father. Looking for him was one of the reasons I found the old mill."

"Why would you be looking for Lucas Dean?"

"Because of what he did to my mother. She managed to escape eventually, but not without having her life ruined."

"Why did she never report it?"

"How could she? She was sworn to secrecy else there'd be revenge."

"By who?"

"Cora Dean. Lucas' wife."

"Really? How did she know your mother then?"

"She helped her. My mother escaped while the coven was conducting a black mass. Somehow she got out – she doesn't remember how because she was half dead after what they did to her, but she bumped into Cora in the woods at about five in the morning. What that woman was doing there at that time I don't know, but she got her some clothes and told her to run and never ever come back. My mother managed, hitching rides until she found the family at an old haunt in Devon. After that they went over to Europe to get as far away as possible from the curse they believed was on them. When I found out what those pigs had done to my mother though, I came back – decided I'd find out who they were and kill them."

"What happened?"

"First I had to get to England and find the place. Then I got lodgings and started tracking down the Deans. I was all pumped up but on the very first day in Woodsend it went badly wrong." He smirked to himself and took another swig of lager. "It was like 'they' were waiting for me…Anyway, I met this woman in the woods and something pretty damn nasty happened shortly after – I got so badly sick I thought I was going to die, and it took me a long time to get well again. Anyway, when I came back a few weeks later to try and find out about her, no one knew who she was. Man, it was weird. I couldn't work out what the hell happened. Had she drugged me or what? So there I was, wandering down to the river to try and work out what to do next, when I saw this girl lying underneath the surface of the water, just waiting to drown and be taken out of the world. I saved her."

"That was Ruby?"

He nodded.

"Ah, so that's how you met! Did your mother describe her time in captivity – did she say what they did to her?"

"Not much. She'd blanked a lot out – but we're talking ritual abuse." He paused while he cleared his mind. "I've blinded myself with drugs all these years just like Ruby. You're right though, they're still committing rape and murder. They destroy people's lives and they're doing something else too – that woman, the one I just told you about – well she's at the heart of it. I could tell you the full story about if you like, although you probably won't believe it coming from someone like me."

"I'm keeping an open mind, Jes. Whatever I need to know…"

Jes eyed him steadily as if weighing up the consequences. Eventually he said, "Okay, I'm gonna trust you with this so you understand what you're dealing with. It's probably best you're prepared for some pretty evil shit because once you get involved they'll throw every low down, nasty trick in the book at you and more besides. They'll mess with your head until you don't know who the fuck you are anymore."

"Okay."

"Right. Well on that first day in Woodsend this woman appeared in the woods. I turned a corner on the path and there she was, just standing there as if she'd been waiting for me. I stopped dead and stared at her like I was hypnotised. She was stunning - with this cascade of shiny, raven hair; all glinting eyes and full red lips. The whole place seemed sort of freeze-framed, all the birds stopped singing and all I could see was her – smiling at me – reaching out for my hand. I wandered back through the trees with her in a dream-like state, and we came out at a cottage. I couldn't take my eyes off her. She had this see-through white top on with her shoulders wriggling out of it, and she kept touching herself - her neck, her hair, her body – while we sat in the garden drinking wine. Next thing I knew we were practically running upstairs to the bedroom. Her skin was warm and soft and tanned; my head was spinning and I was delirious, in a fever, for her. Anyway, I'd got my shirt off, pulling at her clothes, shoving myself into her and it felt like I was going to explode when…are you ready for this?"

"Um…"

"Well, I'm looking into her eyes while I'm you know… when suddenly they turn totally white – like not just the iris but the whole eye – no pupils – nothing. Just all white like they'd flipped round in her head! Next second she morphed into this cackling toothless troll with wild grey hair and wrinkled skin like an ancient hag's. I threw her off and almost fell out of the house with this horrible, raucous laughter ringing in my ears, staggered onto the grass outside and turned back in disbelief. Like, you know, what the fuck was that? Well, I looked up and her window pane was solid black as if it had been painted out. I was, like, did she put something in the wine? What the fuck happened? And then it was like being hit with an overdose of smack - I was running away through the woods but my head was banging and I kept doubling up with stomach cramps. To be honest how I made it back to my digs I'll never know – it was all in a kind of drugged-up blur - the ground kept rearing up and the air was static. I was lurching from tree to tree and there were giant spiders running up the trunks and bloody great bit pythons slithering across the path. Man, it was like the biggest psychedelic trip you could ever imagine…"

"So that was Ida?"

Jes nodded. "Exactly."

"She isn't Ruby's real mother, you do know that?"

"Yeah, they're all inbreeds but that old crone brought her up. What appals me though, and I mean really fucking appals me, is that the old devil himself must be my dad – the one who raped my mother."

"Do you know for sure? He might not have been."

"She was pregnant when she came back to the camp. That's why they'd left her alone that night and she got the chance to escape. She was supposed to marry Nicu, but he wouldn't touch her after that, so she spent the rest of her life alone and had no more children. That old bastard has to be my father. Which is another reason I won't have children and nor should Ruby. I honestly think she's in the best place now, you know. At least she's being taken care of and helped."

"Except she did have a child."

"So you say. She never told me."

"I really need to speak to Cora. Do you think she'll talk?"

"That cowardly bitch looks after number one. Knew what was happening and just let it. Ruby said she'd take her shopping and give her a bath once in a while, but that was all. Cora could have helped her daughters and her granddaughters, yet she did nothing. Meanwhile she's got dear uncle Rick living with her – a bad ass skank who kept a job at the mine until it closed. Now he spends his days in The Highwayman looking for prey. Any woman who drops in there for a quick drink on the way home is asking for trouble. As is anyone walking through the woods on a nice afternoon."

"I need to speak to Cora when Rick's out, then."

"You'll not get a word out of her. She's mother to all three Deans. One of her daughters is now dead and the other is married to Derek. They're all in the coven and she'll not talk."

"Not even for Alice's sake?"

"Course not."

"Jes. If I manage to break this apart, will you testify in court?"

"What do you know about black magic?"

"Um…nothing."

"Thought not or you wouldn't have asked."

"One final question - if you're the son of old Lucas Dean then how come you haven't turned out like the other three Deans?"

"I don't know. Maybe, just maybe – please God – I'm not his."

Toby stuck out his hand. "Thanks for talking to me, mate. I'm going to blast this apart one way or the other."

"I loved her, you know?" Jes said.

Toby nodded, then scribbled his mobile number onto a scrap of paper. "This is going to happen fast now so let's keep in touch."

***

Chapter Twenty-Three

Doncaster Royal Infirmary
Tuesday

When Becky walked back onto the ward she found Anna taking Callum's pulse and she hurried over.

"Is everything alright?"

Anna began filling in his observation sheets. "He's got a temperature again, and tachycardia."

With a pang of alarm, she realised Callum's breathing was rattling quite noisily, and although he was propped up against several pillows he seemed to be struggling for breath. "He's very chesty all of a sudden," she said, grabbing another pillow to put behind him.

"Yes. I'll bleep the SHO," Anna said, bustling over to the nurses' station.

Becky grabbed a chair and took hold of his hand. His health had deteriorated rapidly in the short time she'd left his side. How could this have happened? He was on antibiotics too.

"It's a chest infection, isn't it?" she said to Anna when she returned a couple of minutes later.

"The doctor is on his way."

"Yeah, I saw him in the canteen. Anna…"

The Sister regarded her with a deadpan expression and Becky, tired and worried, blurted out words she hadn't intended, "You know I could do with some help here. Why aren't you more concerned? Why isn't he waking up? I don't understand!"

That woman was all neat and clean, just doing her job, while her own world was falling apart. She looked down at her crumpled clothing and tears pricked her eyes. *How quickly our lives could unravel…*

173

To her surprise, Anna whipped the curtains round them both and drew up a chair. "We don't know why," she whispered. "It's very odd."

Becky stared back. "Anna, you know I'm a nurse just like you – please tell me what you think is going on!"

Anna looked directly into her eyes. "I think trauma. His mind - it does not want to wake up yet. It is my belief he will be okay when the time is right."

Becky nodded. "Really? I see, okay. Well yes, that would make sense."

Anna seemed poised to say more but stopped when the SHO suddenly burst through the flowery curtains. His hair was raked up in a rooster shape and pens, notes, stethoscope and bleeper all seemed to be falling out of his pockets. "Sorry, sorry to keep you waiting…now, how are you, old boy?"

Anna stood up, efficiently relating the necessary information while he listened to Callum's lungs. After a brief examination he said, "Yup. Let's get a sputum sample and I'll write up some IVs. Can we prop him up a bit more and get the physio over?"

Anna bustled away and he turned to Becky. "Are you staying with him again today?"

She shook her head. "I want to but I've been here pretty much ever since he was admitted and I've got to run a few errands. I'll be back as soon as I can, though."

"Okay, well he should pick up soon now we're getting some different antibiotics in."

"But why isn't he waking up? Do you think it's the trauma of what he's been through?"

The doctor shrugged. "Honestly? We don't know. Keep talking to him…there's nothing physiologically wrong that we can identify so hopefully it won't be long before he does."

"Right, well I'll be back as soon as I can – later this afternoon."

Before leaving, Becky had a word with Anna. "You will ring me if there is any further deterioration in his condition, won't

174

you? I won't be long. I really do have to go out for a few hours. I don't want to but there's no choice."

Anna nodded, permitting her face to relax into the tiniest reassuring smile. "Try not to worry, Becky. I will take good care of him."

Becky nodded. "Thank you." Frankly, there was so much that had to be done today she was going to have to trust the woman. And instinct told her she could.

Right, the to-do list as quickly as possible, then. First there were her belongings to collect from home: Mark was staying on and buying her out of the mortgage. He'd messaged to say he was going to change the locks later today and the deadline was lunchtime to collect her stuff. After that the finances would be left to solicitors. She could do without this right now, she really could, but it was best to get it done, and anyway, a person could only survive for so long with one overnight bag.

Once at the terrace she and Mark had once shared, Becky methodically packed her clothes, CDs, books and personal possessions. It filled just two suitcases. Two suitcases for fifteen years of marriage – was that really it? She clicked them shut and lugged them downstairs before, with one last sweeping glance, saying a silent goodbye into the dark hallway and closing the door behind her.

Half an hour later she was standing in Noel's light and airy loft apartment in Leeds Docklands. It had been unbelievably kind of him to let her have the spare room for as long as she needed it. She wouldn't push it, though – Noel was a lovely person but he was also an essentially private man and she would find a rented flat just as soon as she could. Whatever would she have done without him, she thought, dragging her suitcases into the spare room?

God, she was knackered! A tidal wave of fatigue washed over her and she sank onto the bed. Oh for just a couple of minutes couldn't she rest? A ray of sunshine spread across the soft, white duvet and she flopped back. What harm would it do to just lie here for a few precious minutes? Every muscle ached, her whole body heavy, eyelids dropping…Then she'd ring Drummersgate and then

Toby to find out if he'd tracked down Jes and then Celeste's husband to see if he needed any help…. And anyway, it was just for a few minutes…

When she woke up again the light had gone and she was stiff with cold.

Oh no! Oh hell! What time was it?

On the bedside cabinet where she'd left it several hours ago, her mobile lay silently. Puzzled, she grabbed it, realising with a stab of dismay that it was turned off. How odd! She switched it back on and listened to the long list of messages while frantically rushing around drawing curtains and switching on lights. The first was from Toby Harbour. Would she be free to go to Woodsend with him to doorstep Cora Dean tomorrow afternoon?

"Count me in!" she said into the messaging service. "I've just got to sort out some leave for the next few days. Where do we meet? Please call me back as soon as you can."

The next was from Noel. She called back straight away but there was no answer and was just about to try again when he rang. Appalled, she listened to the description of Michael who, only a few weeks before had been her salvation. Yes, of course she would phone Nora as soon as possible. Tomorrow night wouldn't be a moment too soon. She had important news for him too…

"Later," said Noel. "Let's sort this out first."

Next she dialled the DRI. Anna had gone off duty now but the nurse in charge assured her Callum was responding to the new antibiotics and his temperature had come down.

"Oh thank God. Look I'll be there in less than an hour. I've got a few important calls to make first; then I'll have a quick shower and get a taxi – I won't be long."

Grabbing some clean clothes out of a suitcase she dived into the bathroom and turned on the shower. Tomorrow was going to be a very busy day. Good, at last there was progress.

***

Chapter Twenty-Four

Bridesmoor Village

Wednesday afternoon, 29th December 2015

Cora Dean peeked through the kitchen blinds at the couple walking up her driveway and scowled. Oh no! And just when she was in her dressing gown with a TV dinner in the microwave!

When the sharp rap echoed around her hallway she shouted crossly, "Hold on - I shan't be a minute." *Whoever could it be at this hour when it was going dark? Fancy having to go upstairs and get dressed again now; and the dinner spoiled.*

After five full minutes she opened the door, making sure to keep them on the porch. "Yes?"

"Have we got the right address for Cora Dean?" said the woman. Pleasant enough face, early forties, needed her roots doing.

"Who wants 'er?"

"DCI Harbour," said the young man, stepping forwards a little too presumptuously for her liking.

"What's this about?"

"Cora, this is a friendly visit concerning a little girl who's missing in the area," said the woman. "Her mother's in hospital and I'm her nurse. I said I'd try to find her daughter for her and I asked Detective Harbour here to help me."

Cora narrowed her eyes. The man's foot was partially in the open doorway and while she was being distracted by the woman's nice talk, he was ready to push himself into the house. *This was about something else – something they weren't saying yet.*

She thought quickly – Rick had only just left for the pub and wouldn't be back 'til late; Paul and Ida would be at home at this time, as would Derek and Kath. Perhaps it wouldn't hurt to find out what these people wanted? Information was power, after all. Reluctantly she stepped back and let them in. "Only for a few minutes, mind. I've got me tea on."

She showed them into her front room and switched on a bar of the electric fire. "Now then, what's this about? I doubt as I can 'elp you."

The young man perched on the edge of a chair while the woman, who introduced herself as Becky, told her a story, which she could not have articulated more accurately herself. That her granddaughter, Ruby, was the issue of her own son and daughter she knew. That Ruby had been ritually abused she also knew, although she was careful not to react to or endorse the allegations. What *was* news though, was that Ruby had given birth to Alice. She'd thought the child was the result of yet another unfortunate dalliance of Paul's with some tart from the village. Averting her gaze, she did a brief mental calculation …Ruby could have been no more than fourteen, then.

Nor did she know about Ruby's mental health – only that she'd attacked Paul with a knife a couple of years ago and been 'banged up'. The DID diagnosis, and how she'd used it to protect herself, was a revelation. And a shock. Did that mean she might recover memories and spill them out to those in authority?

Behind a mask of indifference Cora's mind worked swiftly: if anyone believed the girl now that she was receiving expert medical treatment, they might come investigating and the family could be exposed. And when they knew their backs were against the wall, they would call on Ida to stop it. And Ida would know it was Cora who had stabbed them in the back. A familiar, old fear flickered inside her: she couldn't go through that kind of madness and terror again, not ever.

"What a load of baloney your mad client's told you," she said. "You've no evidence for any of it. Now if you don't mind…"

Becky raised an eyebrow. "Actually there's quite a bit of evidence."

"Ruby's a certified lunatic – in the nick for attempted murder."

"Is this your granddaughter you're talking about? Not to mention another granddaughter, Bella – no doubt also a certified lunatic?"

"Ruby tried to kill my son and she's been sectioned. That's it."

"Is it?" Becky listed all the incidents which formed the basis for circumstantial evidence, and then began to describe what Ruby went through on a daily basis – her hundreds of alter personalities, the drugs, the memories of ritual abuse that were so bad her own mind could not face up to them. And now Alice would be going through the same thing. She listed all the people who had died or become diseased, and how a lady doctor lay critically ill as they spoke – everyone in fact, who had come anywhere near this beleaguered village. On top of that she added a bluff – the photographs on the detective's mobile phone – the detective who was already telling his story as he lay recovering in hospital.

Cora's face registered no emotion; while the clock ticked solidly on the mantelpiece amid her miniature ornaments.

"I can't help you."

"You did the right thing once, remember?" said Toby. "You helped a young gypsy girl escape from your late husband's satanic cult."

Cora put a hand to her throat. *A weak link, a weak moment, she should have let her die.* "How did you…?"

"Never mind how I know. I'm giving you the chance to save Alice from a horrific fate and redeem yourself into the bargain. We will out this sect and I am sure you would rather be on the right side of the law, so I suggest you save us all a lot of time and tell us what you know. We have photographs, Cora, and we have a police officer's testimony."

She shook her head. Terror had knotted her stomach into a tight ball. *If she said a single word…*

"There's nothing," she said firmly. "Now if you don't mind?" She went to stand by the door, her mind and mouth closed.

As the couple passed she averted her gaze and silently let them out into an evening already glinting with frost.

With the door closed behind them, she walked back into the living room in a daze and sat down. *Think, think, think*...They had nothing. They were bluffing. And Alice would be fine. No one in this village would talk to those two do-gooders, anyway. This secret had been locked in for the best part of fifty years and would die with her boys: anyone who divulged even a fragment of gossip or innuendo regretted it for the rest of their life.

And yet Ruby had escaped and so had Rosella. Rosella – was she still alive and had she come back to point the finger? Surely not or the whole lot of those gypsies would suffer. They'd had warning enough last time. Ruby though – poor, dear damaged Ruby – did the darkness not attack her? Why was she able to talk to the medical staff? How the hell had she survived when no one else had?

And all those babies – never knowing whose they were or how Lucas acquired them – and Paul taking over so the whole nasty business carried on; the coven now protected by people in high places and something even more powerful than the lot of them put together – something that was so frightening she couldn't face it again. Ever. She had *seen* Ida once – *really seen her.* The day after Rosella escaped from Tanners Dell, Ida had paid her a visit; and after that the creeping darkness had never left, appearing to know her every move. There was no way out of this...

Alice! What about Alice, though? Was she Paul and Ruby's like these people said? Her stomach curled with revulsion. Curse the day she'd ever met Lucas Dean.

Silent fury began to bubble and pop in her veins as she sat brooding, stone still, while the clock ticked on and on and on... Her whole life she'd kept her tongue...

Suddenly the blind rage she'd tamped down for the best part of fifty years erupted. Cora bolted upstairs so fast she almost tripped onto the landing, tore into the spare bedroom and flung back the doors to the girls' old wardrobe. There, right at the back in a box of toys was a stuffed rabbit with grimy fur and knots of cotton where its eyes should be. With wildly trembling fingers she ripped open the carefully sewn up pocket at the back and pulled out a key, before flying downstairs and out into the night air.

The couple she'd ejected from her home just minutes before, were still parked up and she waved at them frantically as she ran down the drive, still in her slippers.

Becky buzzed down the window, her eyebrows somewhere in her hair line.

"This Friday, New Year's Day, there'll be a black mass," she blurted out, handing them an intricately engraved key. "Underneath Tanners Dell Mill. They start at three in t' morning – you might catch 'em at it if you're clever and keep quiet. And you," here she glared at Toby, "for God's sake don't tell Ernest Scutts or you won't know what's 'it you. Watch your backs. You don't know what you're dealing with – you really don't."

"Thank you," said Becky, taking the key. "Anyone know you've got this?"

She shook her head, already backing up the drive. "I've had it forty-three years and he never found it, though he took a hammer to the place looking. There were two – ancient contraptions they are – but this is the one they haven't got."

She turned and ran back into the house, locking and bolting the door behind her. Maybe this one last act would save her soul? But before the darkness came for her, which it undoubtedly would, it might be best not to leave that to chance.

There was a drawer full of Tramadol, Dothiepin and Paracetamol upstairs, that she'd kept for just such an emergency. Hopefully God would forgive her.

***

Chapter Twenty-Five

For a moment Becky and Toby sat in the car staring at the tarmac. *Did that really just happen?*

To their right stood a small, stone church, its graveyard somewhat neglected, with overgrown grass and wind-beaten headstones devoid of flowers. There were no posters or service announcements on the noticeboard and weeds sprouted through the cracked path.

"Doesn't look particularly well attended, does it?" Toby observed.

Becky squinted up at the spire. "It's quite old – Norman, I'd say with that square tower."

"I don't know much about churches to be honest."

"I've started to find them fascinating. Oh look…there's a boy standing there."

They both looked over to where a young boy had appeared among the older graves towards the back. "He doesn't look more than about eight or nine," said Becky. "Bit too young to be wandering around on his own, wouldn't you say?"

"I think there's something wrong with his eyes."

He'd started to walk towards them and they both realised at the same time that he was blind, as he tap-tap-tapped his way down the church path, through the lych-gate and out onto the lane.

"I wonder why Cora changed her mind like that?" Toby said, after the child had disappeared from view.

"Very peculiar," Becky agreed. "She was shit-scared though, wasn't she? Do you reckon she's terrified of her own son?"

"I'd say that's highly likely."

Becky turned the key over and over in her hands. "And that's what's kept her silent all these years, I suppose. I'm guessing this spare key was her insurance policy."

"She should've legged it and taken her kids."

"I agree. But then there's the black witchcraft, Toby. You haven't come across it yet, have you?"

"That's what Jes were telling me about last night. I'm still having difficulty with it... I mean, I think Jes must've been poisoned or drugged or summat --there's an explanation for everything in the end."

Becky smiled sadly. "I wish there was. Anyway – big brave soldier – you go to that black mass at 3am on your own then, because you might be alright with it but I'm telling you it scares the crap out of me."

Toby sighed heavily. "Trouble is, all our evidence put together is only hearsay unless Callum wakes up and testifies; and even that's tenuous if the Deans employ a good lawyer. They've got three professionals already to discredit everything we say; and that's if it ever got as far as court, which I doubt because I'm guessing this village is in lockdown – they're all petrified of the Deans."

"There's no choice but to catch them in the act, then, is there? Do you think you could trust Sid Hall with this?"

"Possibly." He looked thoughtful before adding, "And a few others."

"Oh? You'll have to be one hundred percent on that."

He smiled tightly. "I am."

"Okay, well...3am on New Year's Day it is, then. How shall we play it? There's isn't a lot of time."

"That's probably for the best. Let me ring you when I've thought it through. Meanwhile, it'd be an idea to find out exactly where this mill is. You up for a quick scout round?"

"Okay." She glanced at the clock on the dashboard. "I'll have to get back to the DRI soon, though – would you give me a lift please or I'll be really late?"

"Aye, course I will." He started up the engine and began to turn the car round. "Best we park out of sight – bit further down under the trees."

183

*   *   *

The River Whisper gurgled softly, lapping and swilling at the bank where debris and branches caught and snagged its flow.

They tramped along the path in silence.

After about ten minutes, Becky said, "There should be a track up towards the mill soon. Up through the woods?"

"I haven't seen one - it's just solid thicket. Let's keep walking."

Eventually the unmistakeable roar of fresh water bounding over rocks could be heard. "Is that a waterfall?" Becky asked.

"Sound like it. Let's keep going 'til we get to it and work upstream from there."

"Okay, it's odd there hasn't been a track up from here, though. We'll have to find another way in from the village end, I suppose."

"Yes, we need more than one exit, for sure."

"It's bloody freezing. I wish I'd brought gloves."

Then all at once a weir was in front of them, with hundreds of gallons of fresh water racing into the river below; the bank alongside steep, muddy and covered in dead bracken and brambles.

"Up here," said Toby. "Come on!"

"I wish I'd got my wellies as well," Becky said, stumbling onto her hands and knees in the dark. "Aargh, we're really not prepared for this, are we?"

"I was supposed to be going out for a pint later an' all – me shoes are a right mess."

For several minutes they climbed up the embankment, slipping on the mud and grasping at the undergrowth.

"It's gone dark quickly, have you noticed?"

They stopped and took stock. Ahead was Tanners Dell, standing in a clearing of hazy moonlight. Surrounded by forest, the mill's roof had partially caved in, ivy now pushing through it in twisted clumps; the stonework appeared luminescent, its windows

184

sightless sockets; and against a deafening backdrop of pounding water the building exuded a preternatural stillness.

Toby swung round as if startled by someone behind.

"What's the matter?"

In the twilight he looked ghostly white. "Nothing. Thought I felt a breath in the back of me neck." He adjusted his collar. "Spooky place, eh?"

"We're not going in, are we? I mean to try the key or anything?"

"No, not tonight. Come on, let's go – this place is creeping me out. We just need to find a path to the road and get back to the car. Fuck it if anyone sees us."

"No, don't lose your nerve, Toby. We have to know where the paths and hiding places are, then go back the way we came. We can't be seen."

Neither spoke as they crept towards the mill and walked around it. By now the evening was as black as pitch and the lack of a torch was an obvious omission. On the north side a dense wall of forest barred the way, with the moors towering overhead. They skirted around the edge of the trees looking for an exit but there was nothing. "However did that poor gypsy girl escape from this?" Becky murmured.

"God knows."

They worked over to the east side, eventually coming across a narrow track that forked in several directions. "You take that one and I'll take this," said Toby. "Let's see where they go then backtrack. You're right – we can't afford to be seen. Sorry."

"Okay." It sounded like a plan but without a torch, and looking into the army of grey tree trunks, Becky wasn't at all sure. She couldn't put him down again, though. "Okay," she repeated, more quietly now as she picked out a vague trail and tentatively started walking.

The silence was palpable, the path only as wide as one footstep, and the further into the woods she ventured the darker it became. Within seconds it was impossible to see the hands in front of her and she held them out like a blind man. Should she call out

185

to Toby? Better not. Best to just keep going then backtrack exactly the way she came. The only sound now was the soft fall of her footsteps, the blackness thickening as it closed around her in a cloak. She couldn't see a thing and panic stabbed in her chest. So what direction was this then? The path seemed to be tipping downhill now! Then all at once the trail ended, a holly bush bringing her up short. Right, so this led nowhere: time to head back. Turning around precisely one hundred and eighty degrees, she put one foot in front of the other with the intention of doing exactly that, only to find no track only thicket.

For a moment she stood as still as a hunted animal, wondering what to do next, when a breath of air blew into her neck.

Her heart rate sky-rocketed.

Staring into the black forest with her pulse thumping hard, she instinctively put out her hands for the nearest tree trunk, then with her back pressed to the bark she inched around its girth, hoping to see something, anything that would give direction – somewhere to run to. Or perhaps it would be best to lie low and hide? Or should she just yell for Toby and hang it who heard? *What to do? Oh what to do?* The darkness was unbelievable. She waited and listened, holding her breath. Was there ever a place so silent? There wasn't a sound. No one was here. No one…maybe she'd imagined…

But then it came again – unmistakeable this time - a slight sigh.

She sank onto the dank earth, flattened so closely to the trunk it hurt. *Oh God, who was there? There was someone. Once could be imagination but twice… If only she could see. This was it, wasn't it? Oh, she shouldn't have come…* Her fingers scrabbled at the bark behind as if somehow she could escape that way, and that was when she felt it…a gap…a hole. Was it big enough to get into? She felt around inside with both hands now. No, but there was something in there…she pulled it out…a pair of shoes, or what had once been a pair of shoes. Now they were simply small flaps of mouldy leather. This had been someone's hiding place!

"Becky!" someone hissed.

Toby...oh thank God!

Gradually her eyes adjusted to the movement of a figure emerging from the trees. "Over here," she hissed back.

Toby slid down the tree next to her. "I could smell your perfume! Anyway, I found a path back to the village. It comes out just below the houses opposite the church."

"How convenient."

"What about this one?"

She showed him the shoes. "It doesn't lead anywhere except here. It's a hiding place – look someone left their shoes behind. "

"Cora?"

"I'd bet on that. You definitely need her as a witness when all this is—"

A rustle of leaves caused them to clam up.

The silence was so intense, the dark so completely devoid of even a shadow to define it, that they reached for each other's hand. Neither knew how long they waited for the feeling of menace to lift, but eventually a sliver of moonlight threw a shaft of light onto the grassed area in front of the mill. They had been within yards of it the whole time.

"Come on, let's go," said Toby, yanking her to her feet.

***

"I thought when you said, 'Let's go', you meant we were getting the hell out of here. Come on – I don't want to linger," Becky whispered as they crept along the side of the mill by the brook.

"Shhh...keep down low. I've decided we may as well check this out cos I'm not coming back here on my own again."

Becky's nostrils flared and she took a deep breath, exhaling slowly. Never in all her life had she wanted to leave a place so badly. She almost danced on her feet like an impatient child while Toby tried the key in the door. "Doesn't fit."

"There isn't any glass in the windows," she pointed out. "Why would anyone need this key?"

The rush of water behind him almost drowned out his reply. "…must be inside…basement…cellar…?"

"Oh no! I thought you said…"

Toby grabbed hold of her hand and they walked round to the front where the moonlight was strongest. "I can get in through here," he said, pointing to one of the lower windows. "I have to do a recce and see what this key's for. Then we'll go, I promise."

"I'm scared."

"I'll be two minutes. Wait here in the shadows and try not to breathe."

"Thanks. Well hurry up then. I mean it."

"Will you be okay?"

"No. You'd better be really, really quick." She looked over at the woods. Apart from the roar of the tumbling brook the air was still and icy, and a few stars sparkled amid high clouds drifting across the moon. "It's nearly a full moon," she observed. There was no answer and she winged round just in time to see Toby's feet disappearing into the mill.

She kept her back firmly to the wall, constantly scanning the immediate area, alert to the possibility that something horrible might emerge from that bank of black forest. From time to time the moonlight broke free of cloud, casting elongated shadows onto the grass. *Oh for God's sake hurry up, Toby…*

It occurred to her to just run towards the woods and take the path Toby had taken, which led to the village lane, and leave him to it. No, she couldn't.

Was that a voice?

She strained her ears against the backdrop of roaring water. A very faint cry was emanating from… she turned her head… from inside. Louder now, like a child sobbing. She held her breath.

"Becky!"

She physically jumped.

Toby grabbed her hand as he landed on the soil next to her. "Someone's here – come on - run like 'ell."

***

Chapter Twenty-Six

Drummersgate
Wednesday evening

Celeste isn't coming to see me again. Ever. They told me tonight she'd died but I had a feeling anyway, and I know that sounds funny, but I did. I swear. Two of them – Emma and Dr Airy – sat either side of me probably expecting a major kick off. What they don't get is that it doesn't matter because we're spirits and these bodily shells are just that – mortal, ageing, and transitory. But then I'm a certified mad person, so what do I know?

I like this kind of day – slumping in front of the television in the day room with mad old Violet and silly Philly – it's restful. Violet wears a flowery orange and yellow dress, which stretches skin tight over her massive stomach; her hair hangs in greasy, grey strands and her face is all red like it's been boiled. She's been in some sort of institution since she was thirteen because she started stabbing people to see what happened. Anyway, it's okay as long as she doesn't get a knife in her hand, not even to eat with – they give her a plastic spoon. And silly Philly chatters to herself like a little bird with fluttery wings for fingers. She hides things in drawers and scuttles round furtively as if she's a secret agent, looking over her shoulder to see if anyone's watching. It's kind of funny to end up here with the mad, the bad and the dangerous because as far as I know I've never done anything mad or bad.

I can feel Celeste all around me. She has a brilliant warm light like an angel and I know she wants to go to a higher place, but she'll stay with me for as long as she can. It's hard to say how I know she's here – maybe if I describe it as a feeling of comfort, a presence or strength that I didn't have before. A faith! Yes, that's it – a faith. The others inside are quieter too, not just taking over whenever they feel like it, but talking to each other when Dr Airy helps us. It stops us thinking about bad stuff and we know what the triggers are now, like being followed or the smell of wood-smoke or urine. Words too – like people saying they'll pray for me or that I'm a good girl or stuff to do with… No, I've got to stop cos I feel a bit odd.

Focusing on the television now - what they're saying - A home in the sun…

I'm doing this when his silhouette appears in the doorway. I never thought I'd see him again and suddenly I'm back there, floating under the surface of the water with his face rippling on the surface in the trees; great hands heaving beneath my shoulders with the fingers digging in and gasping lungsful of freezing air.

"Hello, Ruby," he says.

"Hello, Jes."

He sits next to me, glancing at me sideways a couple of times with a shy smile. "You took a bit of tracking down this time, I have to say."

"Where did I go?"

He shrugs. "The usual. Only I didn't get to you in time. That's how you ended up here." He looks around the room. "Maybe that's not such a bad thing though, eh? You've had some help, angel girl, and you look ok."

"I'm clean and most of the time I know who I am, so yeah – I'm getting there. How about you? You clean?"

He shakes his head. "Never will be. Hey, I heard about your friend – Celeste, was it? I'm sorry."

"'They' finished her off."

A dark shadow passes behind his eyes. "Ruby, how much do you know about what's still going on? Your nurse, Becky, sent someone to visit me recently and he told me you have a daughter."

"Alice!"

"He said they'd do a satanic baptism and…"

Satanic…I can feel my lip trembling. I'm falling backwards….

"Ruby, you've gone strange." He's got hold of my arms and he's shouting for someone.

191

The next thing I know it's dark and I'm lying on my bed. "Jes?"

"He's gone now," says Emma. "You had a good chat with him, though. Well, Marie did. Shall I tell you what happened because he was very excited – wanted to ring someone called Toby straight away. I didn't get it to be honest, but you probably will."

"My head's banging. I feel sick."

"I'll fetch you some paracetamol and then I'll tell you what was said if you want? Are you up to it?"

I have to sit up and lean over the side of the bed: my entire skull is pounding. "Yeah, I'm up to it."

***

Chapter Twenty-Seven

Laurel Lawns Private Hospital
Later that evening

Noel met Michael in the car park at Laurel Lawns. The man was in a shocking state. Michael had deteriorated so dramatically in the last forty-eight hours he had to be helped out of the passenger seat by both Noel and the younger man he'd arrived with. Tottering like an old man of ninety, he clung onto two walking sticks with bony claw-hands as he tap-tap-tapped his way across the tarmac on match stick legs, which frequently buckled from under him. It was clear to Noel that he'd said his good-byes. This would be his last act of goodwill.

The younger man, dressed in a long overcoat, which gaped at the neck to show a clerical collar, introduced himself as 'Harry Tate.' He had a firm handshake and an arresting persona. Over six feet tall with a large frame, he possessed solid shoulders and a direct blue stare. "I've been given the lowdown," he said as they walked. "Obviously this is all totally under the radar. To be honest I've only agreed because Michael asked me to." He indicated his friend's health, "Well…let's just get it done, shall we? I have to warn you, though, Noel, these things can and do sometimes go wrong. Do you know anything about exorcisms?"

Propped up by the two younger men, Michael had to stop frequently in order to recover his breath. Every step was a huge effort, his bones as fragile as a bird's. He exhaled through dry lips in little whistles, focusing determinedly on the doorway to the hospital while Harry quickly brought Noel up to speed. He explained that he'd studied demonic possessions and the rites of exorcism. However, he had never performed one alone before and never in this country. It was supposed to be sanctioned at a high level and they really should have a doctor and a legal representative present, plus a member of the patient's family.

"We don't—"

Harry nodded. "I know. Like I said, let's just get this over with and pray to God it goes to plan."

Michael stopped, shaking his head. "Have…faith…"

"You're right," said Harry. "But Noel here needs to know how traumatic this is going to be and—"

"I saw *The Exorcist*," said Noel, "and if it's going to be anything like that I'm not looking forward to this one bit."

Harry grimaced. "It won't be, don't worry. But my concern is that it's without the church's sanction and we don't have medical consent and—"

Michael stopped him again. "Stop…wittering…"

Harry nodded. "Fair enough, my friend."

On arrival at the main door Harry turned to face Noel, "Okay, well here's what you need to know because I'm going to be relying on you now. First of all please don't underestimate the power of the demonic. If you do they will attack you and you will know about it and could even be physically harmed. You will need to pray hard throughout and never ever engage with the patient even if it looks like she's appealing to you, calling your name or whatever. Do not interrupt me and do not deviate from your prayers. When I tell you to do something you do it. And you must repeat 'The Litany of Saints' as I read through it. Also, the demons will look for weaknesses and directly attack them so do not be put off – do not respond or show dismay or shame or anger. Do not respond in any way. Hold fast. Finally it's going to take at least two hours and we may have to come back and do it all again. Do you understand?"

"Yes," he said quietly.

The other two looked at him searchingly.

"Yes," he said again, with more conviction than he felt. Looking at Michael he asked, "Are you sure *you're* up to this?"

"I'm well in spirit. And Harry needs me here."

"Okay then," Noel said. "Well, can I just ask one more question before we go in?"

"Of course," said Harry.

"Am I in danger of being possessed? Will it get into me just from being present?"

Harry looked into his eyes. "I can't say that won't happen. It might. You need to have faith and pray hard."

"I'm scared to death."

"Don't show it," said Harry. "Come on – let's do this."

***

True to her word, Nora had informed them correctly: Crispin Morrow was off duty and the locum was not on the premises. The second she saw the three men she motioned them to come round the back way. "She's a lot worse," she said over her shoulder as she hurried down the corridor to the room furthest away from all the others.

The room people go to die in.

As if reading his thoughts, Nora turned to look at Noel when they got to the door, and gave him a half smile. "I know you've seen some sights but you must prepare for a serious shock. I'm afraid there is nothing more we can do, though, except keep her restrained and sedated. Dr Morrow refused to allow a second opinion or to have her transferred to Intensive Care. And he wouldn't allow the clergy in either, even though quite a few of us begged him to reconsider. She has no one, you see? Anyway, that apart, I'm really glad you came." She turned to face Michael and Harry, "I hope you can help her die in peace."

Harry nodded, and then Nora took out her keys and let them in.

She had not understated the situation.

Lying on the bed with her limbs in restraints, Kristy resembled a corpse following a car crash. Her eyes were staring at the ceiling unblinkingly; her skin mottled purple, and her swollen tongue lolled to the side. Plastered back from an oily forehead her blonde hair had been pulled out in clumps, and the dishevelled sheets revealed a body covered in gouges – the deepest of which were on the insides of her arms from repeatedly yanking out her intravenous infusions. Blood spattered the bed and there was an unmistakeable odour of sulphur in the air.

Calmly thanking Nora, Harry walked towards the bed and made the sign of the cross on his own brow, lips and breast before taking out a bottle of holy water from his coat pocket and sprinkling it around the room. Michael sat down by the window and quietly began to pray; and Noel, following his lead, did the same. *This couldn't be happening. It didn't really exist. It was surreal.*

"Okay, now let's begin," said Harry softly.

"Hello Kristy. Let's start with a bit of an introduction. Tell me how you grew up! Were you happy?"

She remained staring at the ceiling, her voice barely above a whisper. "Happy, yes."

"Did you go to church?"

"Yes."

"Were there any problems at home or any illnesses?"

"No," she said, still in a dreamy whisper. "My mother was bipolar – she killed herself when I was six. Dad remarried but died last year from a heart attack."

"You must have been very sad when your mum died?"

No reply.

"Did your dad bring you up?"

No reply.

"Kristy?"

"What made you decide to be a psychiatrist, Kristy? Was it your mum's illness?"

Her body began to stiffen by degrees and her breathing was becoming agitated.

Harry stood up and opened the bottle of holy water, which he signed himself and then Kristy with. At the point where the water came into contact with her skin, it hissed as if splashed on a hot grill. After which everything changed. Within seconds her respiration count began to escalate.

Harry began to recite 'The Litany of Saints.' "Lord have mercy."

Michael and Noel repeated as indicated, "Lord have mercy."

"Christ have mercy."

"Chris have mercy."

Kristy continued to stare only at the ceiling, her chest wheezy and rattling as it battled for breath. Her fists began to clench and unclench, and blood trickled down her chin from a bitten tongue.

"Christ hear us."

"Christ graciously hear us."

The sound of rasping breathing filled the air: faster and faster and faster, to the point of hyperventilating.

Harry continued calmly even as her limbs jerked and twitched.

"Lord have mercy."

"Lord have mercy."

Then quite suddenly it was as if she'd had enough. A primeval roar emanated from her body. It arched back, then with full force began to throw itself around on the bed, violently yanking on the restraints. Then just as suddenly it stopped, and her head snapped round a full ninety degrees to stare directly at Harry.

He looked away, attempting to continue with the process, even as the creature peered intently into his face, a forked blackened tongue flicking in and out between filthy, slimy teeth. A nasty laugh echoed around the room in a chorus of voices and he was struggling to focus when a male voice that sounded like a slowed-down recording, emanated from deep within her chest. "Don't even try, Father. Don't touch her. She's ours."

"I'm not afraid of you," Harry said.

"You should be."

Steeling his nerve he picked up the prayer book and resumed the ritual, moving onto the first Gospel reading, sprinkling more holy water and holding the crucifix up high.

Her fine boned face now began to contort into one bloated and twisted in pain, the forehead pulsating visibly as if something inside was going to burst through. Her eyes rolled back in their sockets and sulphur choked the air.

Both Michael and Noel's prayers increased in vehemence and volume.

Another twenty minutes passed before Harry held his hands up to them to stop for a moment, before commanding,

"Lord send aid from your holy place.

And watch over her from Sion.

Lord hear my prayer.

And let my cry be heard by You."

Once more he signed himself with holy water and did the same to Kristy, holding the crucifix up high. Then he signalled to the other two to recommence prayers before beginning the Rites of Exorcism.

"What is your name?"

A rush of babbled jargon erupted from her chest in a cacophony of indistinguishable voices.

"In the name of Jesus Christ I command you to answer me: what is your name?"

Again came a stream of language unbeknown to any of the men present. Harry shot a glance towards Michael, who shook his head. It wasn't Latin or Hebrew or Aramaic or any language any had come across before.

Kristy's body now started to thrash around so violently it rocked the bed on its castors, banging it down hard on the floor repeatedly. Something was going to break…Something had to break… Her screams of fury were enough to pierce eardrums, the light fitting swung from side to side smashing on the ceiling, and the air temperature plunged to below freezing. Again Harry repeated the command for a name; and again; and again, now walking determinedly forwards holding the crucifix up high. "In the name of Christ I command you…"

Suddenly the crucifix ignited and was swiped from his hands by an invisible force.

At that moment Noel faltered. *This was going wrong…* The cross lay in the corner of the room on the floor, exuding smoke. And the screaming ceased.

Kristy's head now swivelled around to focus on Noel. Her lips curved into a salacious smile. "Arse loving queer boy… Likes to….suck…" The viper tongue flicked in and out of her mouth, the voices inside of her slurping and slithering.

All three closed their ears to the tirade of diabolical abuse that spewed forth, and Harry again made the sign of the cross, repeating his command for a name, now holding the crucifix he wore around his neck on a chain.

Then Kristy stopped again as if re-thinking her strategy. Her head waggled around on its stem before her eyes settled on the cleric.

"In the name of Christ, answer me – what is your name?"

Next second a series of names were projected at him like vomit, "One, two, three, four…Shroud, Lucifer, Cain, Nero…"

She slumped back onto the mattress, a sheen of sweat covering her skin, the chest wheezing and hissing, all traces of physical distortion rapidly subsiding, before her eyes snapped open again and a silky voice said, "Come on Reverend. Now wouldn't you like to put your fingers inside me? You know you would. Wouldn't you like to… finger me…? I've been such a good girl…" She licked her lips and arched her back like a porn star, writhing and moaning as if the throes of ecstasy.

Harry, who had hesitated only momentarily, continued ever more powerfully with the ritual. The demons had divulged their names and now were lost: he was winning. "I cast you out unclean spirits, along with every satanic power of the enemy, every spectre from hell, and all your fell companions; in the name of our Lord Jesus Christ."

Kristy's throat gurgled as if it was full of slime. "He will die in misery and loneliness," she said, looking over at Michael. "He will ache from it. Hell will last for all his eternity. His mistake was to mess with his belief. Demons, say the professor, are merely a part of medieval theology. What a fool you have been, Michael."

She lay on her back again, staring at the ceiling. "You are all blind and in darkness. You are paralysed. You should have played by the rules. You are fools."

The lights flickered on and off, and the cross lying in the corner skittered across the floor as if pulled by a string. Still Harry shouted out the Rites, drowning out everything else, instructing the others, "Pray hard and don't stop."

His voice was strong and it rose yet further to dominate all the hissing and spitting and cursing coming from Kristy as the demons inside tried ever more aggressive tactics. The power within her was snapping the restraints and one of her legs had kicked free. The bed was slamming harder and harder onto the floor and blood was spraying over the sheets, blood vessels slicing into the leather straps as she fought to escape.

Urgency grew with every prayer, reading, blessing and command; but Harry was relentless, minutes ticking into hours, until finally he commanded, "In the name of Jesus Christ I command that you leave."

Her body slumped.

He repeated it. Watched her. Repeated it once more. And then she collapsed.

No one moved or spoke.

For a full five minutes all three stood silently.

Then Harry said the final prayer of deliverance; and slowly, in front of their eyes, Kristy looked up, stared around the room, and began to cry.

Harry slumped onto the window ledge.

Kristy was sobbing heartily now, for her mother, her father, her ex-husband, and for everything she'd ever done wrong that could have brought her to this place.

After a while Harry put a blanket around her shoulders and pressed the buzzer for Nora. Turning to face his colleagues for the first time in four hours he said, "Well, I don't know about you two but I could do with a nice strong cup of…" At the sight of Michael who had fallen on the floor, he rushed forwards, but Michael's skin was already ice-cold to the touch and he no longer drew breath. He turned to Noel, who was standing statue-still. "I think he's gone."

Noel nodded. "Harry, I can't move."

***

Chapter Twenty-Eight

Wednesday Night/Thursday morning

Toby lay wide awake. With every creak of the floorboards or thump of the old pipes in the Victorian terrace he shared, his eyes snapped open again. If only he was back at his parents' place enjoying the comfort of double glazing and new plumbing. These old sash windows rattled in their frames, and since neither of the other two lads were exactly gardeners, overgrown branches now bowed and scratched at the glass. Okay, yes, he got up and put the light on. He was seriously spooked.

The minute he and Becky made it back to the car last night, he'd jumped in and accelerated out of Bridesmoor almost before she'd had time to click her seatbelt on.

They'd got to The Old Coach Road before he spoke. "If we have to go back there on Friday night we're 'aving back up."

Becky, still out of breath from the frantic sprint through the woods from Tanners Dell, was gripping onto her seat as the car roared across the moors. "What on earth happened in there, Toby? For God's sake tell me!"

"Right." He wiped his brow on a shirt sleeve, holding the steering wheel with one hand. The evening was clear and studded with stars, the ground coated in silvery frost. He put both hands back on the wheel and stared hard at the road ahead. "Give me a minute. Let's get off this moor – I hate it up here. They say the ghosts of dead miners roam around and cars go off the road because something leaps out or a sudden fog comes down."

"More likely they go off the road because they've just come out of The Highwayman; but I agree it's not the most comforting of stopping places and I'm way too freaked out to argue."

For a while they sat silently, neither of them looking at the moors, which stretched darkly on either side.

"I keep thinking of Noel," said Becky. "And that sedan appearing out of nowhere. He got the bike up to about 140mph and it was still closing in on him even on corners. And when Kristy was coming back from Woodsend she said this old woman suddenly appeared in her passenger seat."

"Don't tell me anymore."

"Sorry."

Eventually the road began to dip down and the neon glow of town lay ahead. Half a mile after that, they passed a deserted forecourt and then a sign for some dog kennels, after which the road was once again street-lit.

"Now," said Becky, sighing with relief. "Pull over and tell me what on earth you saw inside the mill. If we're going back there I need to know."

Toby parked under a streetlamp next to a twenty-four/seven store. "You're not going back – no way."

"What? But—"

He shook his head. "This has got to be sorted professionally."

She sat quietly. "Tell me what happened."

"Okay, well I climbed into an old kitchen. It were dark, obviously, and I couldn't see much but at the back there's a huge room with a whacking great tree trunk growing up through the ceiling. It's all deserted. Anyhow, I thought that was it and I were gonna come out but then I noticed a really ornate, heavy-duty door – ancient looking with weird carvings on it – and I guessed that the key Cora gave us would fit the lock."

"And it did?"

"Aye. It turned easy. Steep cellar steps as you'd expect and not a jot of light - I could curse meself for not 'aving a torch. Stupid to go down on me own, really stupid. Anyway, when I got to the bottom I could just about make out a huge horizontal wheel but it were really black in there, so I used me cigarette lighter and then I could see a series of archways and tunnels. I couldn't help meself, I just stared and stared at it – there's a bloody great cathedral under there! And I knew someone used it because I could smell fucking weed a mile off, and other stuff… drugs and smoke. Anyhow, that's when I thought I saw summat – like a hooded grey monk floating down the corridor towards me."

"Fuck."

"I ran like 'ell but it were dead slippy and wet so I kept skidding, but I made it up the steps to the door and locked whatever it was down there. So either they had a key or there's another exit. I'm just wondering if that's what Callum found and if he stumbled on that other exit – maybe up at the mine?"

"Like the tunnels lead to a mine shaft?"

"Yes."

Toby's mobile bleeped and they both jumped in their seats.

"You get that," Becky said. "I'll nip in here and get us something to calm the nerves. Hot chocolate?"

He nodded. "Ta." The message on his phone was from Jes. Could they talk urgently?

After that the night had got even weirder.

Toby switched on all the lights and went down to the kitchen in a clinical glare of electricity. Normally he relished being on his own but as luck would have it both the other officers were on night duty. Strong, builders' tea was what he needed, and he flicked the kettle on while his mind retraced events. He wasn't going to be able to sleep with all this replaying in his head anyway.

Jes was adamant they met immediately, so after he'd dropped Becky off at the DRI, he drove to the address he'd been given - a house on the outskirts of Leeds. The street was in the Harehills area and the row of terraces a quiet one. Toby parked outside a tandoori on the main road and walked the remaining few yards, unbolted the side gate as instructed and went round to the back door.

The second he arrived, Jes ushered him into a small kitchen, where four men were sitting around a table. "Take a seat." He handed him a glass and one of the blokes passed along an opened bottle of scotch.

Toby hesitated, then thought better of it. *What the hell. After tonight he needed it.*

"You can kip over if you need to," Jes said, pouring him another. "You've been to Tanners Dell so you'll need more than one of these."

Toby knocked it back, feeling the burn of it chase down his throat, igniting his stomach. It took his breath and he gasped. "Strong stuff!"

A couple of the other men smiled.

"Have you ever been down there – underneath the mill?" he asked Jes.

Jes nodded. "So how about we pool information? I've waited years for a chance like this, and they'll be meeting on New Year for sure."

Toby looked at the other four, one by one. "Perhaps we should introduce ourselves?"

They were Nicu, Tomas, Stefan and Alex: all mid-forties to fifties by the look of them, tattooed, muscular, olive-skinned and hard bitten. "I would trust these guys with my life," said Jes. "And to be brutally honest, we might have to."

It crossed his mind that perhaps he'd fallen down a well into some kind of twilight world. He almost laughed. Toby in Wonderland. Well, there was no coming back from this now, was there? This road had no U-turns. An urgent call was waiting from his sergeant that he'd not yet returned, and here he was in a back kitchen somewhere in Leeds discussing an illicit mission to ambush a bunch of Satanists.

He nodded at each of the surly looking men in turn, and introduced himself while Jes poured out more whisky and a bottle of something with a Russian label on it appeared from one of the holdalls on the floor.

"Drink," said Tomas. "Is good."

The drink flowed, so did the stories. "I've tailed this lot for fucking years," said Jes. "Taken pictures on my cell phone, had videos and given information to various blokes in that village who were more than happy to work with me – hard-assed miners more than ready to rip Lucas Dean's balls off. But every single time I got those pictures back they were grainy and grey. One time all there was on each one was a faceless monk with cavernous holes where the eyes should be. The blokes from the village who helped me…something bad happened to every single one of them. I lost my sight temporarily and worse…"

Toby downed another glass of the clear Russian brew that tasted and smelled like meths.

"It's like that fucking witch is watching you in your dreams. Like she crawls into your mind. And then you get ill, man, like you're paralysed in your sleep and can't lift your head off the pillow. It's called a night crusher. Or you get dreams like you wouldn't believe – you think you're going mad with weights on your chest and black slithering creatures sliding out of the walls, rushing into your face. You can't breathe and you can't call out. I had to get a long way from here more than once. If she knows I'm close it'll all start up again. She smells you out. That's why we have to grab this chance now. Right now."

The other guys nodded. The stories were boundless and included sudden, agonising deaths from cancer; blindness and alcoholism; and they wanted revenge.

Toby shook his head and poured another glass of toxic brew. "No, not revenge. Justice."

Five pairs of black eyes glittered dangerously.

"Jes, you said you'd been to see Ruby. How did that go?"

"Yeah, well she got upset because we talked about her daughter – as you know it was news to me – but another of her personalities stepped in and told me a lot of stuff that stacks up. She remembers watching Ida bottle up her tricks: she takes stuff like hair, nails, blood or even a used condom and maybe whatever that person's guilty secret is, like alcohol or cigarettes…then she'll add a little cocktail of razors and wolfsbane, hemlock, arsenic, belladonna, all nice things…and invoke a curse. The group will then work on their chosen target from a distance and call up demons. It sounds like a load of bollocks but when you realise just how many of our people or people in that village died or had a hideous accident, it's pretty fucking real. And when you've got a local doctor who signs off the deaths as perfectly reasonable and a vicar who endorses it, you get the picture. The witch herself goes after pregnant women or the new-born, which probably explains all those unmarked graves there used to be in the cemetery. Did you know about those?"

Toby nodded. "It's in the diary I told you about – the one the social worker kept during the nineties – she collapsed and died of a brain haemorrhage shortly after finding them. The police didn't have any of this on their records at all."

Jes stared at him for a moment. "You do surprise me! There aren't any unmarked graves there now, though - they moved the bodies."

"Where to?"

Some of the body parts were put in boxes and kept in the caravans but mostly they were transferred, we think to underneath Tanners Dell – there's a whole labyrinth under there. Ruby, or Marie I should say, saw them digging inside the abbey ruins so we think there will be the skeletons of dozens if not hundreds of children, babies and premature births underneath the grounds of the abbey."

Toby stared at him for a full minute while the impact of this sunk in. "We can get them on this. You lot up for a New Year raid?"

**

Several hours later he hailed a taxi on the high street and left the car where it was. No matter how many sheets to the wind he was, there was no way was he spending the night on a sofa sandwiched between a couple of hairy-arsed, rough neck blokes snoring and stinking of home-brew.

His mobile woke him with a jolt just as the taxi driver was asking for cash. For a good few seconds he had no idea where he was, then he felt around in his pockets and paid the guy, stumbling into the icy midnight air and falling into the hallway a few seconds later.

There were eight messages from Sid Hall all marked as urgent.

Superintendent Ernest Scutts wanted to see him first thing tomorrow morning. That fact alone would keep him awake for the rest of the night.

***

Chapter Twenty-Nine

Thursday 6am

Toby walked into Ernest Scutt's office and took a seat opposite the chief superintendent. Outside it was still dark and his head pounded in the unnatural glare of fluorescent-lighting. By rights he should be in bed nursing the mother of all hangovers.

Scutts sat staring at him for so long the atmosphere became seriously uncomfortable. Anyone else and he'd have asked what the hell they wanted because he wasn't in the mood. Instead, he held the man's gaze until his eyeballs burned. Scutts was not an easy man to look at. His nose twisted half way down the bone either from a break that hadn't been reset properly or an unfortunate genetic inheritance; either way he was pug ugly with a protruding jaw that exposed only the lower set of teeth when he talked. A heavy set man with a ruddy complexion, he also exuded a toxic odour of uric acid and stale alcohol, and something else, something indefinable. Not attractive to women, Toby thought, while his mind raced to think what Scutts had on him.

Someone saw me and Becky in Bridesmoor… someone who went to the police… or straight to Scutts.

Eventually Scutts said, "A lady you went to visit yesterday is dead, DC Harbour. Cora Dean. What can you tell me about that?"

The effect was like a slap. "Dead?"

Scutts read from the paperwork in front of him. "Dosed herself up, put a plastic bag over her head and tied a cord around it before hanging herself from the rafters." He looked up. "Any comment? Any light you can shed on the matter?"

God, he was going to be sick. "I…I mean, all that happened was…" The words swam in his head and for the first time since school he was stuttering. "We…we…we… only asked her some questions about h…h…her—"

"Just tell me the fucking truth," the other man snapped.

"I am! I was trying to help a friend. She's a nurse and she's—"

"I know who she is."

He was a schoolboy back in the headmaster's office waiting for his parents to arrive. "Sir, I—"

Scutts leapt from his chair, rounding the desk in a less than a second. "Don't 'sir' me!" He gripped both of Toby's shoulders and shouted into his face. "Now listen and listen good, you little shit."

Whoa! Scutts' breath was rank with halitosis. He was going to be sick – a ball of acid was rising up so fast he had to swallow repeatedly to stop it.

"You do not ever, and I repeat, *ever*, go to Bridesmoor or Woodsend again. The case there is closed. A woman is now dead. There is no case and no reason for you to go, understand? If you disobey me you will find yourself removed from this force and not a soul will help you."

Fear pumped into his veins until they felt like they'd explode. Names of officers who had simply vanished, or been transferred to another division in another part of the country without a word of good-bye, all replayed in his head. It was like suddenly seeing a picture the other way round and realising this was the real one. How the hell did this bloke get away with it? *Unless there were others like him, here in the force, in this building, men he worked with every day?*

Scutts leaned in yet closer, the stench of excreta on his breath making him gag. Toby tried to avert his head, stunned at the words being spat into the side of his face. "Desist immediately or you will be terminated. Don't think you can do a thing behind my back because I will know. You are being most seriously warned, you little prick. Stay out of what you know nothing about. That cock and bull story about helping DI Ross' partner is a pile of shit. It is not her business and it is not yours. Now back off."

Toby nodded.

210

"Now get about your official business and know you are being watched every minute of every day. You will not be able to take a piss without I know what colour it was and how much you passed. Understand?"

He nodded again until finally the other man stood back, skin the colour of beetroot as he wiped a line of spittle from his chin. He started to turn away and Toby's muscles relaxed a fraction. Then without warning Scutts drew back his fist and crashed it across Toby skull so hard the room span and he fell to the floor.

"Whoops," said Scutt. "Whoops-a-daisy."

***

He came round half an hour later to find himself level with a ceramic toilet basin.

Hands were turning him over and a face swam woozily into his. "I heard you had a bit of a fight last night, mate? No wonder you're not feeling too good. Anyway, get a wiggle on – we've got a job to go to."

The sickly ache in his left temple half-blinded him when he tried to stand; the walls collapsing inwards as he staggered over to the wash basins and leaned over. Swaying, he gripped the porcelain rim. Heat rushed into his face and then his stomach expelled its contents in a bilious torrent that left his eyes streaming.

"You stink of whisky," said the cheery voice. "Shall we get some coffee and a doughnut? You'd feel better for it – sugar's what you need. It's low blood sugar that makes you feel so bad after a binge, did you know? And dehydration."

This was surreal. *Who the fuck was this bloke?*

Turning on the cold tap he splashed water onto his face, gulping from the stream before attempting to turn round and look. The instant he did so a wave of black-out pain caused him to stagger backwards and he held onto the sink to stop himself from falling.

"Dear me," said the other man. "We are in a state, aren't we? If I could offer you some advice? Personally I find it best not to go out drinking and brawling the night before a shift, but each to their own."

He's really getting on my tits now. Who the fuck is he, anyway? Have I seen him before, like ever?

With a herculean effort he held tightly onto the side of the sink unit and determinedly looked over his shoulder. The man, in his early thirties and clean shaven, smiled at him with an ice-blue stare and bared a row of tiny sharp teeth.

How in hell will I get in touch with Becky today with this bastard on my case?

"I can't work," he said. "I'm going home."

The other guy frowned. "No, no, no... Sorry you can't do that. Scutts' orders."

"I'm going off sick and there's nothing you can do about it, mate. If you like you can stake out the house all day but I *am* going home."

Lunging for the door it swung into his face alarmingly and he fell back, reached for it, missed, then tried again, and finally lurched into the corridor. Okay, so he was still on the top floor. Gut instinct told him to take the staircase not the lift so he zig-zagged towards it, grabbing hold of the rail before half-falling down the stairs with the other officer still in pursuit.

The moment the front desk came into view he shouted ahead. "I need a taxi to get me home. It's urgent – I'm really sick, gonna collapse."

The desk officer waved his acknowledgement and picked up the phone while Toby slumped onto a seat in the waiting area between an angry woman in a tracksuit and a pissed-off looking woman in a raincoat.

His heart was hammering. This was dangerous. They weren't going to let him just disappear, were they? Shit, how was it going to work out now? And what if his place was already bugged? He thought fast. Okay, right, best to check into a local hotel and get the car back from there. He'd call his mate, Mitch – the guy owed him big time – and get him to leave it round the back with the keys at reception. Nobody stalking him out would know it had happened. One way or another it was vital to speak to Becky and Jes as soon as possible, though, or Friday wasn't going to happen.

***

A mobile phone wasn't safe when your archenemy was a detective, nor was being driven to your destination in a taxi booked by the police service. Through a fog of pain he begged his mind to work properly. He had to keep his wits.

"Can you just drop me here, mate?" he shouted to the driver, bunging him a fiver. The high street was busy with the sales and he jumped out, merging adeptly into the crowds before finding one of the very few remaining phone boxes that worked; and from there he called Mitch.

Mitch had run into a whole lot of trouble in his teens stealing cars and dealing crack, but as lads growing up together on a rough housing estate they had always watched each other's backs and he'd trust him with his life. All he had to do was say what he needed and it would be done – some cash, a pay-as-you-go phone, and the car left as instructed inside the hour. After speaking to Mitch he took some of the short cuts he'd discovered as a truant teen and dodged through shops and back alleys until he found the hotel he wanted – one frequented by older people and families that offered well-priced Sunday lunches, and would be one of the last places a person would look for a single man in his twenties.

There was a room available on the top floor and an hour and a half later he was on the pay-as-you-go phone to Becky with the car parked out back. The paracetamol he'd bought en-route was just beginning to take the worst of the pain off, leaving the dull ache of concussion as he lay on the bed with a cold flannel on his forehead. "Becky, we're in deep shit," he said.

She listened while he related the news.

"You still there?"

"Oh my God, Toby."

"Becky, this has to happen now, and it has to happen as planned or we won't get another chance. I'm fucked anyway."

"No, you're not. We can and will do this."

"There's no 'we'. You have to stay with Callum. He's in a massive amount of danger and you need to be there. I'm organising something right now – there will be enough of us and we'll catch them in the act, I promise. I'll phone you back later but you have to stay there, do you promise?"

"I have to tell you something too, Toby. Noel's in Leeds Infirmary. He lost the use of his legs after being involved in Kristy's exorcism last night."

"Exorcism? Shit, this just gets worse."

"She's a lot better apparently – it worked. She was crying and insisted on leaving in the same ambulance as Noel and Harry. And I'm afraid that Michael died, which I guess everyone expected. I'm really upset about it because if it wasn't for him it could have been me in Laurel Lawns too."

"Ah, that's bad news. I'm really sorry."

"Yes, yes it is, it's lousy. How many more? We're all being destroyed!"

"At least Kristy is better. And you didn't go under, Becky, you survived and so has she."

"Yes, I suppose. I just rang and they said Kristy will probably be transferred to a ward this afternoon, and they've managed to track down her ex-husband. He's coming to see her, which I'm glad about – she was very much on her own in life, I didn't realise. Apparently Crispin Morrow is hopping mad this happened on his day off and he's demanding the clinic sue the priest who did the exorcism; and Noel, and Nora. She's off duty today but I rang to ask how it went and she told me everything. She's scared half to death and convinced she'll lose her job because of it."

"Hang on a minute – sued for saving a patient's life? How does that work?"

"For putting her in danger and doing it without his consent, apparently."

"Unbelievable. What about Noel? Is he okay now? Was it just shock, do you think?"

"I don't know. He had to be carried into the ambulance on a stretcher and this morning he's having tests. He's on the neuro ward so I'll ring again later. I owe him such a lot – I could cry!"

"This is terrible. What about Callum – how's he?"

"Agitated. I've told him everything like I always do, but his nerves are jumping around under his skin and his hands are clenching and unclenching. It's like he wants to be heard, like he wants to surface, but he just can't."

"I wonder if, when all this is over, he'll wake up?"

"I hope so. What about you, anyway? You must be in a terrible state? Do you think you should get checked out at the hospital?"

"No, it were just a nasty slap. I'll be all right when I've rested up a bit. We're going to have to get this done now, Becky, and fast or it gives them time to second guess us. At the moment we just might have the edge."

"I'm truly sorry. I had to ask someone for help and you were the only person I was sure of. I did think twice about it, though. I need you to know that because I knew what was at stake. The thing is, Toby, and this is going to sound wacky, but it's not just some nasty characters you've got to watch out for it's the black witchcraft…"

"I know – I got the low down last night."

She listened as he related some of the horrific stories he'd heard from Jes and the gypsies. "Yes, well it all fits. My guess is Scutts got his information on Cora first hand from Rick; so the Dean boys will know about our visit as will Ida. Toby, don't take this lightly – you will now be a target for psychic attack. I've had it first-hand and believe me it's bloody terrifying. You have to watch out for things you won't believe are happening to you. She *sees* you!"

"What do you mean when you say you had it first hand?"

Becky described what had happened after her accident. "It's been tried again several times recently but this time it didn't work."

"Why? I don't understand – why not this time? What was different?"

She related what Celeste had advised. "It works, that's all I can say."

"I can't do that sort of stuff – it's bonkers."

"So you accept all the stuff about people suddenly becoming ill or blinded, the unusual deaths and bizarre hallucinations; but when it comes to protecting yourself and believing in a higher, divine spirit, it's bonkers? Well anyway, you might change your mind later when it goes dark and you're alone in that hotel room."

"Oh, great! Thanks for that!"

"Well… I've given you the information and now you have it, so-"

"Becky, listen – I've got to go because I need to make some calls and it's going to take a while to set up. I've got a lot of favours to call in and people who are going to have to believe some crazy stuff. I'll ring you later but you must stay with Callum. He's dangerous to them if he wakes up and he's helpless at the moment."

"Yes, of course I will. What about Alice, though?"

"It's not your job. Your job is to take care of Callum and keep him safe."

"Who have you got coming with you?"

"Like I said – I've got a few calls to make. And there's Jes and his family. Just trust me and stay there. I'll ring you when it's all over."

The magnitude of the task ahead hit him after he rang off. There were blokes he'd worked with over the years who would guard another man with their lives – all now in a different force or division – and it was these he had to contact one by one, with each call taking over an hour. Then there were solid friends he'd known since he was a boy. In the end he had a highly-trusted team of

216

twelve; some with firearms licences, some trained fighters and others men who were simply good people compelled to do the right thing.

Then he rang Jes.

"We've got more on the way too– about fifteen of us," said Jes.

"My career's on this now, mate. If we don't pull it off I'm finished."

"No, you're *life is* on it. Sorry, but that's how it is."

"Fuck. How did this happen to me?"

"We've all asked ourselves that one. This is it though, Toby. Don't mess up."

"Of course I won't mess up."

"Is Becky on board with what she's doing?"

"She wanted to come but I told her to stay with Callum. He's the most vulnerable, tied to a bloody bed."

"Yes, he is."

"Anyway she can't run for toffee."

Jes laughed. "Bless her. Right, I suggest we meet outside The Highwayman at 2.30 am and travel in small groups."

"Okay. Everyone wears black head to foot and hiking boots. We'll need some of my blokes at the abbey and the rest of us will go to the mill and cover all exits. This is massively off the radar by the way, and if it goes wrong a whole lot of us are in serious shit."

"We've got knives. And it won't go wrong."

"No – no knives. Leave the arrests to us."

Jes laughed. "You're fucking kidding me. We've waited decades for this."

"One thing. Where will the girl be, do you think? Alice?"

"She'll be with them at Tanners Dell."

"You're joking?"

"Of course I'm not – that's what they do!"

After Toby put the phone down he lay on the bed thinking it all through. Outside it was dark now and a flurry of snowflakes fluttered against the window. What would the next twelve hours bring?

Suddenly he sat shock upright. *Shit! What if they couldn't get up there because of snow?* Bridesmoor was well known for being one of the first places to get cut off in winter. They had omitted to check the weather forecast. Flicking on the television he watched the twenty-four hour news: heavy snow was forecast for high ground. *Oh fantastic! Bloody fantastic!* He switched off the sound and fell back against the pillows. *Dear God and all his angels, we need some help.*

Well what could you do about the weather? Just pray…pray the kind of heavy snow that cut off villages like Bridesmoor didn't come tonight. One more day was all they needed. Half a day even…he closed his eyes, melting into the dull ache that rhythmically throbbed inside his skull. Sleep began to drag him down, his eyelids heavy, and briefly he lost consciousness, surfacing a few minutes later with a start. In the half light of the television he reached for the phone and set the alarm for 2am, forcing himself to double check that it was 2am and not 2pm for sure before finally switching off the remote, pulling the blanket up and giving himself up to exhaustion for a few hours.

You might change your mind later when it's dark and you're alone in that hotel room…

Less than two hours later an arctic chill woke him up.

In the adjoining room a bath was being run; from somewhere else there came the sound of canned laughter, and down the hallway a lift pinged. He glanced at the digital clock: just gone midnight. Damn, it would have been nice to have had another hour at least but he was frozen to the bone. The light had changed too, and for a while he lay observing the silvery outline of the furniture, his attention magnetically drawn to the door. He looked at that door for a long time. No, it was no good, it was impossible to try and sleep now – the chain was way too feeble.

Pulling back the blanket he sat up and peeped through the gap in the curtains. Good, no snow yet. A heavy frost covered the cars down below but the night was starry and clear with a full moon overhead. He started to shiver and couldn't seem to stop. *Flaming hell, this room really was perishing.* His mother would say it was too cold to snow and he smiled as he reached over to switch on the lamp – they use to argue about such daft things. Well that was odd, it had worked earlier. He checked the plug socket – yup, all switched on. He clicked the switch again – still nothing.

Oh well, there was just enough light to see over as far as the dresser, which had a high-backed chair tucked underneath it. He stood up but immediately had to sit down again. It felt as if his brain had come loose inside the cranium and was banging against the skull. After a minute he tried again and stood swaying for a minute, just as a light breeze blew into his cheek. *What the fuck?*

You might change your mind later when it's dark and you're alone in that hotel room…

Fear prickled up and down his spine and he had a word with himself. This was stupid, and stupid and stupid – get a grip! He had a serious job to do in a few hours' time and it was essential to get a few more hours sleep. It was just a case of securing that door so he could relax better. Slowly he walked across the room so his head didn't pound too badly, picked up the dressing table chair and rammed it firmly under the handle. Good, now maybe he could get some rest.

After that he paid a visit to the bathroom, had a pee and drank a glass of water. In the mirror, bleary pin-hole eyes looked out from an ashen face. Man, that was rough. He leaned forwards to examine the stubble and was just thinking about trying to shave with the bic razor provided, when the shower curtain rings clinked. Frowning, his reflection eyed the scene behind. What was that? God, he really was badly spooked. This was…

Then it happened again. He whirled round and yanked the curtain back. There was nothing there. *Oh, for fuck's sake!* He needed to sleep. It was concussion, a bump on the head, all the stories he'd been told… Where the hell was the thermostat anyway? It was freezing in here.

Somewhat crossly he stalked back into the bedroom, not noticing at first, but then the full horror of it hit him.

The chair was back underneath the dressing table.

***

Chapter Thirty

Friday 31st December/Saturday 3am

A light covering of snow glittered like Christmas icing over the moors.

Few words were spoken as a large group of men broke into two factions outside The Highwayman – one would head straight down to Five Sisters Abbey in Woodsend; the other would travel west for Tanners Dell. Under the brilliant light of a full moon and a galaxy of stars, they had to move quickly, darting into the shadows and keeping low until protected by the forest. All had been briefed extensively and knew what was at stake, although Toby suspected the police officers wouldn't have a clue about any dark tricks they might encounter on the way. Well, it might happen, it might not – they wouldn't believe it if he told them; so as long as he had his wits about him – and Jes was definitely well prepared having learned his lesson before many times – they should be okay. A lot depended, he supposed, on whether Ida knew they were coming or not.

Scooting over Drovers Common close to the hedges, he said a little prayer inside – something he hadn't done since he was a child. It was when you knew something else really did exist, he thought, that your world spun on its axis and after that nothing was ever quite the same. An owl hooted and he nearly jumped out of his skin. *Was it that witch or was it just a bloody short-eared, head-swivelling, flat faced bird? Oh dear God, help me not to lose my mind. Help me to find the strength to face whatever happens tonight...*

Under Jes' command, the other group skirted the woods in packs of twos and threes. The north wind cut into their faces and snow crunched beneath their boots, twigs snapping underfoot. The forest branches were piped white and tiny crystals glittered in the moonlight as they tramped along. Once level with the Deans' cottage, he signalled for the troop to stop. A black dog was growling with bared teeth from where it stood tied to a rope in the yard. Crouching low, Jes inched towards it before throwing down a piece of meat laced with enough sedatives to knock it out for a week. The muscle-rippled creature sniffed it, pawing it around.

"Go on, eat it, you thick mutt," he murmured silkily.

Eventually the dog took a bite, before wolfing it down. After a few more minutes the dog whined a little and sank onto its haunches. Then the men crept past. The track was deeply rutted from the wheels of 4x4 trucks, before gradually petering out to a single dirt track. This soon gave way to virgin snow and a hushed silence as they travelled further around to the north east side of the woods. Without the shelter of the trees it was a biting wind that howled over the moors and they put their heads down, until eventually on the left they came to a tiny, sheltered copse containing an ancient cemetery. This was the one Linda Hedges had stumbled on, as had Kristy when they'd each come looking around Woodsend. The Sisters of Mercy had fostered many children in their day, most already ill through poverty and disease, and the graveyard was mostly populated with tiny headstones, now askew and partially sunken, the inscriptions illegible. Walking past at a pace, each man felt drawn to stare at the ring of wrought iron railings around the graveyard, and the small shimmering white stones within. And each was still looking when Jes stopped short and they almost toppled into each other.

In the middle of the path sat a large fox, its black eyes pinpricked with red pupils.

Jes motioned the others to stay back as he reached into his rucksack for the slaughtered chicken he'd brought precisely for these tricks. Flinging it onto the path he retreated, watched and waited.

The emaciated fox was suffering badly from mange, and before long it crawled forwards to inspect the offering. Still with its eyes firmly on Jes it began to drag the chicken back across the dirt, then picked it up in its jaws and shot into the snowy woods. There was a collective sigh of relief and a few minutes later the abbey ruins came into view.

After many hundreds of years, there was little left save a few dry stone walls, an old well and the remainder of a large, ivy-clad archway. In the centre ground it was clear where the division of rooms had once been and Jes indicated where they should start digging. The earth was ice-hard; and in total silence the men unhooked their rucksacks and began to unload a grim cargo of pick axes and spades, amid flurries of fresh snow swooping down from the moors. Around them, the wintery woods shrouded what they were about to do. And what they might find.

***

The other group had kept up a pace and were now entering Carrions Wood opposite Bridesmoor church. Toby split them up at this point and directed them onto separate paths. Tacitly and armed with night vision glasses, each then picked their way through the undergrowth as stealthily as huntsmen, ducking down every few seconds to check they hadn't been seen.

As soon as the mill was in sight they positioned themselves to surround it; and once all was in place, Toby and one other officer darted towards the building. The only sound apart from their own breathing was the continuous pounding of cascading water as, backs to the wall they scanned the darkened kitchen window. As before, all seemed empty.

"Let's go," Toby whispered.

Inside the kitchen the air was icier than a morgue, the stone floor slippery with damp.

"Careful underfoot," Toby hissed.

Padding further in, it was obvious the upper floors were totally deserted. They stood as statues, listening hard to make absolutely sure, before Toby gently tried the cellar door. The handle turned but the door wouldn't budge. He put his ear to the keyhole to be met with hissing silence. Again his ears strained for the slightest hint of chanting or voices but there was nothing.

He and his partner exchanged a complicit glance. Then Toby took out Cora's key and turned the lock. The door swung open and he pocketed the key before leading the way down.

Like descending into a cave, each step took them further into a pit of darkness, the only sound that of dripping water. Underfoot the stones were as sheet ice and each clung onto the railing, until finally they were standing in the blackened vault underneath Tanners Dell.

The huge horizontal mill wheel dominated the basement and provided something to hold onto as they felt their way across the chamber towards the series of archways, which ran the length of the building and beyond. To who knows where, Toby thought. All the way to the mine? Without night vision glasses it would have been coal-face black. With them the place was extremely creepy and it was difficult not to be distracted by the carvings of macabre figures performing obscene acts, which could now be seen in the stone – half-human, half-beast. Various skulls sat in nooks and hollows; and black mirrors, inscriptions and diabolical drawings of demons and devils adorned the cavern walls; the insidious drip-drip-drip of water almost hypnotic in the background.

They both noticed the smell of burning.

"Chasing the dragon?"

Keeping flat to the walls they started down the long, arched corridor, eyes fixated on the smoky gloom at the end of the tunnel. The further they advanced the stronger the sweet, heady scent, and before long there was flickering firelight on the walls. Still, it seemed a long way off and they had much further to go. Venturing further and further underground, Toby realised they must be under the moors by now. This was no basement; but a series of purpose-built underground tunnels with ante-rooms and chambers, like castle dungeons that went on and on… Peering into one of the vaults with the advantage of night vision glasses he baulked at what he saw. Affixed to the slimy wet stone walls was a heavy-duty array of metal chains and clamps. At the far end was an iron chair nailed to the floor and everywhere there was horrific graffiti etched into the stone where victims had scraped out their torment using bones. Several skeletons still lay slumped where they'd died and decayed. *Good God*! With an incline of his head, he kept the other man from seeing it. They had to keep moving.

Then at last – the haunting sound of a trance-inducing chant – and shortly afterwards they turned the final corner.

"Opium," said Toby as they stationed themselves on either side of the archway.

The other man whispered. "Summat else an' all – summat disgusting!"

"Don't breathe it in," Toby hissed. "They hypnotise themselves with it."

The chorus of voices had escalated now, echoing around the chamber in a guttural, animalistic frenzy of excitement.

"They don't sound human," his colleague hissed back.

Toby shook his head, his heart banging hard as they peered into the vast chamber.

A ring of people in domino robes and masks were holding hands while walking round and round on an intricately engraved floor. A huge inferno of a fire lit up the room and shadows leapt around the walls as the chanting rose to a crescendo. Some of them were roaring like wild animals, howling and screaming. The dancing became manic with robes flung off to reveal the sweating naked flesh of mostly overweight, wrinkled, saggy old men. Using voices laced with malice and hate, they were repeatedly chanting a specific incantation: "Poison her soul, wither her mind, leave no trace of her behind, let their cry be in pain, let them lie and go insane…"

The name: Rebecca

"Rebecca. Rebecca. Rebecca".

The man at the head of the circle then held high a macabre doll made of what looked like straw and hair before throwing it into the flames. A feverish cry of triumph went up and then quite suddenly the naked figures fell to the floor in a hiss of submission. A grotesque creature had emerged from the shadows.

Toby's eyes nearly popped out of his head.

The creature wore the mask of a horned goat and an elaborate cloak of feathers and fur. *Was this for real? Wasn't this just some kind of stupid adult games party for the thrill-seeking deranged?*

And yet he was riveted to the spot, mesmerised by the figures crawling around on the floor like snakes, writhing about in a complicit act of inhuman wretchedness, the willingness to participate like some kind of contagious disease. And at the same time he understood with a stab of abject horror that no, this wasn't a stupid adult party because in the middle of the circle lay a bundle of something in a sack, and that something was alive, crying and struggling to get out.

The ceremony now rapidly reached its climax and the horned figure held a knife high above its head, steel flashing in the firelight, the terrible image flickering across the far wall, as it threw back its head and let out a bestial, blood-hungry scream of triumph.

"Fuck, it's a sacrifice," said Toby.

They ran in.

Vaguely he remembered grabbing the animal in the sack and running from the room just as mayhem broke out. In a melee of confusion there were men shouting, "Freeze!" and people thrown to the floor. It looked like the entire police service had suddenly turned up.

Toby reeled. Where the hell had all this lot come from?

A tap on his shoulder gave him the answer as he backed out of the room with what turned out to be a trembling puppy in his arms. Sid Hall's face glowed above his torch like something from a B movie. "I've not worked in CID all these years without knowing a thing or two. Got you covered, soft lad."

It was a grim scene. Fifteen adults, all men bar one, being filed out of a desolate old mill in the early hours of New Year's Day. With their hoods yanked back they kept their heads down as each was handcuffed and led through the woods to the police vans and ambulances waiting on the lane. A sole cameraman snapped each of their snarling faces as they emerged blinking in the moonlight, and several were lifted screaming and grimacing onto stretchers.

Toby met the full glare of Ernest Scutts' rage as he was shoved none too gently into the back of a van. Scutts paused long enough to hurl a rounded, blackened gob of spittle in his face and hissed, "You don't know what you've done, you little snot. We raised Lucifer. And if you don't believe me you soon will."

"Oh fuck off," said Toby. "I'm not in the mood."

Word came from the abbey there could be dozens of small corpses buried there. It would take days, if not weeks, to unearth them all and then a team of forensic scientists would have to be involved. The area had been cordoned off as a major crime scene.

"What a way to start the New Year," Toby said to Jes as they stood watching. "Are you all right, by the way?"

Jes grinned. "Never better. I heard Paul Dean had his balls accidentally detached from his scrotum during the fight."

Toby stared after him, as the man then turned and vanished into the night with a jaunty wave, the dark outline of his retreating figure stark against the now fast falling snow.

***

Chapter Thirty-One

Doncaster Royal Infirmary
New Year's Day

WHERE ARE YOU?
ON MY WAY. DRIVING!
CALLUM'S TALKING!!!
THERE IN TEN
DID U GET THEM???
YES
SERIOUS?
YES
I'M DYING HERE – TELL ME WHAT HAPPENED
JUST PARKING UP

In the end it was almost midday by the time Toby burst onto the ward, ashen faced and splattered in mud from his hiking boots upwards.

"Sorry, it's chaotic – every room at the station is full of chief police officers, lawyers, the press…" He sank onto a chair unable to keep the grin off his face. "We fucking did it, Becky!"

"Nice work," said a familiar voice.

Toby glanced over at Callum. Although he still had an oxygen mask in situ and was struggling to breathe, his eyes were open and he could talk. "Well it was good of you to turn up, DI Ross. Better late than never, eh?"

Callum groaned as he tried to sit up more. "Ouch! Ouch! Oooh… Ha, bloody ha. Tell you t' truth, Toby, I can't remember a thing. I were just telling Becky the last memory I've got is running like hell down a track through the woods with a pile of blokes after me. That's it."

"It's just fantastic to have you back, mate, it really is."

"Got the kids coming this afternoon, as well. They had a bit of a skid on black ice the other day, but they're on t' train now so…"

"Ah, that's brilliant news."

Callum tried to smile but winced, his facial tissue still bruised and swollen.

"Toby, no offence but I can't believe you pulled this off," Becky said. "Everything feels better too - look at the light coming through the windows!"

Stardust was dancing in the air, sparkling in the January sun.

She turned to him, alive with excitement. "I'm dying to know what happened, but first, I want to tell you that Noel is going to be okay. He still has a lot of numbness in his legs but they say it's a temporary paralysis and he'll make a full recovery, thank God. And Kristy's been moved to a normal ward. Apparently her ex-husband is there now, so…you know, it's odd isn't it? I mean extremely odd…" She shook her head. "But it really is like a spell of darkness has been lifted. The last few weeks have all been in a kind of half-light – I've been plagued with fear and worry, constantly watching my back and expecting the worst to happen to the people I love and care about."

Toby sat forwards with his elbows on his knees, enjoying watching Callum breathe. "Never in a million years would I have believed in all this dark magic stuff. Never. But it touched me last night and I've never been so shit-scared in all my life, Becky. By comparison, what we did a few hours ago rounding up a nasty bunch of sadistic paedophiles was easy."

"What happened?"

"And I'm sorry I didn't take you seriously when you told me what to do to protect myself. All that white light stuff? I locked me sen in t' bathroom for two flaming hours this morning."

"Why?"

He told her and she blanched.

"Anyhow, it worked so…"

"It certainly puts a new dimension on life when it happens to you, doesn't it?" Becky said, patting his shoulder. "Either that or we just go mad."

He nodded. "God, I'm shattered. I still couldn't sleep though. I'm not sure I'll ever sleep again."

"You will. Now for the love of God would you please tell us what happened. Oh…" She waved to Anna. "Anna, can I bring some coffees in please – would that be okay? Only this police officer's been up all night – he's done an amazing job - it's going to be in the news today."

Anna's face twitched very slightly. "Okay. But I bring them to you."

"Wow," said Callum when she was out of earshot. "You've really charmed *her*."

Becky smiled. "Let's just say we have an understanding. Now spill, Toby, or I will be forced to slap your legs. Very hard!"

He spilled.

"Ernest Scutts!" said Callum, taking off his mask for a minute. "Flaming Nora! I'd heard stuff about him being a nasty bastard – couple of blokes disappearing off the Force – that sort of thing – but paedophilia and Satanism?"

"And the rest," said Toby, elaborating further on the torture chambers and graves.

"Who else was there in the coven?" Becky asked.

"The ones you'd expect – Paul, Derek and Rick Dean; the GP – Crispin Morrow; Kathleen Dean; Reverend Gordon. On top of that there are those whose names you won't know yet but they're currently under arrest – let's just say one is a highly prominent lawyer specialising in child abuse; another is a private school teacher for kids with special needs; there's a couple who've worked in a children's home for over thirty years; several members of the police service both locally and from further afield, and most shockingly of all… well it was to me – a senior paediatrician. "

When Anna came back with a tray of coffees all three were sitting in stunned silence.

"Thanks, Anna," Becky said, handing Toby his. "That's really kind of you."

Anna lingered. "Is everything okay? I just heard the radio."

"Do you know, Anna, I don't think anything will be okay again, really, but at least the rot's stopped. Well, that is… Oh my God, I've just had a thought."

Toby had his cup half way to his lips. "What?"

"Well in the line-up of arrests you didn't mention Ida."

Toby flicked an apologetic glance at Anna and she took her cue. "Shout me if you need anything. You want a private room? Side ward?"

"God, no!" Callum nearly choked. "I had bloody terrible nightmares in there… dead people coming out of the walls and stuff. I couldn't shout or move or anything. It were 'horrible. No, they're haunted, they are. Please don't make me."

Anna grinned. "I think that is the drugs talking, Callum."

"If only…" Becky muttered under her breath as she walked away.

"There were only one woman there and that were Kathleen Dean," Toby continued. "She had these strange, pale eyes like glass – late forties but looked older, haggard like. There definitely weren't anyone fitting Ida Dean's description, though."

Becky frowned. "She's the one who does the curses. She would have been there…the question is, did she escape, do you think? And if so how and where is she now?"

Toby looked blank. "I'll get a search out for her. But I'm telling you we had that place surrounded and there were a team up at the mine and combing the moors; plus more over at the abbey. When we got them the entire area was floodlit and—"

"But those tunnels could come out at a mine shaft. She could've got out that way like Callum did?"

Toby shook his head. "I'm not saying there isn't another exit but me and me mate raided their parade when they were in full throttle and we got everyone there. Well…maybe she ran or flew or summat…"

"What – turned into a bat?" Becky laughed. "Shit – she probably did as well!"

"Well, we'll not catch her if she's done that. If she's a normal human though, we will because there are hundreds of officers up there now combing the place. The old mine, the moors, the tunnel exits, and knocking on every door."

"The child that was found - was it Alice?"

"Ah, this is the bit that's difficult."

"What do you mean? Surely she wasn't the sacrifice? That's not what I understood was going to happen to her?"

"No, it were a puppy they were gonna stab to death, poor thing. Oh God…" He covered his face with both hands for a minute. Eventually he looked up, unable to hide the smudges of tears. "They probably couldn't get a baby in time. I feel sick to me stomach at what those bastards 'aver been doing."

"Was Alice there? Please don't tell me she's disappeared with Ida."

"No, we got her. She's safe."

"Where?"

"She were in another room, like an ante-room or summat… Drugged up because she were just lying there with her eyes wide open and frozen… I can't…" He looked away, wiping tears away with his sleeve.

"No, okay." She patted his shoulder. "She's alive though?"

"Yes. She's got a child protection officer with her and she's in hospital."

"Badly traumatised like her mum, I suppose. Hopefully one day she'll be able to give evidence though…"

"I doubt it, Becky. This is what I meant about the difficult bit."

"Why? What do you mean?"

"They cut her tongue out."

***

Epilogue

Drummersgate
August 2015: 1.11 am

It's a really hot and sticky night. Not a single balmy breeze, and here we are lying sweating on the bed with no need for sheets.

There's a slight weight on the bed as if someone has just sat next to us and after a while I see her; kind of like a ball of haze.

"Lighter in the spirit than in the flesh," she giggles.

Her voice sounds like she's talking from the bottom of a pond and it takes a bit of tuning into, like fiddling with a radio for a signal. Eventually I hear her better. I've learned not to try too hard – just to get an impression – and we talk in our minds.

"Celeste?"

A warm glow inside tells me I'm right.

"I'm going to be your spirit guide," she says.

"I didn't know I had one."

"Everyone has one, maybe more than one. But they know you won't be allowed to find help so I've been given the job and we'll work like this. I'm delighted."

"There's so much I want to ask."

"And so much I want to tell you, child. But first there is a message. It's for Becky…can you get this to her …?"

Celeste's voice fades out and then shouts, fades and then shouts…I have to practice this better…

"Do you want me to take over now, Ruby?"

"No, Eve. I'm doing this."

"But I want to talk to Celeste. I want to ask her loads."

"No. I am the host and you will stay there."

"Celeste, are you there? I need to know how Alice is. They say she's being looked after but will I see her? When will they let me see her?"

There is a lull and then the hazy shape grows and radiates more strongly. "Yes she is getting well. You will see her... have to use your energy... you have to develop it... There is a message for Becky..."

"What is it?"

"That's better. It's difficult...finally got through to you... I've been around but your energy has been draining away in here. It makes you vulnerable..."

Again her voice fades.

And then suddenly it's back with a yell. "I am being told to tell you this. Becky...paint her new house in white and yellow and all the colours of summer. White and light everywhere... Lilith sees her."

"I don't understand. "

"Tell her to find out about Lilith – the demon, Lilith. Becky is with child, dear."

Acknowledgements
Glossary of Terms

The author of this book would like to add that a considerable amount of research was undertaken in order to broaden her knowledge of Dissociative Identity Disorder (DID), which affects many people, and in 90% of cases can be attributed to child abuse. Thank you very much to those who helped with this research.

RSA: Ritual Satanic Abuse

DID: Dissociative Identity Disorder (previously known as multiple personality disorder) is thought to be a complex psychological condition that is likely caused by many factors, including severe trauma during early childhood (usually extreme, repetitive physical, sexual, or emotional abuse).

PTSD: Post Traumatic Stress Disorder

Dystonia – A syndrome of abnormal muscle contraction that produces repetitive involuntary twisting movements and abnormal posturing of the neck, trunk, face, and extremities. (Farlex Partner Medical Dictionary © Farlex 2012)

Haloperidol – an anti-psychotic agent

***

Father of Lies – Book 1

A Darkly Disturbing Occult Horror Trilogy: Book 1

'Boy did this pack a punch and scare me witless..'
'Scary as hell...What I thought would be mainstream horror was anything but...'
'Not for the faint-hearted. Be warned - this is very, very dark subject matter.'
'A truly wonderful and scary start to a horror trilogy. One of the best and most well written books I've read in a long time.'
'A dark and compelling read. I devoured it in one afternoon. Even as the horrors unfolded I couldn't race through the pages quickly enough for more...'
'Delivers the spooky in spades!'
'Will go so far as to say Sarah is now my favourite author - sorry Mr King!'

***

Ruby is the most violently disturbed patient ever admitted to Drummersgate Asylum, high on the bleak moors of northern England. With no improvement after two years, Dr. Jack McGowan finally decides to take a risk and hypnotises her. With terrifying consequences.

A horrific dark force is now unleashed on the entire medical team, as each in turn attempts to unlock Ruby's shocking and sinister past. Who is this girl? And how did she manage to survive such unimaginable evil? Set in a desolate ex-mining village, where secrets are tightly kept and intruders hounded out, their questions soon lead to a haunted mill, the heart of darkness...and The Father of Lies.

http://www.amazon.co.uk/dp/B015NCZYKU
http://www.amazon.com/dp/B015NCZYKU

Magda – Book 3

The dark and twisted community of Woodsend harbours a terrible secret – one tracing back to the age of the Elizabethan witch hunts, when many innocent women were persecuted and hanged.

But there is a far deeper vein of horror running through this village; an evil that once invoked has no intention of relinquishing its grip on the modern world. Rather it watches and waits with focused intelligence, leaving Ward Sister, Becky, and CID Officer, Toby, constantly checking over their shoulders and jumping at shadows.

Just who invited in this malevolent presence? And is the demonic woman who possessed Magda back in the sixteenth century, the same one now gazing at Becky whenever she looks in the mirror?

Are you ready to meet Magda in this final instalment of the trilogy? Are you sure?

***

The Owlmen
Pure Occult Horror

If They See You They Will Come For You

Ellie Blake is recovering from a nervous breakdown. Deciding to move back to her northern roots, she and her psychiatrist husband buy Tanners Dell at auction - an old water mill in the moorland village of Bridesmoor.

However, there is disquiet in the village. Tanners Dell has a terrible secret, one so well guarded no one speaks its name. But in her search for meaning and very much alone, Ellie is drawn to traditional witchcraft and determined to pursue it. All her life she has been cowed. All her life she has apologised for her very existence. And witchcraft has opened a door she could never have imagined. Imbued with power and overawed with its magick, for the first time she feels she has come home, truly knows who she is.

Tanners Dell though, with its centuries old demonic history...well, it's a dangerous place for a novice...

http://www.amazon.co.uk/dp/B079W9FKV7
http://www.amazon.com/dp/B079W9FKV7

***

The Soprano:
A Haunting Supernatural Thriller

'It is 1951 and a remote mining village on the North Staffordshire Moors is hit by one of the worst snowstorms in living memory. Cut off for over three weeks, the old and the sick will die; the strongest bunker down; and those with evil intent will bring to its conclusion a family vendetta spanning three generations.

Inspired by a true event, 'The Soprano' tells the story of Grace Holland - a strikingly beautiful, much admired local celebrity who brings glamour and inspiration to the grimy moorland community. But why is Grace still here? Why doesn't she leave this staunchly Methodist, rain-sodden place and the isolated farmhouse she shares with her mother?

Riddled with witchcraft and tales of superstition, the story is mostly narrated by the Whistler family who own the local funeral parlour, in particular six year old Louise - now an elderly lady - who recalls one of the most shocking crimes imaginable.'

http://www.amazon.co.uk/dp/B0737GQ9Q7
http://www.amazon.com/dp/B0737GQ9Q7

***

Hidden Company

An eerie, supernatural thriller set in a Victorian asylum in the heart of wales.

1893, and nineteen year old Flora George is admitted to a remote asylum with no idea why she is there, what happened to her child, or how her wealthy family could have abandoned her to such a fate. However, within a short space of time it becomes apparent she must save herself from something far worse than that of a harsh regime.

2018, and forty-one year old Isobel Lee moves into the gatehouse of what was once the old asylum. A reluctant medium, it is with dismay she realises there is a terrible secret here - one desperate to be heard. Angry and upset, Isobel baulks at what she must now face. But with the help of local dark arts practitioner, Branwen, face it she must.

This is a dark story of human cruelty, folklore and superstition. But the human spirit can and will prevail...unless of course, the wrath of the fae is incited...

http://www.amazon.co.uk/dp/B07JQYQ7R8
http://www.amazon.com/dp/B07JQYQ7R8

***

Monkspike

A Medieval Occult Horror

1149 was a violent year in the Forest of Dean.

Today, nearly 900 years later, the forest village of Monkspike sits brooding. There is a sickness here passed down through ancient lines, one noted and deeply felt by Sylvia Massey, the new psychologist. What is wrong with nurse, Belinda Sully's, son? Why did her husband take his own life? Why are the old people in Temple Lake Nursing Home so terrified? And what are the lawless inhabitants of nearby Wolfs Cross hiding?

It is a dark village indeed, but one which has kept its secrets well. That is until local girl, Kezia Elwyn, returns home as a practising Satanist, and resurrects a hellish wrath no longer containable. Burdo, the white monk, will infest your dreams....This is pure occult horror and definitely not for the faint of heart...

http://www.amazon.co.uk/dp/B07VJHPD63
http://www.amazon.com/dp/B07VJHPD63

***

If you have enjoyed reading Tanners Dell, please would you leave a review? It would be very much appreciated by the author. Thank you!

—

Lightning Source UK Ltd.
Milton Keynes UK
UKHW020134251022
410994UK00022B/883